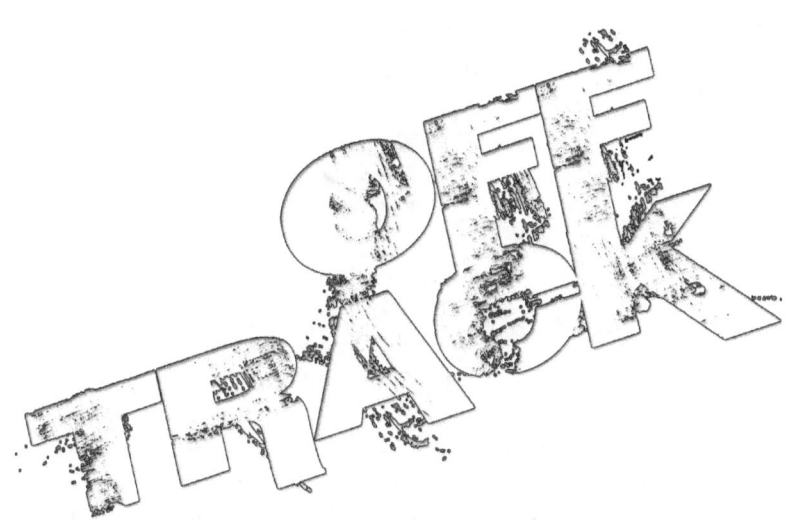

MICHAEL J. HULTQUIST

OFF TRACK

By Michael J. Hultquist
2nd Edition 2018
1st Edition Trade Paperback 2011

All Rights Reserved

Dark Recesses Press
657 Craigen Road
Newburgh, Ontario
Canada K0K 2S0

Edited by Jodi Lee
Cover Art © 2011 Stephen Blundell

Library & Archives Canada ISBN
978-1-988837-11-6

DEDICATION

To all the fathers.

Table of Contents

CHAPTER I

What Kind of Cowboy Do You Want To Be?

Four Years Ago.

Gary Sanderson huddled in the dim corner of his bedroom, rocking himself to an invisible rhythm, skinny arms wrapped about his knobby, scarred knees. He gripped the handle of the gun he'd taken from his father's underwear drawer, not daring to let his finger stray toward the trigger. He found the gun the previous week when no one was home. When he found it, the idea bled into him that he might need it one day. He just didn't think it would be so soon. He had no idea if it was loaded, but he hoped to God it was.

He hated his father and wished he were dead. He feared the drunken, brooding, violent bear of a man. Gary was twelve years old and small for his age with wisps of blonde hair that fell out of place too easily, a boy too thin and too quiet for the kinds of thoughts running through his head. Even though he'd imagined killing his father before, he never had the means to do it until now, which frightened the life out of him. It was never a plan before, never so real.

Through the floor vent, his father shouted and his mother screamed. The sounds dug in, ripped open his skin like shards of glass. His parents fought daily, religiously, mostly because his father was a belligerent drunk and came home looking for a fight. The man hated the way dinner was cooked, or he hated the way the laundry wasn't finished up, or he hated the way Gary didn't get good grades, or he hated the way you looked at him or didn't look at him. He was a man born to hate things and that made Gary hate him.

The fight this particular evening started out in the normal fashion. The pork roast was burned because his mother let Gary help her in the kitchen. She told him to remind her when it was 5:30 so she could remove it, but he forgot. At a quarter to six, she hurried into the kitchen and snatched it out of the oven, but it was already too late. It didn't look bad to Gary, but he could tell by the way the muscles in her face tensed and the paleness in her cheeks that she would pay for those fifteen minutes with more than she cared to.

That was what made him think of the gun.

His father stumbled in at just after six with a lurching crash against the front door and a dreadful scowl. He headed straight for the fridge. He liked Wild Turkey with a dash of coke in it, and there was never a lack of it in the house. He kept four full bottles in the top kitchen cupboard, lined up like loyal soldiers.

Something gouged into Gary's heart. He didn't like the scowl his father wore. It meant he'd had a bad day and the fighting would be worse than usual. And his father was already drunk. He left work every day at 3:30 to hit Tilly's Town Pump down the road immediately afterward. He'd stay there drinking Wild Turkey and coke until close to 6:00, come home and eat, then sit in front of the television until he passed out in the brown and yellow loveseat no one else was allowed to sit in. It smelled like urine anyway, so that was no problem for Gary. Sometimes his father laughed at the television, but mostly he yelled at it, his voice so garbled Gary could only make out the swear words. And mostly he started in on Gary or his mother about something.

Tonight was the pork roast.

"Don't even tell me I have to eat this crap." His teeth clenched together so hard they might shatter.

"I'm sorry." His mother's timid voice broke a little. "I left it in the oven a little too long."

His father slowly pushed the plate to the center of the table and took a deep breath, as if letting them both know the Herculean effort it took for him to remain calm in such an upsetting situation. Gary exchanged a quick glance with his mother. She shrunk back against the counter, ringing her worn hands. Her eyes darted with worry. It was going to start.

"I only ask for one damn thing!" His father's face boiled bright red with blood. He slammed his fist down on the table and threw his fork at the wall. The prongs stuck into the drywall just above the stove. There were other, older marks there as well.

Gary flew up from his chair and positioned himself between his father and mother. A jackhammer pounded away in his chest. It was the first time he'd ever done such a thing. "It was my fault!"

His father only glared at him. His eyes were red slits glowing with anger.

"Go to your room, Gary," his mother begged. Her eyes pleaded with him.

Gary felt her fear, the wild, raucous fear of realization. He tried to ignore it. He didn't want to see her take the pain again for something he had done.

"Don't even start, you little shit," his father growled. "Get the hell out the way."

"No." Gary defied his father for the first time in his life. He felt the blood run from his face. "It was me. It wasn't Mom's fault. She told me to remind her when the roast was done, but I forgot."

"Go to your room!" his mother screamed.

Gary didn't move. His knees trembled like loose cornstalks holding up a scarecrow, but he didn't move away from her. He wouldn't leave her this time. His father's eyes darkened and met Gary's, like a spear plunging into his flesh, searching for something.

His father's mouth twisted open to say something, but then he hesitated. His head cocked once to the left a notch, as if some track in his mind had reset itself. His face reddened further.

"Are you eyeballing me?"

"No." Something clenched in Gary's frame and paralyzed him. The tone of his father's voice made him cringe.

"Don't you dare eyeball me," his father said. "You know what the drill sergeants did to us in the Army if they caught us eyeballing 'em?"

Gary didn't want to know. Confrontation barreled up on him like a freight train, but he couldn't muster the strength or wisdom to pull himself away. He felt if he let his eyes slip away from his father's at that moment, he would never be able to do this again, and his father would win like every other time. He couldn't let that happen to his mother again. He couldn't let that happen to himself.

His father lumbered slowly up from the table and took one step forward. His shoulders were as broad as a locomotive. His eyes burned like coals. Thick stubble peppered his face, matching the marine-style haircut on his head. He hovered within inches of Gary's face, standing a good foot over his son, glaring down with practiced intensity honed specifically to intimidate. Gary cringed at the stink of whiskey on his breath.

"They made us go to the snake pit." A queer smile grew on his lips, like a cannibal about to enjoy his prey. "You know what the snake pit is?"

The question sapped the moisture from Gary's throat and clenched his neck in an invisible vice. "No."

"Believe me, you don't want to know."

His mother gripped Gary's shoulders. "Would you please go upstairs? Please?" She pleaded more desperately this time, quivering, saturated with fear.

"Shut up," his father grumbled and broke the stare. "Gary's a big man now." He spun to the side and whipped his arm around. The back of his hand connected with his mother's cheek with a dull *crack* that sounded almost cartoonish.

For an instant, the blow stunned Gary as if he'd been struck himself. He'd seen his mother struck before, but never this close up, and it had never been so directly his fault. His muscles tensed and he considered buckling down and rushing his father, but before he could respond, his father whirled back and struck Gary full force in the face. The fist connected dead on with his cheekbone. A million stars erupted in his eyes. Before Gary even realized what happened, he was sprawled along on the floor, gaping up at his angry father.

"That's for getting ideas in that stupid head of yours, now get the hell up to your room."

Gary rushed up the stairs, beaten and afraid. He waited by the floor vent in his room, but not before he took the gun from his father's dresser drawer. The image of his mother crying filled him with hatred, drowned out every thought.

On the dresser in front of him stood *Butchy the Cowboy,* the six-inch figurine his grandfather on his mother's side gave him when he was five.

"Some cowboys do things that are bad," his grandfather told him, "but some cowboys always do what's right, just like an English knight. What kind of cowboy do you want to be, Gary?"

Gary glared at the figurine. It stood strong, ready to draw its pistol. He clenched his fingers around his father's gun. The slick metal practically vibrated in his hand.

What kind of cowboy do you want to be?

Gary thrust Butchy into his back pocket. He couldn't see through the puffed bruise of his right eye, but he felt it all the same. He carried the dead weight of the gun with him and inched down the stairs, step by step, following his mother's terrified screams. Her strained voice echoed off the walls and bled through the pores of the house. For years those screams defined the house. They oozed at every moment, even through the silence. It seeped into Gary's ears.

His thoughts, in those moments, weren't his own. The world wasn't real to him anymore. The air felt strange, as if swirling around him like a giant whirlpool, floating him toward some inevitable force intending to smash him to bits. Then it rushed him head on.

At the bottom of the stairs, he stumbled to the entrance of the kitchen and poked his head around. His mother leaned on her knees before his father, her hands clamped onto his pants leg for support. She pleaded with him, crying like Gary had never seen her before, molten tears pouring through her eyes and streaming down her raw face. His father struck her hard across the cheek and the slap echoed against the walls like a hand on wet concrete.

Gary fingered the gun and lifted it slowly. It was cold and hard in his hands, and so much heavier now. It was an anvil. He felt as if he wasn't really there in the room, as if he were watching the events through an old black and white, 1950s television screen. He distantly heard his father yelling something at his mother, but the words were gibberish. They were part of the air. He breathed them.

His father reached to the counter and took hold of a dark yellow clay ashtray, the one with the words "I Love You, Mom" painted in thick red acrylic around the edges. Gary made it the year before and gave it to his mother for Christmas. The surface had the dull sheen of porcelain and looked oddly comedic in the big man's hands where perhaps a baseball bat or a crowbar or some other heavy weapon might have been at that moment.

His father raised the ashtray and slammed his mother across the face with it. The crack of bone split the room like thunder. His mother groaned as her breath escaped and she slumped to the ground.

He gasped and betrayed himself. His father spun with a maniacal scowl. He drew his fists up and he began to bark something, but then he saw the gun. His eyes fixed on it. A semblance of sanity trickled back in.

"What are you doing with my gun, Gary? What do you think you're going to do with that, you little shit?"

Gary glanced numbly at his mother lying motionless on the floor. Blood seeped from her forehead where the broken ashtray left a long and painful looking gash.

The world spun beneath his feet as if his head were connected to a giant pendulum. Gary raised the gun and pulled the trigger. It was loaded. The sound of it exploded in his ears like the echo of a slammed gavel. His father fell back to the ground, dead.

The hospital was cold. The chill of it soaked into Gary's bones like the sharp, dead burn of dry ice. His neighbor, Mrs. Farrelly, stood behind him, taking up nearly half the room in her kimono, reeking of stale perfume and cigarettes. She had reported the gunfire and lumbered over to see what happened after the police arrived. She waited the whole time, her barrel shaped body looming like an oil painting on the wall, the portrait of a dead woman staring. She volunteered to accompany Gary to the hospital so he wouldn't have to be alone, but more likely to get the goods on the gossip so she could spread the word to all the neighbors.

Gary's face felt like a piece of hot sausage had been sewn into the skin around his eye and cheek where his father struck him. He kept that eye closed, or he saw two of everything which made him sick to his stomach. He was vaguely aware of a blue uniformed police officer in the hospital room with them, hovering somewhere near the doorway like a wraith, but he couldn't take his eyes from the rumpled figure of his mother lying in the sterile bed in front of him. A plastic tube protruded from her mouth. It looked unnatural to him, like a robot trying to crawl into her throat. A machine next to the bed clicked and whirred in rhythm to her breathing.

A young doctor with olive skin and tired eyes adjusted the machine and checked his mother's pulse at the wrist. He lifted her eyelid and shone a dull beam into her eye with a silver pen light. A quiet, white cheeked nurse stroked his mother's hand and glanced over at Gary, her face long with pity.

Mrs. Farrelly's incessant gibberish whisked in and out of Gary's ears, some of it meant for him, some of it meant for the cop in the room, some of it meant for herself.

"...so sorry you had to see this...I've never seen anything like this before in my whole life...always knew something like this would happen...he was just a time bomb waiting to go off...he was a terrible alcoholic...felt so sorry for the woman all the time...it's always the children who suffer most...don't know anyone that could take care of him...."

The barrage of twaddle rattled from her mouth and thudded all around him like jagged stones. He didn't like the woman, never liked her from the moment he caught her spying on his family through her living room curtains, pretending she wasn't really there but watching, watching all the time.

Butchy jutted out of his back pocket, ready to draw. He still felt the weight of the gun in his hand, the cold of the metal, the kick after he pulled the trigger. His hand ached from it.

He wondered what was going to happen to his mother. He already knew what happened to his father. There wasn't a doubt in his mind the man was dead. The bullet struck him directly in the chest, but that wasn't what made Gary so certain. It was the look in his father's eyes after the shot—the grim, lifeless stare of a corpse, looking, but no longer seeing. He had never seen death before. He wondered if he'd see it again.

All of this could have been avoided if he had only pulled the trigger a moment sooner. What if he had fired the gun when he saw his father lift the yellow ashtray? What if he had killed him just a second earlier than that? His mother would be all right now, and he wouldn't be watching her with a plastic tube crawling out of her throat and a machine forcing air in and out of her, telling her to live when there was no way she would ever want to live this way.

But what if he hadn't killed him at all? His awareness of the cop in the room grew. Gary had done something horribly wrong, hadn't he? When it was all said and done, hadn't he killed someone?

What kind of cowboy do you want to be?

Gary knew what kind of cowboy he was. He was the murdering kind. No way around that. He killed his father and it didn't matter what the reason was. Gary would be a killer forever.

The machine's beeping rhythm quickened and a siren sounded. His mother shifted violently in the bed. Her back arched and her eyes flew wide open toward the ceiling. Gary saw the fear in her. It was a fear he'd never seen in her before, a fear worse than the kind he felt with his father. He wanted to cry for her because he knew what that fear was for, the fear of death.

The doctor waved his arm and the nurse slid the shade around the bed. Mrs. Farrelly groaned and tightened her grip on Gary's shoulders, causing him to wince as the sharp tips of her dry, yellow stained fingers stabbed into his muscles. The cop sidestepped closer to the door. He clearly didn't want to be there.

Numbness swept over Gary. He knew what was happening but couldn't feel it. He was a zombie. He wondered if something was wrong with him. He wondered if it would always be this way.

An hour later, the doctor declared Gary's mother dead. It was done. Mrs. Farrelly blathered to herself, and it pained Gary because not once did he remember seeing the woman talk to his mother or remember talking to her except to hear her complain about him walking in her grass. What right did she have to cry when he couldn't? Where did she get permission? She tried to draw Gary to her, to hug solace into him, but he yanked himself free of her drooping slabs of flesh and kicked the wall. Compassion bloomed in her face.

"Just let it out," she said, which carried his anger to the tip of the mountain.

"Fuck you."

He ran out of the room, hooked a stack of magazines off the waiting room counter with his fingers and flung them across the room. The cop chased him and tried to calm him down, but Gary pushed him with everything he had, threw blind, angry fists at the man and would have killed him if he could have. The cop embraced Gary in a bear hug so tight he could hardly breathe, but he thrashed just the same, doing everything in his power to break free from the cop, to break free from everything around him.

But he couldn't break free. From that moment on, Gary was alone in the world.

The next few weeks were a blur. He met with a representative from Child and Family Services who mumbled when she spoke and smelled like mashed pea and ham soup. For the first few nights she dropped him into a dark and musty halfway house where ragged shadows crept along the dark wood of his room. The walls were naked and too thin, and he heard the woman in the next room crying until all hours of the night. She had a deep, wrenching wail that sounded like he felt.

He went before a judge with an overweight, middle aged lawyer sporting a greasy ponytail who liked to call Gary "sport" a lot. Gary didn't understand most of what was happening to him. The prosecutor argued that Gary was in full control of his mental faculties at the time of the killing and said Gary should get the proper medical attention and counseling an abused child needs. That prosecutor, as far as Gary understood, wanted to see him go to a special kind of jail where young boys lived and received some special mental treatment, and when he turned eighteen, he would be moved to a real prison. His own lawyer argued that it was too harsh a punishment for a boy his age. The gunshot was his only way out in both defending his mother and saving his own life from such abuse.

"And just look at his face, your honor," he said. "The little sport was fighting for his life."

Gary understood that much of it, but what he didn't understand was why his lawyer took him aside before the trial and told him to say he didn't remember any of it. "Just say you remember your father beating you that night, and the next thing you remember is hearing the police breaking down your door. Can you do that, sport?"

That's what Gary did, and they all believed him, even through the secret wink of his greasy, pony-tailed lawyer.

Gary felt horrible about it, about the lie, mostly because he wanted to be punished for what he'd done. He thought it was what he deserved. He killed his father and he let his mother die. Why should he go free?

Only he didn't go free. Soon after the trial, a police car whisked him away and a scowling cop told him to pack his things from the halfway house. The next morning, they brought him to the Radcliffe Juvenile Detention facility in Lake Marion, Illinois.

He was told he'd have to live there until he was eighteen years old, at which time he could leave and live anywhere he wanted to live, but not before then. Maybe if he was a good kid they'd let him stay in a foster home, but they doubted it. The social workers told him there was nowhere else for him to go. The judge ordered it, and even if the judge didn't order him to Radcliffe, no one else wanted him. The only living relative who might have taken him in was his Uncle Karl, his father's older brother and part time party buddy, and he said he'd just as soon spit in Gary's eye than take him in after what he'd done. So Radcliffe it was, and the whirlwind began again.

Radcliffe was an enormous beast of a complex standing tall on the largest of a set of hills for miles around. A steel fence surrounded the expanse, making the place as oppressive as a Russian military installation.

He was first greeted by a security guard who carried a billy club strapped to his hip and sported long, pork chop sideburns, neatly clipped, but intimidating all the same. He helped Gary tote in his gear, and dropped him off at a dank administration area. Soon a robust blur of a woman named Mrs. Sanchez, calling herself his counselor, rushed him away first to his new room, where he left his few belongings, then to a briefing room, where a different security person told him about "the rules" with a threatening glint in his eye.

Radcliffe tolerates neither fighting nor insubordination, Gary was told, and if he did his best to keep his nose clean and get along with the staff and others, this place could be comfortable as home. But if he rocked the boat, they could make things miserable for him, if Gary caught his drift.

Gary said he did. Tears welled up, which he successfully fought back.

After this, Mrs. Sanchez set up a schedule for Gary. He would begin his counseling with her in two days, and they would meet three times a week at regular times. He would go to school on site from 8:00 A.M. to 3:00 P.M., and he would work in the kitchen during the evening meal on a rotating schedule. This was his new life, and he was told to get used to it.

Curious eyes followed him everywhere, from place to place, piercing the stifling walls of Radcliffe. They burned into the back of his neck with a mixture of wonder and anger. He wanted to cry, but wouldn't let himself. He would be strong even though he didn't want to be in this ridiculous hellhole of a place. He feared what might happen if he showed weakness in a place like this. He would be a fortress. He decided nobody was going to get in. He would close himself off and simply exist in this new place. He would do what he was told, and when he was eighteen, he'd leave and start over again.

Screw everyone, he thought. *Screw the whole world. I'm half dead already, and I'm nothing but a killer. I deserve everything I get.*

CHAPTER 2

Good Riddance to Radcliffe

"Hey, birthday boy," Officer Kellar said as he passed through the kitchen.

Gary paused with his mop and gave the man a quick salute, knocking the long blond strands of hair out of his eyes. At sixteen years old, he'd grown a full six inches since his arrival four years ago, though he was still shorter than most of the guys his age. Just in the past year he'd gained nearly fifteen pounds in muscle, giving him a lean wrestler's body that deceived most people. He was short at five foot six, but he was sturdy, like a little fire hydrant.

"Hey," Gary said cautiously.

Officer Kellar was an amiable man, and Gary liked him more than most of the guards, but he was still a guard. Gary never saw him without a smile, and he never tried to act tough around the boys in Radcliffe like the other rent-a-cops tended to do. With Officer Kellar, what you saw was what you got. He had a jovial barrel of a belly hanging over his belt and jowls that wiggled like Jello when he laughed.

"When I was your age," Officer Kellar said, "I was living in California, just off the beach. That was a good place to be sixteen."

"A lot better than this place, huh?" Gary said.

Officer Kellar chuckled. "I suppose so. And I was about as skinny as you, too. Yep, those were the days." He continued on his way while drawing his pants up a little tighter around his blubbery waist. "Damn, Gary. You could eat off these floors."

Gary dipped the mop and wrung out the soap. "What can I say? I was born to mop."

The ancient bucket squeaked in protest as Gary dipped the mop in for another swoosh. His scuffed gym shoes squibbed through the dampness.

"So you'll be leaving in a couple of days?" Officer Kellar said.

Gary nodded. "Yep. Finally."

"I got to say hello to your new foster parents last time they were here. They seem like nice people."

"Yeah. I think they are."

Gary had a few reservations, but he did his best to ignore them. He was happy to be leaving two full years before he turned eighteen, and they seemed like nice enough people. His real worry was that they weren't going to like him enough to hold onto him. He'd heard too many horror stories.

"Well," Officer Kellar said. "Best of luck to you. We'll sure miss you around here."

Gary popped his customary salute and continued on with his mopping duties.

In nearly four years, he'd come to know the kitchen better than any place in Radcliffe. He knew he wouldn't miss it when he finally unburdened himself of the dark dungeon of a home, as he had come to think of it, but he wasn't afraid to admit a sense of pride in keeping the kitchen in shape, in part at least. There weren't too many things to take pride in at Radcliffe, so he was thankful for the kitchen. It was a pleasant distraction from the 'daily drab' around him, as he and his friends had come to call it.

On his shift, he kept the place clean, but he also helped organize the place. Much of the fulltime staff had come and gone, while Gary was one of the few constants in the kitchen. He knew where everything went and even helped to implement a written booklet of procedures and inventories.

His counselor, Ms. Sanchez, commended him on the initiative he took when he began to organize that particular project, but he could tell it didn't completely offset her concern for his overall progress. She never said it in so many words, but her worry about some of his behavior loomed in every glance she threw his way, in every unblinking stare during counseling sessions. She had been with him since the beginning, and although he couldn't be certain, he figured it bothered the hell out of her that she couldn't get into his brain. He couldn't help it, though. He didn't like to go there.

More than once she'd remarked he wasn't helping himself a whole lot by not allowing her in, but he shook her off as best he could. His problems would go away in time, he figured. So far they hadn't, but talking about them sure wasn't going to do anything but make it worse.

When he was nearly finished with the floor, the door opened and then closed quietly behind him. Careful footsteps entered, squib-squibbing along the freshly mopped concrete. It wasn't the tapping shoes of Officer Kellar. They were sneakered feet, like his own. Gary pretended no one was there. He set the mop into the bucket and pushed it down, then twisted the handle loose from the head. His body tensed. He knew who it was. He'd been waiting for this confrontation.

Willie, Karge, and Big Ben marched toward him. While gangs didn't necessarily form up in Radcliffe, this trio came as close to one as could be in a strict juvenile detention ward, and most people stayed away from them.

Willie was from Kentucky with a long scar on his neck everyone liked to speculate about. Most people thought someone tried to kill him down south, but they didn't succeed because Willie was too tough to handle. He was a big kid for his age and bulky from spending his time lifting weights in the gym. They threw him in Radcliffe for stabbing his grandmother with a screwdriver and stealing her car.

"I told you you weren't leaving without saying goodbye, little punk ass," Willie said.

Karge and Big Ben stood dutifully behind, each of them bigger and stronger looking than Willie, but it was clear who the leader was.

"Come on, Willie," Gary said. "Don't start this shit now. I'm leaving in a couple of days."

Willie slammed his fist into his hand. "What did you say to me? I own you."

"I already told you it wasn't me," Gary said. "I didn't take shit out of your room."

Gary slipped to the side of the room, still holding onto the mop handle. The bucket rolled along with him on squeaky wheels. The others formed a half circle around him, forcing Gary's back to the wall. Gary knew it wasn't the break-in that got Willie in his present uproar. He'd had a thing for Gary for nearly two years when Gary refused to back down to his mindless bullying.

Willie snarled. "So now you're going to start making shit up? Is that what you did when they found out you killed your Daddy?"

Gary's face flushed and the familiar burning in his chest flared that came when his temper stepped up. He hated that. He hated it when somebody brought up his father for one, but he hated it when someone did it just to piss him off. Sadly, it always worked. Gary tightened the grip on the mop handle and braced himself.

"You know what you are?" Gary said. "You're like a little girl. You know it wasn't me that took shit out of your room. You just want it to be me because I'm smaller than you are and you think you can take me."

Hot coals shoveled into the engine of his chest.

"I can take you with one hand tied behind my back." Willie slammed his fist into his palm again.

Gary glared at Karge and Big Ben. "Yeah, right."

"Man," Willie said. "They're just here to watch me mop the floor with you. So let's do it."

Willie lunged at Gary. His face was a throbbing mass of anger, twisted and red. He drew his fist back, eyes focused on Gary's eyes like a bull rushing a tiny matador. If Gary hadn't been prepared, the bull might have struck him down immediately.

Instinctively, Gary brought the handle up and jabbed. The end of it caught Willie dead center in the solar plexus. Willie's eyes popped wide open in shock as his breath escaped him.

Without surprise, both Karge and Big Ben rushed Gary, their huge, over pumped arms flailing like dumb zombies. Gary swung the mop handle like a baseball bat, connecting with Karge's head. The blow resounded with a reverberating 'hunk,' and Karge fell to the ground, stunned.

In the commotion, Big Ben managed to get his arms around Gary from behind and lifted him up, squeezing him into a bear hug. Gary's breath escaped and he tried to slam his head back, hard as he could, but could only strike the top of his assailant's head, which did no good. Ben swung him with a huge grunt, and tried to slam Gary down in a poor imitation of a WWE wrestling move, but Gary twisted once and landed on his feet with Ben still holding him. Gary shoved backward with his legs, giving all he had. The force threw them both into the back wall. A quick elbow to the groin released Big Ben's grip long enough for Gary to rush for the mop handle. He dove, sliding along the floor.

Gary snapped the handle in half over his knee and held the pointed end against Willie's neck, tracing the scar with the tip of the splintered wood. "Back off, or he's fucking dead! I'll shove this thing through his neck, I swear to God."

Willie grabbed for the stick, but Gary pressed it down harder. The force drew a small line of blood. "Is this how you got your scar, Willie? Fighting kids smaller than you?"

"Dude, you're going to kill him," Big Ben said.

Gary almost laughed. "Come on. You know all about me, don't you? I'm the kid that killed his old man, didn't you hear about that? Why shouldn't I kill him?"

Both Karge and Big Ben stood frozen, aghast. Gary wondered briefly how they could be so stunned at this, considering what they had just tried to do to him. Willie glared up with hatred. It was so much like his father's eyes that day.

"Why shouldn't I kill you?" Gary said to Willie.

Willie's face scrunched up. "Fuck you, Daddy killer."

Something in him snapped. The world went white. He existed in the interior of a hot sun. Without thinking, he raised the handle up, poised to strike down at the boy on the floor. His muscles tightened and, for the first time in nearly four years, he felt he could kill someone again. What right did this person have to live, Gary thought? Why should he be allowed to treat others like this? Why shouldn't there be someone to kill the bullies that deserve to die anyway?

Had he made the decision? He didn't know, but at the moment he felt ready to plunge the jagged edge of the mop handle down into Willie's throat, the back door opened.

"Hey, what's going on back there?" It was Officer Kellar.

Gary lowered the handle and Willie shot to his feet. Karge and Big Ben loosened.

"Nothing," Gary said. "Just a little going away party, that's all."

Officer Kellar watched as Willie and the others left the kitchen. When he saw Gary was alone, he started for the door again.

"You sure you're all right?" he asked.

Gary picked up the pieces of the mop handle, straightened his hair. "I'm all right, thanks."

When Officer Kellar was gone, Gary knew he wasn't all right. His body shook while the anger circulated through his veins like a drug. The inside of his chest burned as if molten steel ran through him.

He had almost killed another person today. How could he have let that happen to himself? What good is a person who kills another person anyway?

He didn't want to think about it anymore. He was leaving soon, and everything was going to change.

Gary returned to his room to finish packing. He hadn't accumulated many things over the years in Radcliffe and much of it he didn't even care to keep, but it was enough to fill up an hour or two of time. He wouldn't miss the tiny room at all. It was no bigger than the room he had when he was twelve but this one had to fit two beds and two desks, not to mention a whole other person and his stuff.

The ragged walls were cinderblock and concrete partially covered up with dark wood paneling and the floors were concrete with a dingy, thinning throw rug he figured must have been there since the 70s. Radcliffe also had an incessant musty smell that permeated the rooms like an invisible smoke. It crept into his clothes over time and he smelled it everywhere he went, even the kitchen, which sometimes had some powerful smells of its own.

The county gave him three plastic bags to stuff his clothes into, but his new foster parents, Don and Gail Morgan, brought him a large, tan, leather suitcase to use. He looked forward to living with them, especially with Gail. He'd met with them on three separate occasions during the interview process, and recently spoke with Gail again when she drove up to drop off the suitcase. She was kind enough to him. He figured anyone willing to take in a foster child from a place like Radcliffe must be kind straight out, but she had a presence that made him feel at ease with her right away. She said she had never been a mother, but Gary thought she would have taken to it easily.

Don was a quiet man prone to stolid staring, but it didn't matter to Gary. Most of the guards in Radcliffe were the same, and Gary didn't take offense to it. Some men were just this way, and it didn't make a person bad. Gary was pretty quiet himself.

He opened the suitcase and packed his jeans first. They barely took up the bottom layer. His shirts and underwear took up another layer, and his socks padded the sides, leaving plenty of room left over.

At the bottom of his top drawer sat several rolled up pieces of paper he thought he might take with him, but thinking twice, he decided to leave them there. He unrolled them to take one last look. They were his drawings from last year's Art class. One of them was a charcoal sketch of a black bear with a tumultuous waterfall streaming behind it. He had the bear halfway emerged from the cave. Looking at it now, it didn't look all that bad to him. Another was his first attempt at drawing a dragon, but that one hadn't fared so well. The last one was a picture of his mother he tried to draw with some cheap pastels. The art teacher had raved to the class about how wonderful the picture was, how he had made some excellent choices of colors and strokes, but he didn't like the way it turned out. It might have been a good drawing, but he could never share it with his mother, which made it all the more bitter.

In the end, he threw them all into the trash, including the one of his mother, and made himself forget about them.

He reached into the back of the bottom drawer and felt something hard there. He pulled it out and stared at it. It was Butchy, the cowboy figurine his grandfather gave him. He'd completely forgotten about it, but looking at it now, it reminded him too much of things he'd tried to forget, and some of the unwelcome heat flashed in his chest. Butchy hadn't changed at all. He wondered if he had either. He gripped the figurine, wondering why he felt he couldn't leave it at Radcliffe, chiding himself because the answer didn't matter. He couldn't leave it there. It was part of his past, there to serve as a reminder of things he had done. With Butchy, he would never forget.

The door opened on its whiny hinge and his roommate, Hector, strutted in. Gary shoved Butchy in his pocket. Hector clapped Gary on the back and plopped onto his bed. He'd lived with Gary almost a year now, so he was allowed to do that.

"So, big bad Gary's leaving town tomorrow, huh?"

"Day after."

Hector was only fifteen, but he was streetwise in a way Gary never would be. Hector was quick with a smile and always confident, bragging, though Gary thought it was a front to hide something deeper. They never talked about it, though. No point in talking about shit like that.

"Dude, you're sixteen," Hector said. "You only got two more years before you can leave on your own. Why don't you just wait it out?"

"Are you kidding? I have to get out of this place. I hate it here."

Hector locked his fingers behind his head and leaned back on the wall. "Yeah, but a foster home? Dude, that's suburbia. You'll never fit in there. It's too different. They're all crazy lunatics out there."

Hector was a city boy and Gary expected his attitude, but part of him wondered if he was right.

"Like we're not all crazy lunatics in here?" Gary said.

Hector laughed. "Yeah, but at least we know it."

"You're the perfect example."

Gary grabbed Butchy from his pocket and shoved him into the suitcase, then covered him up with clothes.

"Just don't let those suburbios screw you up." Hector tapped his index finger on his forehead. "Stay strong in the head."

Gary sat on the chair and faced Hector. "Nothing out there is going to screw me up like this place does. Not anymore."

"I don't know, man. You were pretty screwed up when you got here, weren't you? What if it happens again?"

Gary trembled again. He didn't want to think about that shit, and besides, he knew things would be different with a normal family. His blue eyes flashed. "It's not going to happen again. Ever."

Hector must have seen something in Gary's face because he backed off. "Hey, that's cool. No problem. Good luck."

Wise decision, Gary thought.

He stood to leave then and Gary continued his packing, but Hector stopped at the doorway. He produced a folded up piece of paper from his pocket and tossed it onto Gary's bed.

"Happy birthday, man."

"What's that?"

"It's a special goodbye note, roomie."

Gary smiled. "Thanks."

"Later."

When Hector was gone, Gary opened it up and smiled again. The note read, "Be like me. Stay cool. Hector."

Typical Hector, but certainly good advice. Stay cool out there, especially with all the big changes coming his way.

The door opened again and he was about to call out, "Yo, Hector!" when his counselor poked her head in.

"Can I see you in my office?"

Gary nodded. He didn't like the tone of her voice, which was a bit too serious, and usually didn't mean good news either.

Gary shifted uncomfortably in the plastic green chair Mrs. Sanchez provided for 'her young boys,' as she liked to call them. Her office was one of the least comfortable places he'd ever been. If she truly wanted to help 'her young boys,' she might start by giving them somewhere softer to sit, a cushion, a beanbag, anything but a hard plastic chair that by all rights had once been somebody's lawn furniture.

But uncomfortable furniture aside, Gary understood his counselor wanted only the best for him. Even now, she wore the same distressed look she always had when she spoke with him, as if she, too, bore his pain.

She took the seat behind the hulking oak desk and crossed her weighty arms over her chest. She was an overall large woman with round shoulders that stretched the seams of her clothing. She kept her espresso colored hair closely cropped to her head, often cutting it near the length of some of the boys in Radcliffe. She always wore dresses or skirts with dull black shoes.

"So how do you feel?"

Her mud colored eyes scrutinized worse than usual. He shifted in his chair. He was a worm wriggling on a fisherman's hook. "Fine."

"All packed up, then?"

"I guess."

He braced himself for the real point of the meeting. He had met with her regularly since he came to Radcliffe and there was always a point to the meeting lurking somewhere in the subtext of her questions, some dramatic issue waiting to leap from her lips. How could it not be dramatic? She knew what happened with his mother and father. She thought it ate him up inside. She had said so on more than one occasion. He didn't care what she thought. He did what needed to be done to survive. He kept the promise he made to himself when he first got to Radcliffe. He didn't let anyone in. No sense in changing things.

Mrs. Sanchez produced a manila folder from a drawer and laid it in front of her. She pulled out picture of his younger self, a smudged Polaroid standing against a faded brick wall. The vacant look in his eyes made him shudder.

"I know you've earned the right to leave here," she said, "and that you've convinced Dr. Fielding you're okay to do so, but I have my concerns."

Dr. Fielding was the head social worker honcho and Gary had met with him a few times over the last month to discuss foster care.

"About what?" Gary asked. He did his best to sound nonchalant.

"Look at this." She sifted through the file, fingers tripping over various papers and forms. "How many fights have there been? Seven? Eight? You had one just last week."

The encounter from earlier in the evening flashed in his mind and he knew it would never get into her records. So many of them didn't.

"I didn't start any of those," Gary countered. He rubbed his bangs back over his head. He didn't want to sound angry, but it came out as such anyway. "Half the kids in here are nuts and start fights just to do it. It's like they're bored or got something to prove. And they always go for the small guys because they think we'll just lie down and take it. I don't take it."

Mrs. Sanchez tightened her arms over her chest. "I see. You had absolutely nothing to do with those fights. It's always somebody else's fault. Do you even know how many times I hear that in a day?"

"I'm sorry," Gary said. The anger in his voice turned to worry. "But I'm not lying. Please don't try to keep me here. Haven't I been here long enough?"

"I don't want to keep you here any longer than you need," she said. "I just want to make sure when you leave, you don't come back again. We both know you don't want that. Your foster parents are taking a big risk on you. Give them a reason to have faith."

He chewed his lip. "I won't screw up. I don't want to come back here. There's nothing but violence in this place. And hate."

"It's not the place that's violent," she said. She touched her hand to her head, then her heart. "It's what's in here and here."

He shook his head. "This is the kind of place that'll kill you if you don't kill what's in here and here first." He pointed to his own head and heart.

He usually didn't contradict her so directly. A wave of guilt sprung up in his head, so he decided to shut his trap. He sat in the ensuing silence, waiting to be dismissed. When she did, he rose from the chair and headed for the door.

Mrs. Sanchez sighed, as if giving into an argument she couldn't win. "Gary?"

"Yeah."

"You don't really believe what you just said, do you?" she asked.

He didn't hesitate for an instant. "In here I do."

Gary waited for Don and Gail to arrive at the front of the building. A stiff security guard followed him from his room, heels clopping along the scarred linoleum, not so much as a security precaution but as a gesture of formality. This was Gary's official send off. Such an end to four lousy years. "Thanks for nothing!" he wanted to yell.

Mrs. Sanchez was there also, but they hardly spoke more than banalities, discussing how nice of a day it was, and wasn't it nice to be outside on a day like this? It was sunny and cool and mild. The blades of green grass on the grounds poked up like tiny daggers.

Gary ignored her. He took deep breaths and let the coolness of the air tickle his lungs. It was delicious, invigorating and pointed with nostalgia to the days of his early youth, when he was at his happiest, before everything turned bad like cancer. He remembered running in the lawn in late March as a child, the air much like now, so cool it almost stung his skin yet reminded him of how alive he was. The scent of lilac surrounded him.

He hadn't felt like this in ages. If he were alone, he would have let it all out, broken down and cried for it, but not in front of his social worker. He wouldn't have done it in front of anyone, so he shoved the thought away and reminded himself this wasn't the time for celebration. He had to be strong and not screw up.

He'd been outside often in his tenure at Radcliffe, off grounds for field trips and volunteer details, but each time before he left with the knowledge he would be back, that Radcliffe owned him. He had no freedom to roam before, no freedom to grow and change. He had no hope.

Now he did. He glanced back at the cold and impersonal stack of rocks he'd known as home for nearly four years and contemplated it all. Had Radcliffe helped him in any way? Had it changed him for the better? He didn't think so. His father hurt him in a way no one could ever hurt another, but was tossing him into a violent concrete hole with the likes of Willie and Karge and Big Ben supposed to help him?

It had made him worse. But now was his chance to change that. Things would be different outside the walls of Radcliffe. Leaving the place gave him hope. A mixture of giddiness and nervousness bubbled in his stomach. He was going to be, dare he think, "normal". At least he would have the opportunity to be. He'd go to a regular school, hang out with regular friends, get a regular job, and do regular homework. Maybe he'd even find a girlfriend. He'd do whatever 'normal' people did.

In his mind, he was leaving everything bad about himself behind, and what better place to leave the bad stuff than Radcliffe, the center of all bad stuff? For once, he'd be in a place where no one would know about what he did, except for Don and Gail, but he wouldn't talk about it with them and they wouldn't force him to. They'd already talked it out during their earlier visits together when they were deciding whether or not to take him in, and Gail said she understood. She said he could talk when he was ready.

He doubted he'd ever be ready.

In the distance, the Morgan's Dodge Ram motored through the iron security gate and headed toward him. He hoisted up the tan suitcase and gripped it tightly at his side. Mrs. Sanchez lingered nearby, so he did his best to contain himself. He didn't want her to know how excited he felt.

Gail popped out of the Ram first and embraced him, squeezing his shoulders. She rubbed her hands vigorously over his back. He tried to hug back, but it didn't feel natural for him.

She pulled back, revealing kind green eyes. Her hair was close-cropped and blonde, feathered and parted down the middle. Her lips were pink with lipstick and her face powdered with blush. She wore a sky blue windbreaker and new jeans, and she smelled faintly of perfume. It was nice. She reminded Gary of an updated version of a 60s sitcom mother, like Mrs. Cleaver for the new millennium.

"Finally, huh?" The creases around her eyes crinkled up to smile with her lips. Her voice was soft and happy, genuine.

Don strode around the front of the truck and offered Gary a stern handshake. He wasn't a large man, but a working man. His shoulders were wide in a way that suggested hard labor and his hands were dry and calloused. His hair lay unkempt atop his head, like a bushel of straw, as if he'd been driving fast with the window rolled down. He wore a southwestern style shirt. Without a word, he took Gary's suitcase and tossed it into the back.

"You'll just need to sign the final paperwork." Mrs. Sanchez held up a clipboard.

Don scribbled his signature into the forms.

So many forms. All they'd done the past month was fill out forms. Who knew going into foster care could be so confusing?

"Set to go?" Gail asked.

Gary sighed with relief. "More than you know."

Forms completed, Don jumped back into the driver's seat and started off. Gary snuggled into the back seat and relished the cold of new leather against the back of his legs. This was the beginning of it all, of his new start.

He took one final look back at the building, a visual goodbye, or a good riddance. Mrs. Sanchez watched him go, her face like stone. The pity in her eyes flashed like a lighthouse beacon, warning him, calling him back. He hated that.

He sneered at the old place. *I'll show you. I won't give you the satisfaction of coming back to you. Ever.*

CHAPTER 3
Winsbury, Illinois – Escape to Suburbia

Heaven. What other word to describe it? The sun through the window warmed Gary's skin. Heaven to be in a car, going anywhere. On the highway, trees and wild grass zipped past in a green, panoramic blur. It hypnotized him. He found himself smiling to the wind, wondering how long it had been since he'd felt so completely uplifted.

Don't get too excited, he reminded himself.

This was only the beginning of a new journey for him. Everything was brand new to everyone. Things still might not work out. For all he knew, the Morgans might tire of him in a week and decide they didn't want to deal with a foster child anymore. They could toss him back to Radcliffe with a word, and he knew it could happen if he screwed up. He'd seen it happen before. He didn't expect it to happen, but he wasn't taking any unnecessary chances with his hopes.

Still, a part of him wanted to revel in his new freedom, so he let that part of himself roam free through his head. He was out of Radcliffe. That was reason enough to celebrate. He thought of everything he had left behind and couldn't think of a single thing he'd miss. Maybe the kitchen, but it hadn't exactly been a labor of love. He might miss Officer Kellar, but Radcliffe wasn't exactly the kind of place he'd want to know a person anyway. Hector was the only person he'd come close to calling a friend, but it just wasn't the right place to maintain a real friendship. He'd blocked himself off in Radcliffe, hidden parts of himself away he didn't want anyone to see. He hoped he might learn to change that someday, but it certainly wouldn't have happened there. He knew that much about himself.

Gail swiveled in the front seat and leaned her elbow up, facing him, green eyes twinkling. "We'll be home in less than an hour. Are you all right back there?"

"Great, thanks." Gary couldn't help smiling again.

She gripped the back of the seat with her small hands. "We're happy you're coming to stay with us. It's going to be good for everyone. You just wait and see."

Gary nodded. "Yeah. I think so."

He allowed himself to open up a little more to the idea that everything *would* be all right. Why wouldn't it? What sort of trouble could he get into if he did everything he was supposed to?

"We'll have fun." She spun back around to the front.

Gary cracked the window and drew in a deep breath. In the rearview mirror, he caught glimpse of Don watching him nonchalantly. Don hadn't spoken yet, at least nothing of actual relevance, and it was part of the reason Gary's reservations crept in. He couldn't tell how Don felt about taking in a foster child, but he was doing it, so why would there be a problem?

But his eyes said something else to Gary. They didn't look happy. Not angry or mean, just not quite happy.

Nostalgia washed over Gary as the truck pulled off the highway onto Main Street. The town was Winsbury, Illinois, and even though it had been four years, it felt a lot like where he used to live before Radcliffe. The streets ran in straight, narrow lines, ending in calm islands of grassy neighborhoods, protected by trees and neatly trimmed bushes. The curbs were clean and swept. The cars parked along them sat new and gleaming, without a rusty junker in sight.

Darkness might loom down any of those avenues, but not on this day.

Ain't no cowboys hanging around these streets.

A few miles into Winsbury brought them to Washington Street, where a right took them past an old fashioned bowling alley and laundromat, then a video store and a faded green brick grocery store. They passed beneath a small copse of willow trees, their leaves rolling in the breeze, and emerged at the bottom of a hill.

The truck climbed and the faint horn of a train sounded in the distance. Train tracks ran down along the houses to the left of the street and he smiled. He enjoyed trains, not toy trains or models like some children or collectors enjoyed, but real trains, massive, powerful machines that crisscrossed the continent. They were unstoppable things, juggernauts. He'd always felt it in his bones, there was no way Superman could stop a speeding locomotive. No way.

Finally, the truck slowed and stopped at a small white house with a decorative wooden fence. It was a two-story house with new vinyl siding and a dark, shingled roof. A freshly painted porch jutted out the front. Two wicker chairs sat lazily beneath the overhang.

To Gary, it was something out of an old TV show. *The Brady Bunch* maybe, or *Little House on the Prairie*.

He carried his bags inside and stopped to marvel at how neat the whole place was. Growing up, his mother kept a neat home (mostly to keep his father from complaining about it), but this home was museum clean, hospital clean even. Seeing a small row of shoes efficiently lined along the wall near the door, Gary slipped his own off and lined them up with the others.

From behind, he sensed Gail's relief at not having to ask him to remove his shoes.

She quietly led him up the stairs to his new room. It was small, but nearly as large as the hole he'd been assigned to in Radcliffe, and this was all his own. A twin bed with a yellow flower print comforter sat in the right corner of the room. The walls were bare and featureless, painted baby blue. A thin birch dresser that still smelled of new wood sat against the closet wall, and Gary guessed they recently purchased it just for him.

"Sorry about the flowery comforter," Gail said. "It's all we have right now, but we can get you another one later."

Gary dropped his bags. "Oh no, that's all right. I like it."

Gail smirked. "Uh huh. You're too kind, but don't worry. I won't make you sleep with flowers for long."

He didn't mind, but he didn't argue. Anything was better than Radcliffe, even flowery comforters.

Gail opened one of the dresser drawers and pulled out a stack of clothing. "We got you some new jeans and shirts for school. You can wear whatever you want, but we thought you'd need something new. Let me know if anything doesn't fit."

He picked up a primly folded shirt and inspected it. It was a dark green polo with tiny flecks of yellow and gold spread throughout. Nothing he would have ever picked for himself, but certainly better than anything the state would have provided him.

"Thank you."

"I'll let you get settled in. I'm making dinner and we'll eat at six. See you then."

Gail gone, Gary unwrapped his new clothes and held them one by one against himself. He was sure they would fit, but *wow!* One of them had flowers on it worse than the bedspread. Did she think he was going on a trip to Hawaii? Standing there in his new room with his new clothes in his new home, he couldn't stop himself from chuckling.

He set the clothes neatly back into the dresser, separating the shirts for one drawer and pants for another. He unzipped his bag and stuffed the innards into the remaining drawers. From the bottom of the suitcase, his mother's picture looked up at him, one of the only times he'd ever seen her smile for real. He set it gently on top of the dresser and hoped Gail and Don wouldn't mind him keeping it there.

And finally, he felt the last item calling out to him, good ol' Butchy, waiting to take his place in the room, waiting to remind Gary of everything in his life that brought him to this point.

What kind of cowboy do you want to be?

Gary shoved Butchy to the back of his sock drawer and did his best to forget about him.

The maddening aroma of pot roast wafted through the house, following a trail up the stairs, and finally reaching Gary's nose. It tugged at him like in a Tom and Jerry cartoon. His stomach grumbled in protest to his refusal to rush down the stairs and gobble up the whole thing himself. He resisted temptation and spent his time straightening things in his room, organizing his clothes by drawers, and staring out the window into the manicured yard. At six o'clock—*finally six o'clock!*—he went slowly down the stairs in one of his new shirts and waited at the kitchen door.

Gail stood at the sink, draining white rice into a Pyrex bowl. The roast took center stage on the table, sliced and juicy. Beside it sat a gravy boat with thick brown gravy, a bowl of steamed broccoli and cauliflower, mashed potatoes, and bread and butter.

A homemade meal.

"Sit right there." Gail motioned to the center chair with her elbow. "I went a little overboard with the food, but I wanted you to feel plenty welcomed."

He sat and swallowed the saliva from his overactive mouth. He'd eaten fairly well in Radcliffe, even better than most since he worked in the kitchen, but there was never anything like this, not even on Christmas. Cafeteria food had a way of looking and even smelling like real food on the outside, but it invariably dropped into his stomach like a brick once it passed his lips.

"Don should be here in a minute." Gail set the rice onto the only bare spot left on the table. "Then we can eat."

"Thanks."

By the looks of the kitchen, Gary would have never guessed someone had just cooked such an enormous meal within it. Aside from the finely set table, there was no evidence. No dirty dishes sat in the sink waiting to be washed, no crumbs had fallen onto the floor, and no counters wore the drips and stains he would have expected to find accompanying such a feast. The kitchen was like the rest of the house, gleaming in its splendor of cleanliness, betraying nothing. Even the window dressings were crisp and pressed.

Don finally strode in through the back door, his hungry eyes swallowing the table.

"Looks great." He washed his hands in the sink with soap.

He sat next to Gary and Gail took the other end. Gary waited. He set his napkin in his lap and pinned his arms primly to his side. At Radcliffe he would have dug in and been done long ago, and probably half way back to his room by now, but here he hadn't an inkling of how to act. Were they going to pray? Were they supposed to wait for Don? Or was it ladies first? Or... *or....*

"Dig in," Gail said and Gary gave a mental sigh of relief.

Don took small portions so Gary followed his lead. He seized a small end piece of the roast and added a single spoonful of everything else in neat, tiny piles around the meat.

"You can take more than that if you'd like." Gail hadn't even started to add anything to her plate yet, instead opting to watch Gary. He couldn't tell if her smile meant pleasure or amusement. "There's plenty of it."

Gary gladly reached in for more and doubled his portions. When Gail finally began to fill her plate, Gary went to work, taking small and slow bites at first, but ultimately giving into his own ravenous hunger by shoveling large scoops into his mouth. When his plate was empty, he suddenly realized both Gail and Don were watching him, and his face flushed with embarrassment.

"Now that's what I call an appetite," Don said.

Gary swallowed. "I'm sorry. We didn't have anything like this in Radcliffe."

Gail straightened proudly in her chair. "That's the perfect compliment. Thank you." She waved her hand at the center of the table. "Go on. There's more to eat."

He took more of everything and ate more slowly this time since his stomach was not quite so demanding.

Don cleared his throat and leaned his elbows onto the table. "Is your room all right?"

"Excellent," Gary said. "Thanks."

"Good," Don said but Gary could tell this wasn't just going to be dinner conversation. Don's forehead creased. He fixed his eyes on Gary. "Now that you're here, we'd like to lay down a few ground rules."

"Don't you think we should wait until after dinner?" Gail asked.

"I think now is a good time," he said, but after a small exchange of eyes with Gail, he deferred some. "Is that all right with you, Gary?"

Gary nodded. "Sure."

"Good." He tried to smile, perhaps to soften the message and not seem so stern, but it wasn't as effective as he might have hoped.

"Look, we already know about what happened with your parents, and we know all about the trouble you had at Radcliffe."

Gary shifted in his chair. He expected this conversation to occur at some point during his stay, but it made him uncomfortable nonetheless.

"We're not going to hold any of that against you," Don said. "This is your chance to start over again. I'm a big believer in that. Ask Gail."

"Thank you," Gary said.

"If you follow the rules here," Don said, "everything should go fine. You'll go to school every day. No ditching. And there will be no fighting. If we get wind of anything like that, you'll go back to Radcliffe, no questions asked. Got that?"

"Yes, sir."

Don's gaze met Gary's with an intensity that meant business, and Gary looked down at the table, thinking of his father's reaction to 'eyeballing.' He'd had a hard time looking into people's eyes since then.

Gary set his fork down. His appetite dwindled all of a sudden.

Gail set her napkin on the table. "Don't worry. We're not trying to run a prison here. This isn't Radcliffe. We want you to be happy, but we also want you to be safe. You are our responsibility now. We just want to help you."

"I know." Gary took a deep breath. He had wanted to say something to them since he first met them at Radcliffe, and now was his chance to do it. "I really appreciate your letting me come to stay here with you. It really means a lot to me and I promise I won't let you down."

Gail patted Gary's knee. "We know."

Don remained a solemn statue, giving nothing away.

Gary sat on the edge of the porch and watched the sun settling down along the tree line beside the railroad tracks. In twilight, the roofs glistened yellow and white, casting rippling shadows through the trees along the lawns that flowed like a green ocean. The sky was crisp and blue, just beginning to purple toward the horizon. The street was much like Winsbury's main street, with clean pavement stretching down past the hill and onward to infinity, rows of cookie cutter houses lining it like film props. Every lawn was connected in a green blanket like golf turf, with not a blade out of place.

An old man with silver hair and a light blue windbreaker ambled along the sidewalk on the far side of the street, whistling a melancholy little tune. A bouncy terrier scuttled out in front of him, attached by a thin leash. The dog sniffed near a tree, squatted, and plopped a turd into the grass. The old man reached casually into his pocket and produced a clear plastic baggie. He slipped it over his hand, reached down, picked up the turd, then pulled the plastic baggie from around his hand, wrapped it right up into a neat little package, and slipped it back into his pocket. Then he moved on down the road.

Gary watched him go in wonder. It didn't seem normal, but why wouldn't it be? Why shouldn't people pick up their dog turds in such a nice little neighborhood as this? It made sense when he considered it, and that was probably why the neighborhood looked the way it did. The people who lived here cared about where they lived and they didn't want to see it blemished with dog turds.

He considered the town and Don and Gail. Mixed emotions circled his head like a cloud of gnats. He understood Don's seriousness. It wasn't unlike the methods used in Radcliffe for newcomers, two parts authority, one part intimidation. You had to show them who was boss early on and let them know the stakes. Keep them a little afraid and set up respect from the get go.

He respected Don and didn't want to disappoint him, mostly because he didn't want to go back to Radcliffe. But understanding it didn't mean it didn't crawl around under his skin a little. Don's animosity toward him was obvious, though Gary had no idea from where it stemmed. Maybe he didn't want Gary there. Maybe he felt Gary needed a strict home as a transition from such a strict environment. He could think of a thousand reasons why Don might have started out hard on him, but he decided not to dwell on it. It was what it was, and he'd take every opportunity he had to prove to both him and Gail they'd have no reason to regret their decision.

Across the street and to the right, a girl emerged from a squat yellow and brown house. She looked about his age. Her dark brown hair hung in thin, wavy strands down to her shoulders, mostly obscuring her face. Her jeans were loose and faded, bunched up around her ankles and her thick, gray sweatshirt was far too large for her to wear. She looked a bit grungy to Gary. She carried a small set of clippers and moved to the far end of a row of bushes, then proceeded to prune a bush of sickly roses growing there.

Gary watched her. She pulled her hair back behind her ear, and although he was still rather far away, he could tell she was beautiful, like his mother was beautiful, in a subdued sort of way. Beautiful in a way that goes unnoticed until it shocks you into asking yourself, "How could I have missed that all along?"

She gave him that impression by the way she walked with her shoulders drawn slightly forward and her hair hung low, hiding herself. Maybe it was the way she worked quickly in the yard, hurrying to finish her tasks so she could get back into the safety of her home. He didn't know, but he hoped he could meet her. Someday, at least.

Her task finished, the girl wiped the clippers off in the grass and skittered back into her house, letting the door bang loosely on its hinges behind her. He watched her go and continued to stare at the house in a dreamy wonder, his mind a muddled blur of the day's events when an abrupt 'ahem' drew his attention.

The neighbor woman from the house on the right stood on her porch, hands planted firmly on her hips, staring. She wore a plastic bag over her hair. Spatters of red dye leaked from beneath it, onto her forehead. Her neck was abnormally thick for her scrawny, aging body, giving Gary the impression of a gargoyle. She wore a long, daisy print dress that looked older than she was.

She shook her head at him, then spun on her heels and headed back into her house.

Just letting me know she saw me and doesn't like me already.

Gary leaned back, setting the square pillar of the porch between him and the neighbor lady's house. He didn't like the way she looked at him, or her obvious glare of disapproval. It made him feel like a dog turd blemishing the otherwise quiet and normal neighborhood, and even though he knew he wasn't normal, he desperately wanted to be. He wondered if he could 'normal up' before some giant plastic covered hand reached down and scooped him away.

The first night in his new foster home wasn't quite as comfortable as he hoped. Gary didn't realize until then how the cold walls of Radcliffe had crept into his bones over the years. He hated the place, sure, but it was familiar territory, and familiar things are, well... *familiar.* They don't surprise you when you aren't looking.

When he first arrived at Radcliffe, every sound startled him, every shadow crept into the corner of his eye, every whisper drifted under his door. During his first month, he considered suicide almost nightly and would have done anything to escape the dank prison, but slowly the feeling dissipated and he stopped thinking about endings and started thinking about just getting by. The whispers under the door came less and less often, and the shadows revealed themselves to be nothing more than tricks of light.

The real threats were the Willie's, Karge's, and Big Ben's of the place, but he grew used to such things. He learned how to fight, to protect himself without getting busted all the time. Sure, Mrs. Sanchez knew he fought and confronted him, but not nearly half of them were reported and certainly not the serious ones.

But now, in his new suburban bedroom at Don and Gail Morgan's house, he had something entirely new to get used to. Silence.

There was no more Hector snoring away in the bed across the room, no more *click clack* of guards' heels tapping down the hallway outside the door. No echoes reverberated through the concrete floor from some unknown origin.

It was disquieting. He folded his hands behind his head and stared at the ceiling, counted a few sheep, but it didn't work for squat. Whoever thought of counting sheep anyway? He let his mind wander on more pleasant things, things to look forward to. He learned long ago not to get his hopes up. If you always expected the worst, you would never be disappointed, but weren't things different now?

He let himself dream. He imagined walking along the halls of his new school, slapping hands with some of the other kids, shaking hands with teachers that liked him and didn't look at him like he was a pitiful boy that shot his father dead. He imagined himself sitting on the porch in the twilight, like earlier tonight, only this time the neighbor next door didn't shake her head with disdain. This time she smiled grandly and gave him a bow and a wave and thanked him for helping her mow her lawn. Such a pleasant thought.

He imagined himself walking past the gates of Radcliffe and glimpsing the heads of the place there along with an entourage of guards swinging their clubs as he stopped and offered them his middle finger. This particular fantasy he liked the most.

It could happen, he thought. Realistically, he looked forward to a new school, a real school with other kids who weren't known for stealing and fighting and going off without warning. Mostly, he looked forward to being around people who didn't know about him.

The more cautious part of him stepped forward and nudged the dreamer. *You can dream all you want but it doesn't change what you are, and what you've done.*

I know, I know, he replied, *but what they don't know won't hurt them.*

But it might hurt you.

Gary didn't respond. He didn't want to think about it, but his cautious self persisted.

Ignoring it doesn't make it go away either, it said. *A past is a past and sometimes it can come back to bite you in the ass.*

Shut up, Gary told himself, but to no avail.

Don't get your hopes up.

He shut his eyes into the palms of his hands. He didn't want to listen to that cautious half, but he couldn't help it. He knew it was right.

Gail tapped on Gary's door at 6:00 A.M. and asked him if he was ready to get up. He rubbed the sleep out his eyes, startled.

"I'm sorry," she said. "I have to get you an alarm clock. I'll pick that up today."

"It's all right." His muscles ached from the new bed. It felt like he'd just fallen asleep and now it was already time to get moving. To say he was tired would have been a terrible understatement.

"The bus stops at seven on the corner. Here's your stuff." She opened his closet.

It surprised him to find her so wide awake at such an hour, 'bright-eyed and bushy-tailed' as his own mother would have said. She wore a long blue dress and her face was done up with light makeup, as if ready for a social event. She had stuffed his book bag with books, notepads, and other assorted supplies. From the pocket of one of the zippers, she produced a small piece of paper. "Here's your class schedule. I picked up the books for you last week. You're all set to go."

He smiled. She had done so much for him already. He remembered the whirlwind of paperwork the month before leaving Radcliffe just to get into his new school, the proof of custody forms, residency, health, dental, and a slew of others.

"Thank you," he said. "I really appreciate it."

"Then you better get in the shower. I had to sign you up for a zero hour class."

With that, she closed the door and he stood up, took the class schedule in his fist. *Zero hour?*

His first class started at 7:30. Gym. Yuck. He wondered who on God's Earth would allow a Gym Class to be scheduled for 7:30 a.m., but he bit his lip and sucked it up. Hell, it would probably do him some good. Better than falling asleep in algebra class.

He showered quickly and even that was perfect. No other naked bodies crowding the place and no wondering if the guy next to you is staring at your privates. The bathroom was all his own and he sat on the edge of the tub for a moment just to relish the fact. Silence in the bathroom. What a concept.

He popped on his trusty pair of old jeans, thought twice about it and slipped them off. He put on a new pair of pleated khaki Dockers Gail purchased for him and donned a green button down shirt with a strange looking tree print design on it.

It wasn't exactly his style of attire, but it wasn't so bad, he supposed. He didn't want to hurt Gail's feelings. He flung the book bag over his shoulder and heard another rap at his door.

Gail poked her head in and craned her neck gleefully. "Oh, those clothes look so nice on you."

Gary blushed. "Thanks."

"I'm so glad," she breathed, "I wasn't sure if you'd like those sorts of clothes."

"Oh no, they're great," Gary lied. "I really appreciate it."

She ducked out and he followed her down the stairs. She led him to the kitchen and opened the top cabinet. "Cereal?"

"No, thanks," he said.

But Gail insisted. "Oh, come on. You know you're hungry. Besides, I didn't know what you'd like so I went ahead and bought all the popular ones. Too many, probably."

She stepped aside to reveal seven or eight boxes of assorted cereals aligned in orderly rows. Nice selection. Gail's thoughtfulness amazed Gary. She grabbed a bowl and spoon for him, as he grabbed a random box from the shelf and came up with Cheerios. *Good enough*, he thought.

While he ate, Gail leaned forward in her chair with her chin resting on the palm of her hand, gently rocking her foot back and forth. She half watched him eat and half stared out the window, all the while a strange little smile curled up around the corner of her mouth. It made him uncomfortable.

When he was finished, she snatched up his bowl and rinsed it in the sink. "You sure you don't want any more?"

"No, thanks." He paused awkwardly. "Thanks though."

At the front door, she straightened his collar and pushed a loose lock of his floppy blonde hair behind his ear.

"There you go," she said. "Perfect."

Gary felt another blush coming on, and the mere fact of blushing in front of her made him blush even more. Thankfully, she didn't seem to see it, or she didn't react to it. He found it strange the way she looked at him, almost like he was a doll she was dressing up for a child's tea party. But it felt nice and reminded him a little of his mother. He liked to be reminded of her in that way. What a rare thing to think of his mother without picturing her in the kitchen lying on the floor in the final hours of her life.

"And don't forget you have to meet with your new counselor after school today. Only on Mondays."

Gary nodded. "Yep. I think it's even on my schedule." He checked to make sure and there it was, hand printed: *Meet with Ray Travis, Counselor, room 117.*

"Have a good day," she said, as she let him go.

CHAPTER 4
A New School

Outside and standing on the wooden planks of the porch, he pulled the door closed with a gentle 'snick.' The chilly morning air stung brusquely, and he tightened the book bag over his shoulder. He felt slightly nervous about going to school for the first time here, but he also looked forward to getting a move on. Time to start living again.

The warm sun pressed his cheeks, and he turned his face upward. Only a few clouds spread thin across the still sky. Almost the perfect day. The faint scent of freshly cut grass floated on the air.

He glanced across the street to the brown and yellow house, hoping he might see the girl emerge with a book bag of her own, but nothing. She probably had regular class hours and none of this zero-hour stuff.

The bus stop wasn't far down the street. Several other kids stood like tired zombies, statues erected to permanently wait for the bus. He couldn't tell for sure from the distance, but he counted six or seven of them.

He was about to step off the porch when Don's truck backed up from the garage and into the main part of the driveway, blocking his path. Gary saw his warped reflection staring back from Don's dark and tinted windows. Don rolled down the window. He slung his arm out and paused a long moment. With a nearly imperceptible nod of his head, he gave Gary a small wave and smiled. "Have a good day at school. Stay out of trouble."

"Will do."

Don headed away. Gary watched the truck rise then fall over the edge of the small hill, finally disappearing out of view. He tightened his grip and reset the book bag on his shoulder.

He waited on the corner for the bus with the other students, most of them his age or younger. He supposed the older kids would be driving their cars to school, and he would have too if he had a car, if he could drive for that matter. That was another thing to look forward to, getting his license.

When he was 11, his mother let him take the wheel of their El Camino in the mall parking lot, so he remembered how it felt to turn the wheel and press the pedals. As long as it wasn't a stick he'd be all right, and now he had the opportunity to make it legal.

Two boys, both of them as gangly as basketball players, stood at the curb, joking about something. One of them snorted and said "Stupid bitch," and snorted again. Then they both snorted. The behavior made him feel like he was back in Radcliffe for a moment.

Three girls huddled together at the stop as well. One looked all of thirteen and wore a shiny blue sweater vest, which reminded Gary of Catholic School. The second had a nose ring and a purple streak in her hair that dangled down the right side of her head. The third one wore blue jeans that screamed 70s and hung in ragged ends over a pair of polished clods.

Nobody looked directly at Gary, and he didn't expect them to. They only side glanced him warily. That was the way it was with people. He learned this early on. *If you want to avoid confrontation, don't look other people in the eye. That's the way it is with dogs, too. You stare at an unknown dog's eyes long enough and he'll jump up and snap you in the nose.* People could do worse.

He hoped he'd see the shy girl from across the street, but no such luck. He supposed he'd meet her soon enough, but the bus stop would have been the perfect opportunity. It would have been his 'in' to start talking to her. It was always good to have an 'in' to help start up a conversation.

When the bus finally jostled up, he followed the rest of the students through the narrow doorway and filtered down the aisle. Wary, tired eyes followed him, and he kept his head down. He didn't want to attract any attention to himself.

He found a seat four from the back and slid in, leaned against the cold window. The air smelled of stale cigarettes mixed with old soap and faint perfume.

"Hey, asshole," someone yelled from behind him.

It sounded like it was directed at him, but he didn't turn around. *Ignore it, and maybe it'll go away,* he figured.

"Hey, asshole!" the same voice said with more force this time. It pinged the back of his head like a stone.

He turned his head toward the voice, but then another student one seat back yelled out, "What the fuck are you calling me an asshole for?"

He relaxed and settled back into his seat. Paranoia, maybe, but it got his blood pumping, even if they weren't talking to him. He pictured a tiny little Mrs. Sanchez sitting on his shoulder, waving her finger and nodding her head at him.

"It's what's in here and here," she said.

He smirked and 'poof' she was gone.

Behind him, the last three rows spat out curse words and lit cigarettes and laughed with gooney hysterics Gary would never have been able to muster at such an hour. They were obnoxious, but he was used to it and beyond. At least he didn't feel any physical threats. That was always a plus in any situation.

He certainly wouldn't miss the physical worries, the fear of being struck when you weren't looking, or getting smacked for something you didn't even do. In Radcliffe, the stupidest argument, the tiniest glance, or even walking the wrong way could have resulted in a brawl. Radcliffe was for society's misfits, the idiots who couldn't get along with others.

No more. Maybe he'd even be one of the idiots in the back of the bus one day, belching and spitting on the floor. He doubted it, but at least now he could if he wanted to.

The bus arrived at school. The entire ride couldn't have been more than a mile and a half with all of two whole turns, not including the turn into the parking lot.

The school was different than he expected, which was a relief. He half expected a mini version of Radcliffe—dark, stifling walls without the gates—but he was pleasantly surprised. It was a two-story, light red brick building with large, painted windows and huge letters on the front reading "Winsbury High School, Home of the Eagles."

He loosened the collar on his tree print shirt and headed toward the building, schedule in hand.

The inside of the school gleamed as much as it did on the outside. He crossed the threshold through one of four pairs of doors with the tired crowd of students and first noticed the long glass trophy cases lining the front wall. Golden statues glimmered from within, jumbled in mismatched sporting categories. Prizes for football, basketball, wrestling, volleyball, and swimming mostly, with a few others peppered the rest. Staring at them, he caught his reflection in the polished glass. A wave of self-consciousness washed over him. He unbuttoned another button on his shirt and took a deep breath. Probably just a bad case of the nerves.

When the crowd of zero-hour students finally dissipated, he found himself in the center of the main atrium, surrounded by pristine brick and glass, schedule clutched in his fist. Gym class. He hurried down the main hall, face buried in his schedule and as he turned the corner, he didn't see the two larger fellows coming straight toward him.

"Watch it." Gary received a not-so-gentle shove. It stunned him and he flopped to the side, bouncing into a locker with a resounding bump.

There were both a good head taller than him, and wider to boot. The first one had tanned skin and long greasy black hair trailing down to his shoulders. Gary couldn't tell the nationality, but he looked Spanish or Greek, maybe.

The one who shoved him was a bulky thug of a guy with close cropped stringy brown hair and a thick mustache. Gary didn't often see kids around his age with mustaches, not even in juvie. Obviously this guy must have been held back a few grades. He reminded Gary of an evil Wyatt Earp.

'Mustache' let loose a dry chuckle. It was obvious they were seniors who enjoyed messing with the younger students. "Yeah, watch where you're going, egghead."

43

Gary picked up his book bag, which had fallen to the side. He kept his eyes on the two in a side glance, not attempting to incite any rivalries, but to make sure they didn't try anything on him when he wasn't looking. He straightened his bag and started back down the hall away from them.

"Gee, that's a pretty shirt," the greasy-haired one called.

This time Gary felt the anger percolating. He stopped and half turned his head, not looking at the guys but waiting. He pursed his lips in a pout, jutting out his lower lip slightly. It was a sign of disrespect at Radcliffe, jutting out the lip in defiance, practically calling someone a girl. He doubted they'd know what that meant exactly, but the intention was clear.

"What the hell you looking at?" Greasy-hair sneered.

Gary felt for a moment he wouldn't mind telling them what he was looking at, but wouldn't that be a great way to start the new day at school? Even if he did, he knew there wouldn't be a fight. These guys didn't seem like the kinds of guys who would fight in the school hallways. They might wait for him after school somewhere, but they wouldn't do it in plain sight. Gary didn't want to give any reason for trouble.

"Nothing," he said. "I'm just new here. I'm lost."

Greasy-hair and Mustache didn't say a word as Gary hustled toward the Gym. He figured he'd see them again, but he wasn't worried. He wasn't going to fight anymore or do anything to jeopardize his new life. No matter what.

Gym class wasn't so bad. Gary didn't think he was going to mind it for his zero-hour class. The teacher was Mr. Reynolds, a leathery skinned man with looping peppered hair and faded sweat pants. He had everyone run a couple laps before things started, much to the grumbling of a few select students, which he answered with a few extra laps.

Running wasn't such a horrible thing. He didn't feel comfortable in his new gym clothes and his knees were knobby, but running never bothered him. With every lap as he passed Mr. Reynolds sitting on the end of the bleachers, he caught a look from the man. It was probing, searching. Maybe he wanted to see what the new student in his class was made of, and Gary did his best to keep up with everyone. He didn't want to pull ahead or fall behind. He just wanted to stay in the middle, blend into the walls as much as he could.

With laps done, they did pushups, sit ups, and a bizarre exercise he'd never heard of before called a 'burpee' that consisted of squatting down quickly, thrusting your legs out behind you into an almost pushup position, then pulling them back in, standing up, and starting over again. It got the heart pumping.

Finally, when the exercises were finished, Mr. Reynolds wheeled a cart of basketballs from the storage room and told everyone to go to it. Some students formed groups and played teams, but Gary didn't feel comfortable asking anyone if he could join in. In fact, he didn't feel comfortable at all with a basketball. Radcliffe had a court in the gym and he'd played a few times, but he had a horrible time getting the ball into the basket, so whenever a game broke out he always made sure to be somewhere else.

He took one of the balls and headed to the far end of the court where the majority of the students without partners milled, lazily lobbing balls up and only rebounding the shots bouncing in their general direction.

Gary took a spot next to a lanky student with bright yellow spiked hair, shot once at the basket and missed. No one noticed the shot, or him for that matter. They all seemed concerned with looking busy in front of the teacher, which was fair enough to Gary.

The yellow haired guy drew the ball back and took a fairly decent shot Gary figured was going to swoosh right through the net, but it bounded up just off the rim and flew off to the right.

Attempting to be social, Gary cleared his throat and bounced the ball in his hand a few times. "Nice shot."

The yellow haired guy muttered a quick "thanks" under his breath.

Gary couldn't tell if the kid was put out or just nervous about talking to people.

While Gary took his shots, Mr. Reynolds watched from the edge of the bleachers. Gary didn't think he was being paranoid when he observed Mr. Reynolds watching him more than anyone else. He did his best to ignore it, but he couldn't shake the 'eyes on the back of his head' feeling that made the hairs stand up on the back of his neck.

Five minutes before the end of class, Mr. Reynolds wheeled out the cart and blew the whistle dangling about his neck. Everyone stopped, took whatever ball might be nearby, and headed for the cart. Gary reached for a ball but someone else snatched it up before he could get to it, so he stood there, wondering what he should do now.

Mr. Reynolds made the choice for him.

"Gary Sanderson." His voice was morose, disinterested.

Gary's nerves bunched up. Mr. Reynolds motioned toward the locker room and Gary followed him in. Inside, the gym teacher hooked a left into a cubbyhole of an office and sat on the edge of his desk.

"So you're from Radcliffe. Is that right?"

Gary's throat went dry. "Yes sir."

Mr. Reynolds' head bobbed in thought and not once did his eyes leave Gary's. Gary looked away, uncomfortable.

"Your file says you were there four years."

"File?"

"Your file," Mr. Reynolds repeated. "Four years is a long time for anyone, isn't it?"

"I guess so."

The whole mention of the file made him nervous. He hadn't considered the fact that Radcliffe would send his file along to his new school, although it didn't surprise him now that he thought about it. It made sense, didn't it? Wouldn't they need to know where he'd been the last four years, what he'd studied, what his strengths and weaknesses were? Everything he'd done?

If Mr. Reynolds knew, then all of his teachers knew.

"Well," Mr. Reynolds went on. "I'm sure you won't have any trouble fitting in. Just keep your nose clean and your chin up and things will go all right for you here."

Gary scratched at his neck. He wasn't sure what to do with his hands. He had no pockets in his gym shorts. "Thank you."

"Go on now. Shower up."

And then Mr. Reynolds smiled at Gary and rapped twice on his desk. Knock on wood. Gary didn't know for sure, but he figured Mr. Reynolds liked him.

With his hair still wet from the shower, Gary wound his way through the strangely spotless hallways of Winsbury High until he found room twelve in the B building. He poked his head in and glanced down at his schedule, which said *English – Mrs. Torrence.*

Mrs. Torrence stood at the front of the class wearing a white silk blouse and a pair of black pleated pants that hung too loosely on her thighs. She looked too young to be a teacher. He liked her jet black hair and the distracting twitch she did with her eye, like a super fast wink.

She waved Gary in with a friendly gesture, inviting. "Take a seat." She turned back to the room.

He slipped in and felt immediately awkward. Everyone else was already seated and he was the last student to arrive. Everyone else had more time to get there since it was the first class of the day for most of them, not having zero-hour to contend with. And those who did have zero-hour probably didn't have to come all the way over from the gym.

The class was interspersed in a sea of bright, faddish clothing, similar to the kids who rode the bus. It was radically different from Radcliffe's bland uniforms. One girl in the front row eyed him with thinly veiled suspicion, her head tilted slightly forward as she chomped on a huge wad of gum.

He found one seat available on the far wall, four seats back from the teacher. Not bad. It was near the window at least. He might have preferred to sit in the back row where blending into the background would have been easier, but this would do. He moved through the rows of about thirty students and slipped his book bag into the slot under his chair.

Mrs. Torrence waited for him to finish, and when the bell rang, she spun dutifully around to the chalkboard, snapped up a piece of chalk, and wrote *Mr. Flood's Party, by E. A. Robinson.*

She spun back to the class and opened the textbook on her desk. "Open your books to page 211. I hope everyone did their homework last night."

Gary fished the English book out of his bag along with a notebook and a new pen. He opened it to *Mr. Flood's Party* and began to scan the words. It was a poem, one he'd read before but didn't entirely understand. He'd read poetry in his classes in Radcliffe, but this was a long one compared to the other stuff. He remembered one having something to do with a red wheelbarrow and some white chickens, but that was about all.

"So why is the poem called 'Mr. Flood's Party' if Mr. Flood is alone?" Mrs. Torrence asked.

A silent rumble rippled through the rows. It was worse than gym class, a sea of exhausted faces, including his own.

He lowered his head and scanned the poem further, but it didn't seem to get him anywhere.

"Hey, what's your name?" Came a whisper.

He raised his head and saw the kid in front of him, his half turned face pointed toward the window. He spoke through the corner of his mouth, a caricature of a secret operative in a spy flick.

"Gary," he whispered back. He tried to go back to his poem, but the whispering continued.

"So where you from?"

He groped for words. "Uh, up state," he said off the top of his head, which wasn't untrue. "I just moved here."

He'd have to come up with something a bit more creative in the future. He didn't want to suddenly blurt out, "Hey, I'm from Radcliffe, you know?" What a surefire way to scare people off.

The kid in front of him gave him a sort of half nod and turned toward Mrs. Torrence, who was in the middle of something about *'Auld Lang Syne,'* but before long he turned his head back. Gary figured the kid was bored or hadn't read the poem, and didn't care much about it.

"So where do you live?" the kid asked, but this time, Mrs. Torrence flung a little *ahem* toward him and propped her hands onto her hips.

"So Stan, what do you think the relevance of 'Auld Lang Syne' is in the poem?"

Stan twirled eyes front and flipped a few pages of his textbook. "Uh, uh," he stuttered.

"That's what I thought." Mrs. Torrence went back to her lecture.

Gary laughed quietly to himself and didn't hear another word from Stan for the remainder of the class.

In the hallway after English, Stan popped up from out of nowhere and slapped his hand onto the flat of Gary's shoulder blade. "Hey, my man Gary."

Stan was a small kid, only an inch or two shorter than Gary but much skinnier. He had to be fifteen or sixteen to be in Gary's classes, but his oval baby face made him look even younger. He wore a dark blue designer jean jacket with round metallic studs sewn along the arm seams and a tight black muscle shirt hanging loose where it should have fit tight. His left ear was pierced in two places, and a thin silver chain hung between the holes in his earlobe. He had stark green eyes and wore thick gel in his hair, which raised it up in spikes.

"Hey," Gary said back.

Stan whirled around to Gary's side and gave him a friendly little nudge with his elbow.

"Sorry about getting us busted in there." He drew his voice out with a strange, emphatic drawl. "I just get so bored reading that poetry crap, and I got to do something else."

Gary nodded. He knew what Stan was doing. It was in how he dressed and how he talked. He was making a presentation out of himself to the new guy. It didn't bother Gary. He'd seen it time and time again in Radcliffe, and he'd done it himself in the past. New arrivals at Radcliffe invariably did what they could to fit in.

Some of them acted tough, like they were the newest, hottest shit since Vin Diesel, but those were the ones who got their asses kicked right off the bat. Some of them tried to be funny, and sometimes they got along all right, as long as they didn't go over the top and start disrespecting some of the hotheads. The smart ones, in Gary's opinion, were the quiet ones who stuck to themselves. You couldn't tell what was going on in their heads so you just left them alone. Who knew? They could be psychos.

Stan was a mixture of the first and second variety, which was odd to Gary, but he supposed this would only be the first of many things oddly different outside of Radcliffe. He didn't mind the act Stan was putting on, mostly because Stan exuded a natural friendliness and had an obviously energetic personality.

"I hear you," Gary said.

"So uh, I guess I'm sort of like the welcome wagon," Stan said. "Seeing as how you're new and all, how would you like to attend a sweet little gathering this Friday night?"

Gary paused. He highly doubted Gail and Don would allow him to go to a party so soon.

Stan seemed to sense his hesitation and added, "Come on, plenty of fun, plenty of girls."

"Well, I'm not sure...."

"That's cool. It's a bonfire, though, and I don't think you'll want to miss it. Party of the year and all that."

"I'll have to check with my foster parents, I guess," Gary said.

Now it was Stan's turn to pause. "Foster parents? Holy shit, man. Did you just break out of Radcliffe or something?" He laughed and gave Gary another playful slap on the back.

Gary's face flushed. How easy it was for the slip of a tiny little word to get the whole Radcliffe thing started. "Something like that."

Stan's eyes widened with the strangely pleasant revelation. "Shit, I was only joking. I didn't realize you were really in juvie. Damn, what'd you do? Kill a nun or something?"

Gary pulled a couple of steps quickly ahead of Stan, hurrying away. Adrenaline spiked through his veins. His anger piqued and he hated it, but he also felt embarrassed, and that was worse.

"It's none of your business," he said.

Stan hurried up to his side, the grin gone, replaced with a more serious expression. "Hey, bro. I'm sorry about that. I didn't mean to get all up in your business like that. I'm just making conversation."

Gary faced his new acquaintance. He didn't want things to start out this way, so he did his best to relax. He extended a hand to Stan, and Stan took it with a firm grip.

"Don't worry about it," Gary said. "Friday sounds all right. I'll have to see if I can make it, though. Seriously. I'll let you know."

"That's cool. See you back in English."

Gary followed the locker numbers, hoping he would eventually come to his own locker so he could unburden some of the contents of his book bag. Stan spun around and headed back in the other direction. Stan was all right. He actually reminded him a little bit of his Radcliffe roommate, Hector, but without the suave demeanor.

He wondered if they'd be friends. Something in his gut told him they would be.

Room 117 lay practically hidden at the end of a dank, oppressive hallway at the far end of the school. It was a quiet hall, still, like a heart paused between beats. When Gary's last class of the day, Algebra, was over, he followed the numbers all the way across the campus until he approached Room 25 and saw the hallway.

The last set of fluorescent lights at the end of the hallway was out completely, and the second set in the middle had only one lit that sputtered, blinking chaotically at the shadows.

He saw an open door down there, a gaping mouth waiting for him. He adjusted his bag and shuffled toward the door, wary of the dark hall. He imagined things jumping out at him, ominous shadows with glaring eyes and the glints of knives ready to ram into his skin. Shake it off, he reminded himself.

He ran his fingers along the wall lockers. They felt like cold, corrugated cardboard. With every flick of the light above him, the polished floor blinked dully.

He stopped before the door and poked his head around the doorjamb. Inside sat the man he was supposed to meet, a slim, pony-tailed man of about 30 sitting at the desk. His legs were up, resting on the desk in front of him. His feet were enormous for his size, clad in dirty white sneakers with stark, new, white laces. He flipped a deck of cards nonchalantly in his hands, deftly shuffling.

"Mr. Travis?"

The man swung his large feet off the desk in a swooping arc and set the cards down on the corner. "It's Ray, or Counselor Ray, actually," he said. "Gary, right?"

Gary nodded.

"Come on in, have a seat." Counselor Ray waved at the chair in the center of the office. The office was little more than a broom closet with chairs and a desk. There weren't even pictures on the walls, just cold yellow painted brick someone probably thought would brighten up the dungeon.

Gary sat and dropped his book bag to the side of the chair. Counselor Ray leaned forward and swept up the cards in his surprisingly short fingers. But they were dexterous fingers. He split the deck with one hand and shuffled. Gary watched with interest. He'd never seen anything like it before and it disarmed him.

But when he noticed Counselor Ray staring at him with amusement, he crossed his arms and settled back into his normally rigid pose.

"So how are you, Gary?" Counselor Ray set the cards aside.

"Fine."

Ray smiled agreeably. "You're probably wondering why you need to see a counselor now that you're out of Radcliffe, am I right?"

Gary said nothing. He had been wondering, but didn't think too hard on it. It was part of his new reality after all. But then Counselor Ray said something that drew Gary's interest.

"You know, I spent some time at Radcliffe myself a while back."

Gary perked up. "Really?"

"Yep. Two years, actually. I was bad news, did a lot of drugs when I was pretty young. When it got to huffing, my parents said 'enough is enough'. So that's where I went."

This got Gary thinking about the type of kid his counselor could have been, but he still said nothing.

"I lived in the B wing the whole time," Ray said.

"I was in A, near the kitchen," Gary said.

The new counselor let out a severe belly laugh that startled Gary. "Oh, that must have been punishment enough, sniffing Radcliffe kitchen food for four years."

Gary couldn't help but laugh with him because it was true. Working in the kitchen was all right, but living so close drove him up a wall sometimes, for the good smells and the bad.

"So you had some pretty rough stuff happen to you before you got there, huh?" Counselor Ray asked.

Gary tightened. *Here it comes. This guy gets all nice with me, then drops the old counselor bomb. Tell me about why you killed your father, kid, tell me about your mom.*

Gary crossed his arms and looked away.

Ray backed off. "I just want to let you know, during our sessions, you don't have to talk about anything you don't want to talk about. I'm basically here to make sure you're doing all right and give you someone to talk to. All right?"

That's good. Gary nodded. He looked back at the counselor and noticed a manila file folder on the desk.

"All right," Gary said, "but you'll be reporting on me back to Radcliffe, right?"

Ray tapped the folder. "Part of the job. Got to be honest."

"Sure."

Ray picked up his cards and began shuffling them again. "You like cards?"

"They're all right." Gary shrugged.

"What about Spades?"

"I've never played that one."

"Rummy?"

"I used to play that a long time ago, but I don't remember all the rules."

"Well what games do you know how to play?" Ray asked.

"War and Go Fish are about it. Oh, and Blackjack."

Ray paused. "Now that's a strange combination. War, Go Fish, and Blackjack. Here." He dealt out seven cards each. "I'll refresh your memory with Rummy."

Gary won the round with kings and fives. The rules came back to him quickly. He used to play with his mother some nights before his father's drinking went overboard. They would sit at the kitchen counter or across the coffee table in the living room while they watched her favorite shows. He hadn't remembered it until now.

"You're a natural," Ray said. He didn't deal another hand. "I don't want to keep you too long, so today's session is over. I just wanted us to get a chance to meet and let you know what these sessions were going to be all about."

"Thanks," Gary said.

"All righty, then. See you in a week?"

Gary scooped up his bag and headed for the door.

"Just a second." Ray stood, bounced around the desk, and pulled something out of his pocket. It was a business card. "If you ever have any problems, just give me a call. Really. I'm here to help you."

Gary stuffed it into his pocket and headed back through the dreary hall, liking Counselor Ray a lot more than he ever liked Mrs. Sanchez, although he wasn't setting this opinion in stone just yet.

CHAPTER 5

A New Job

His first counseling session behind him, Gary hurried toward the final school bus. Most of the students had gone home already, but a few stragglers like himself remained, members of student clubs, after school committees and the like.

He propped the strap of his book bag over his shoulder and let it bump against his back as he walked. It was heavy with books and homework. The sharp corner of his English textbook nudged into the inset of his spine. Plenty of reading to do tonight, but he didn't mind it so much.

Outside, only one bus remained, waiting patiently at the curbside with quiet drone faces staring blankly out the windows, mesmerized by nothingness. He decided he didn't like the bus, and since it wasn't much of a walk, he took the opportunity to see some of the town firsthand. He didn't think Gail would mind his choice. He had a strong curiosity and wanted to get a better look at the downtown area he drove through when he first arrived in Winsbury.

He headed through the circular bus turnaround and started down the doublewide sidewalk, his eyes following the neatly manicured grass along the edges. The grass in Winsbury amazed him. He'd never seen such perfect grass anywhere in his life. Not that he'd been many places, but still. Perhaps it was just another way perfect people manifest themselves.

Cars zipped past him through the streets, many of them high schoolers killing time. Not a jalopy in the bunch. His father always drove old wrecks, kept them running for a year or so before dumping them off and picking up another wreck. It was a cheap way to get around, but they were often loud and obnoxious with rumbling, punctured mufflers and whining engines in desperate need of oil.

He walked half a mile until he crossed into the downtown area, the outskirts starting at a quaint, little beauty salon with pink window treatments and a freshly painted pink door. Through the window, he noticed two old ladies with curlers tightened in their hair, chatting away like old women do, their heads propped beneath gigantic dryers.

Mick's Chevrolet took up the entire southwest corner, complete with garish neon signs shouting from every showroom window, such as 'Super Low Financing,' 'Test Drive Today,' and 'No Trade-Ins Refused!' Several used Fords and other models filled the lot, all with new paint jobs but probably clunkers.

Across the street stretched a long row of smaller stores, from the corner 'Avalon Pharmacy and Convenience Store' to a narrow 'Winsbury Library Extension Location,' 'The Game Room' hobby shop, 'Rocky's Pizzeria,' 'Main Street Café,' and finishing off the side of the block with a big slab of a building with a sign reading 'Industrial Chemical Supplies.' The faded red brick of many of the buildings reminded Gary of a movie he'd once seen set in the 1920s. They must have been around a long time. A neon bowling pin poked up from the next building over, and half of a grocery store sign from behind the pharmacy.

He crossed the street toward Avalon's and took a left, looking through the windows of the shops nearby. Avalon's windows were jammed with newspaper ads and specials worse than the Chevy dealer so he couldn't see much inside. The library was dead, save for a bored looking woman sitting at a desk in the far back staring blankly at a newspaper. She fiddled with a tiny pencil, probably agonizing over a difficult crossword puzzle. The hobby shop had some interesting things in the window, among them a slew of fantasy novels about John Carter of Mars.

He'd never read a fantasy novel, but he thought he might like to and figured maybe he could return to the library one of these days and get himself a card. It would be nice to read something different for a change. Dragon stories could be interesting.

Rocky's Pizzeria had a squat red and white striped overhang above the main window with gold lettering stenciled in a semicircle on the glass. The blinds were closed, but in front of the blinds on the bottom left corner, someone had propped a 'help wanted' sign.

Gary's eyes lit up. What an excellent opportunity. He'd considered that he could get a job when he finally sprung out of Radcliffe, but so soon? He wasn't even sure if Don and Gail would approve, but he was sixteen after all, and he wanted to prove to them he could be responsible. Besides, a restaurant would be the perfect job, considering his previous job in the Radcliffe kitchen.

"Maybe I'll get it, maybe not," he said to himself, "but you never know unless you try." With that, he adjusted the book bag on his back and headed in.

The gold plated bell dinged above the door, then once more when the door closed behind him. Initially, Gary thought Rocky's Pizzeria would be a dive, but an interesting one. The walls were the same solid, faded red brick covering the outsides of the buildings. A stuffed moose head hung from the left wall above a soot covered fireplace. Four wooden booths lined the wall next to the large window overlooking the street. No patrons were present, but Gary figured the high backs of the booths would give them plenty of privacy if any showed up. Five other tables were congregated in the center of the floor, all set and ready for someone to come in.

The wooden floor looked like it had been recently swept clean, but the remnants of what looked like a gigantic peanut explosion remained. Bits of shells lay wedged in corners, in the nooks and crannies of the tables and even the walls. But it wasn't displeasing. It actually felt sort of homey, and he liked that about the place.

A man appeared out of the back wearing a dull white apron and a puffy chef's hat. He looked older, maybe in his early fifties, but solid, like a fire hydrant. He stopped half way between the back and Gary, poised himself then nodded politely.

"Welcome to Rocky's." The man already held a menu in hand and extended it. "How can I help you, kind sir?"

Gary adjusted the book bag on his shoulder. "I saw the sign in the window."

He snapped the menu back and cast a critical eye on Gary. "The help wanted sign?"

"Yeah."

"Oh. So you're looking for some work?"

The friendliness Rocky displayed when Gary might have only been a customer was now replaced with a more cautious, authoritative air. Gary felt it.

"Yes, sir."

"Come on in then," the man said. "I'm Rocky, by the way, proprietor and all that jazz."

Gary followed Rocky, keeping a close grip on his book bag, watching the stiff strut of the restaurant owner.

"You ever work in a restaurant before? What kind of experience you got?" Rocky's voice was gruff, like a stone rattled around in his throat.

Gary paused, attempting to choose his words wisely, then proudly affirmed, "I used to work in a kitchen."

Rocky nodded and scratched his chin with skepticism. "Kitchen? Where was that at?"

He didn't want to say where, but he also didn't want to lie about it to an adult, especially when he was asking for a job. If the truth came out later, where would that leave him? Besides, if it was going to be a problem, then he didn't want to work there anyway.

"Well, it was Radcliffe."

Rocky nodded. He had gray, penetrating eyes that were a little watery and they never left Gary's face. Gary did his best not to look away.

"Uh huh, I see," Rocky said. "Radcliffe. Don't see too many Radcliffe boys around here. What were you in for?"

Now it was time to lie. "Well, it was for fighting and stuff."

Rocky raised an eyebrow. "Fighting and stuff? Sounds pretty serious."

Gary repositioned his bag on his other shoulder and was ready to tell Rocky, 'thanks for your time, but I'm sorry I wasted it' when Rocky took off his hat, revealing a close cropped bristle of gray hair, sort of like a wire brush.

"I don't think we have to worry about too many fights in this place," Rocky said. "Do you think you can work your way around a grill?"

Gary smiled with surprise. "Grill? I thought this was a pizza place."

Rocky returned the smile and lightened, becoming once again the man who met Gary at the door. "It is, but wouldn't you know it I sell more burgers than pizzas half the time. Lately it's turkey burgers, damned health nuts. Come on."

He led Gary past the cash register and through a paint chipped door into the backroom.

Rocky slapped his hat onto the hook at the side of the door along with two or three other crushed paper hats and at least a dozen aprons. He jammed his left hand into his pants pocket and gestured with his right hand. "You said you've been in a kitchen before, so I guess I'm not showing you much that's new. You got the pizza oven over there, the grill, the deep fryer, the sink, the storage bins. Any questions?"

Gary surveyed the kitchen. Despite his initial impressions of the place, it wasn't so bad. A few spots could have been a bit cleaner and better organized, but it wasn't the grimy, grease trap he expected.

The pizza oven was an old beast of a machine hulking along the side wall. It stood over six feet tall and had two cast iron doors that opened downward. It was dark metal, although several shiny spots glistened along the surface where Rocky must have scrubbed it over the years. Gary wondered how many pizzas you could cook at one time with such an oven. Or how many of Gail's roasts?

The grill wasn't in the best shape. It sat opposite the pizza oven with a narrow aisle between them. It was a flattop griddle with small pools of congealed grease sunk into the corners. Beneath it were two cabinets Gary guessed held cleaning supplies and utensils. Above it, two wire shelves held containers of spices, oregano, thyme, red pepper, salt, cilantro, and more. Parts of the red floor tile between the oven and grill were faded from wear.

The deep fryer was a closed metal box crowded into a corner, and Gary didn't want to see what the inside of it looked like. There was no deep fryer at Radcliffe, but he had a good idea of how they worked and what they did, and he had a funny feeling this one would be quite nasty.

Given some time, he figured he could help clean the place up proper and organize things.

"So what do you think?" Rocky asked.

Gary pursed his lips. "It's a nice kitchen. Not bad."

Rocky wrinkled his eyes at him. "Is that your educated opinion?"

Gary flushed. "Well, I..."

"Just kidding." Rocky turned back to the door. "Come on, I'll show you the register."

Another move through the back door found them behind the counter. Rocky clanked a few buttons on the register and the drawer popped open with a muffled ding. It was an old register, a bulky thing Gary guessed was made somewhere around 1950.

"There usually isn't much cash in here." Rocky lifted the plastic tray that held a few tens, fives, and singles. "I like to keep the large bills under here. None there right now."

He closed the drawer and pointed to the keys at the top. Gary leaned in closer to get a better look and caught the faint but distinctive scent of peppermint booze on Rocky's breath.

"You ring up everything right here. It's pretty simple. I won't bother going through the prices with you since I forget them half the time anyway. You can use that list there, or just keep a menu open."

A penciled list on curling paper hung on the drawer below the register, out of plain view. At the top of the list was a burger for $3.00. Not bad.

"Not much else to tell you. The job is mostly flipping burgers when it gets crowded. Maybe you'll ring up a few people, hand out some menus. It's a pretty easy job, just a little too much for one man to handle some nights."

Gary nodded.

"The pay's minimum wage. I hope that's not a problem for you. There'll be some tips, but not much."

"That's all right," Gary said.

Rocky smiled. "Damn straight, then."

One of the front drawers was partially opened. A lance of adrenalin stabbed his heart. Inside was a gun.

Rocky must have noticed the look of horror on Gary's face because he slipped over and slid the drawer closed.

"Don't worry. Not that anybody's going to be needing that thing while on duty, but it's better to be safe than sorry, if you know what I mean. And in case you were wondering, I do have a license for it."

Gary stammered, unsure of what to say. "I wasn't wondering."

"Sure you were," Rocky said. "I saw that look in your eye. You're not going to take it and rob the place blind, are you?"

Gary flushed again, this time with dread. He didn't know why he felt that way. He just did. "I would never—"

"I'm just kidding. You don't seem like the cowboy type."

Another pang speared through Gary's heart. He thought of Butchy stuffed in his sock drawer. He did his best to hide the horror on his face.

"So," Rocky said. "When do you think you can start?"

This shocked Gary's attention back to Rocky. "I'm not exactly sure. I have to talk to Don and... my foster parents, I mean, about it. I think they'll say yes, so hopefully it will be soon."

Rocky patted him on the back and led him to the door. "Damn straight, then. I'll keep the sign up in the window just the same, but rest assured, the job is yours if you'd like it. You seem responsible enough."

Gary shook the man's hand and felt good about the comment. He wanted to be responsible now, and this was the perfect opportunity to show Don and Gail he was or could be, but mostly he wanted to show them he was worthy of their time.

He left Rocky's and the door dinged behind him. He headed straight back to Don and Gail's place, a new energy in his step, excited about the possibility of getting a new job.

Things Start Falling Into Place...

Gary came over the hill on Washington Street, approaching home, and the front door cracked open. Gail's head poked out. She met him at the front door with a proud, curious smile that made him want to blush again. When she saw him coming up the walk, she stepped out onto the porch and waved.

"How was your first day at school?" she asked him.

"Not too bad. I only got lost about four times. Maybe tomorrow it will only be three."

Gail held the door open and he went through, slipped off his shoes, and set them neatly in the corner with her pair of black pumps. The sharp scent of Pine Sol stung his nose, and he wondered if she spent the entire day cleaning.

"I want to hear all about your day," she began, wringing her hands together like an excited child. "But I want Don to hear all about it, too, so why don't we wait until dinner?"

Gary nodded. "All right."

"Do you have a lot of homework? I'm sure you've got a lot of catching up to do."

"A little. I guess I could work on some of it now before dinner is ready."

She gave him a rub on the shoulder. When she touched him, it warmed him. It made him feel pleasantly cared for.

"Good idea," she said. "We're having Mexican for dinner. I'm making tacos. Viva la food!" She snapped her fingers like a Flamenco dancer, twirled once on the balls of her feet, then darted toward the kitchen with soft laughter in her breath.

Gary watched her go, wondering if he could have picked anyone more perfect to live with. Maybe a bit cheesy at times in a way that made him smile, but perfect nonetheless.

"And I'm off." She went about grabbing a frozen slab of ground beef from the freezer, preparing the lettuce and shredded cheese.

Gary went to his room and unpacked his book bag. He didn't have an overwhelming amount of homework, but he did want to make sure he didn't fall behind early on, so the opportunity to study now was a welcomed one. He leaned back on his bed, propping his pillow behind his head so he could lean in the corner. That was always his favorite position to study or to read. The clanky metal bedrail at Radcliffe had always made it a somewhat uncomfortable position, but this new bed was made of Birchwood and the railings were much shorter. They didn't interfere with him at all. Now he could settle into his nook anytime he wanted to.

He wanted to tell Gail about his job opportunity, but she said she wanted to wait to talk to him at dinner, so Don could hear it all. He found that interesting. He wasn't sure how to read Don yet, and he supposed it was Gail's way of getting the two of them to open up a bit more to each other. Opening up wasn't an easy thing in Gary's mind.

It wasn't that Don was a bad person. Gary just couldn't understand why Gail made such an effort with him while Don loomed in the background, apparently displeased with the situation, waiting to pounce with a disciplinary speech. It made him think of the shadows lurking in corners and under doors at Radcliffe.

Gary knew Gail was the main instrument bringing him to this place in his life, but he couldn't understand what part Don had in it all. So far, it seemed like Don had no desire to keep a foster child. But that made no sense. How could Gary have been there if it was the case?

The real reason for the difficulty, Gary figured, was the similarity between himself and Don. They were quite a bit alike. They were two versions of the same type of person, quiet, maybe hard to get to know, preferred to be alone. Mrs. Sanchez always said this about him, and Radcliffe had a lot of guys this way. It made him wonder if Don ever spent time there himself. Maybe he'd find out someday.

He studied Algebra first, completed the assignment rather quickly, then settled down to read through *Mr. Flood's Party*. He read through the whole poem once, then read through it again more slowly, scrutinizing the words. Every other line rhymed, that was obvious, but when he read it out loud, under his breath, it didn't sound like it rhymed, which amazed him. It flowed naturally, beautifully.

Pretty cool. He wondered why the teachers at Radcliffe hadn't taught more of this stuff. He remembered reading *The Raven* by Edgar Allen Poe a few years back, but the tedious instructor hadn't made it sound nearly as interesting as he could have.

Mr. Flood's Party by E. A. Robinson was about some drunk guy heading back home to Tilbury Town, talking to himself about how much the town had changed. Gary read the last four lines again, and a sense of sadness crept up on him.

> *There was not much that was ahead of him,*
> *And there was nothing in the town below—*
> *Where strangers would have shut the many doors*
> *That many friends had opened long ago.*

He considered the old man in the poem. It reminded him of the pizza place owner. Rocky might be like him, some drunk guy with a sad look in his eye.

He closed the book when the wonderful aroma of simmering taco meat slid under his door. His stomach gave a few grumbles to let him know what it wanted, and he almost laughed at how loud the grumbles were.

Jeez! You'd think a tiger was stalking something in my belly. Or maybe it's an alien burster getting ready to break through my chest.

His imagination sprang to life and he leapt up from the bed, clutching his abdomen, hacking and twisting as if a gigantic creature were breaking through his skin, then fell back to the bed laughing.

When he looked up, he saw the clock on the dresser. Five minutes to six o'clock. He smiled again, thinking of Gail. The clock hadn't been there this morning, and he remembered her saying she was going to get him one soon. He sat up, checked the alarm setting. It read 6:00 am. She even set it for him.

What a nice lady. He readied to head downstairs to eat. *I guess I'm lucky.*

Gail was finishing up the tacos when he entered the kitchen. The table was again set perfectly, not a thing out of place, with even a chili pepper print potholder centered on the table to match the taco theme. Gail turned off the burner, set the pan on the potholder, then gave the basement door a soft rap.

"Time to eat," she said. "Have a seat."

Gary felt like a starving animal. The meat made his mouth water. Ever since he arrived at their home, he'd been hungrier than a lumberjack, but he didn't want to come off as a slob. He thought he should be gracious, thankful, and gentlemanly.

From the basement, Don emerged like a bear from a cave. When he saw Gary, he nodded officiously. "How's it going?"

"Great."

Gail plopped a couple of spoonfuls of seasoned ground beef into a taco shell and passed it to Gary.

"Fixin's are right there," she said.

And there were plenty. He piled on a spoonful of sour cream, followed by some salsa, lettuce, cheese, and finally a slice of something green that might have been avocado, although he wasn't sure because he'd never *had* avocado, but knew sometimes people ate them on tacos.

He took a small bite and the flavor exploded in his mouth. His stomach immediately begged for more. Before he knew it, he'd eaten three of them and then he remembered to breathe.

When he looked up, both Don and Gail were staring at him, clearly amused. "I'm sorry."

Gail waved her hand in the air. "Oh please. I'll bet Don used to eat like that when he was your age. Isn't that right?"

Don grinned. "Oh, I think I probably demolished a few tacos in my day."

Gary felt better. He started to reach for another taco shell, Gail tapped him on the hand.

"So?"

Gary froze. "What?"

"Aren't you going to tell us about your first day at school?"

She cocked her head, waiting. Don set his napkin down as well.

"It was a good day." He recounted some of the highlights of the day.

In reality, he couldn't recall any particularly interesting moments, but it was his first day and Gail was becoming increasingly interested in his telling the story, so he added all the detail he could think of.

When he was finished, she leaned her elbow on the table. "Did you meet any friends?"

"Oh, yeah." He realized he hadn't mentioned Stan. "There's a guy in my English class named Stan. He seems all right, I guess. He invited me to a bonfire party this Friday."

At mention of the word 'party,' Gail took her elbow off the table and shot a glance toward Don, who frowned.

"Party, huh?" Don said. "I'm not sure about you going to a party yet."

Gary set his hands in his lap. "I told him I wasn't sure if I'd be able to go, so it's no big deal. But I'd like to, I guess, if that's possible. But it's okay if you say no."

Don's face darkened. He took a deep breath, sighed. "You haven't even been here a week yet. I think you need more time to settle in before you start going to parties."

Gail handed Gary a plain taco. He started to eat it without putting anything on it.

"I understand." He took another bite.

They sat quietly and Gary felt vaguely guilty about the ensuing silence. He didn't like to be the reason for moments of silence like this, so he opted to bring up the job.

"I walked home today and went through the downtown." His muscles tightened with anticipation of their reaction. "There was a help wanted sign in a window." Both Don and Gail perked with interest. "It was Rocky's Pizzeria. He needs someone to help in the kitchen. He said it would be a few nights a week and maybe some weekends."

"That's wonderful news," Gail said.

"I'll just be bussing tables and maybe making burgers and pizzas on slow nights. If that's all right with you."

Gail said nothing, waiting for Don's reaction.

After a long pause, Don assented, although it wasn't without wariness. "All right. As long as it doesn't interfere with your schoolwork. If your grades aren't up to par, that'll be the first thing to go."

"Yes, sir."

They all readied for another taco, and when Gary reached for a new shell, Gail patted his hand.

"Good job." She winked at him with a twinkle of pride in her eye.

After dinner, Gary felt he could have easily stuffed another two or three tacos down, but it was clear Gail and Don were finished eating so he excused himself from the table.

He flopped back on the bed in his room and read through *Mr. Flood's Party* three more times, then cracked open his Algebra book one more time to make sure he understood most of the gibberish scrawled across the pages. It would be some tough going for him in the Math department, but he'd muddle through.

After an hour, his eyes started bugging out of his head. He rose, stretched his muscles out, and went to the window for a look-see. He parted the curtains a few inches and gazed out across the street toward the shy girl's house. Nothing. The house lay dark in the purple evening.

Standing there, his mind wrapped up in the darkness, a ripping sound from the hallway distracted him. He peeked through the door.

Nothing there, but the ripping sound grew more distinct.

He stepped into the hall and leaned on the oak banister, cocking his head slightly toward the noise. It came from the end of the hall, from the room there, through the closed door.

He went there, he leaned closer. The ripping sound was gone, but now he heard swishing, splashing, then the tink, tink, tink of a spoon on porcelain. Then silence.

He was about to turn away and head back to his room when he convinced himself to tap on the door. He knocked twice, softly.

Footsteps approached from the other side. Reflexively, he moved back a couple of steps. The door flung open. Gail stood there wearing a tattered, smeared smock.

"I didn't bother you, did I?" she asked.

"No, not at all." He tried subtly to peek into the room.

Gail stepped aside to give him a better view. "Come on in. I would have invited you in sooner, but I thought you were still studying."

He entered and noticed first the back of a large canvas on an easel. A small desk sat to the right side of the room covered with paints, papers, and dark colored jars with paintbrushes poking out at various angles. A dozen or so other paintings in different stages of completion lined the left wall along the floor.

"So what do you think?" she asked.

"Wow. You like to paint?"

Gail smirked and set her paintbrush into a small jar of water, swooshing it around. "I try to, but that's the fun part. You always get better as you go along. Want to see what I'm working on?"

He followed her around to the other side of the canvas. He was surprised to find a fairly accurate painting of a barn. She started with the outline of it in lighter yellow colors, then filled in the outline with a wash of browns. She had just started working on some of the detail with darker browns and oranges, dabbing with ripped cloth, when Gary interrupted her.

"That's really great," Gary said. "I didn't know you were a painter."

"There are a lot of things you don't know about me. Do you like to paint?"

He paused, but finally told her no. He thought for a moment he might tell her about some of the drawings he'd done at Radcliffe, but he didn't like the scenarios playing out in his head upon consideration. She'd probably ask him what sorts of things he liked to draw, and he'd inevitably wind up talking about his mother. That was how it was most times with adults.

Gail must have sensed his hesitation because she cocked her head and put her hand on his shoulder. Gary didn't know why, but her touch disarmed him.

"I guess I always wanted to," Gary said, "but I just never did. I probably can't."

Gail pulled her smock over her head and handed it to him. "Here."

She took her canvas down, set it against the wall with her other paintings, and opened the closet door. She removed a packet of shiny new canvas paper, ripped off a piece and clipped it to the bare easel.

"There you go," she said. "Go ahead and paint something."

Gary stared blankly at the empty canvas. "I don't know what to paint?"

"Just follow your heart, and I'm sure it will be beautiful."

He regarded the canvas dumbly, considering the size of it. It was small, yet so huge. He was more used to drawing on paper leaning over a desk, but his creative muscles murmured in his brain with hints of ideas, demanding to be heard.

Finally, an idea clicked. It was the poem, *Mr. Flood's Party*.

He dipped his brush into a dark brown paint Gail had prepared and began to create an outline first of a hill, then of a small tree at the base of the hill. He took a new brush up from the desk, dipped it into some dark orange paint and started working on the outline of an old man standing atop the hill. Finally, within a few minutes, his outlines were finished, complete with Old Eben's jug and the town below.

Gail stayed at his side the whole time, breathing softly, the warmth of her emanating. He glanced at her through the corner of his eye, wondering what she might be thinking of his new creation, feeling a mixture of excitement and discomfort. He couldn't tell which of those feelings was stronger at the moment.

She leaned in toward him and brought her hand up to her chin, considering the work.

"Holy cow," she said. "I have to admit that I thought you'd come up with something creative, but I really didn't expect it to be this good."

"Really?" Gary said. "Can you tell what it is?"

"Sure." She ran her hand over the lines he painted. "This is a man carrying a bottle or a jug of something, and there's a little town at the bottom of the hill. And that's a tree."

Gary blushed. "Wow."

"That really is a great start. I'd love to see more from you. You can use this office any time you want, whether I'm here or not."

"You don't mind?"

"I don't mind the slightest bit, and I encourage it."

He dipped his brush into another glob of burnt orange and spread it into the hill. Gail watched him.

"Painting has had an enormous impact on my life," she said. "I think it's important for people to have a creative outlet for expressing themselves. And sometimes for letting things out, if you know what I mean."

Heat swept against the inside of Gary's chest. Was she just trying to use painting to get him to start talking about things? Things he didn't want to talk about?

He supposed if he had to talk to someone about his mother and father, Gail would deserve the most to hear about it, considering how kind she had been to him so far. But it didn't change the fact that he wasn't ready to talk. He doubted he'd ever be. Besides, this felt sneaky.

When he first met Don and Gail in Radcliffe, she brought up some of the things that happened to him. She said she had, of course, read through his file and wanted to help him. If he ever wanted to talk about anything, she said, he could feel free to bend her ear a little. Gary nodded politely, but he doubted he'd ever talk to her about it. He didn't want to talk to anyone about it. What's done is done, he felt. Wasn't that the best philosophy? Why dredge up the past when you have the future to look forward to?

Gail put her hand on his shoulder, waiting perhaps for him to say something, but he instead set the brush down and removed the smock.

"Thanks a lot." He handed the smock to her. "I think I should probably do a little more studying before it gets too late."

Gail sighed so softly it was almost imperceptible. "That's okay. But I'm serious about wanting you to use this office as often as you want, as long as you're painting. Got it?"

He forced up the corners of his mouth into a smile, though it took some effort. "Got it."

He headed for the door. Gail cleared her throat and leaned against the wall.

"About Friday," she began. "I want you to go to that bonfire."

This took Gary completely by surprise. "Are you sure?"

"I think it's important for you to go. You've been cooped up for so long, I think it's time you socialized some, met some new friends your own age. What do you think?"

"What about Don?" Gary asked.

"I'll deal with him. You just plan on going to the bonfire. But I don't want you out late. Let's say 10:30? No, 11:00."

Any twinge of discomfort Gary felt before was now completely gone. "Thanks. I appreciate it. I mean, really."

When he left, bubbles of excitement percolated in his stomach, not only for the bonfire, but for the painting he had begun.

At just after 9:30, the urge to paint crawled into Gary's head and gnawed at him like termites at his sawdust brain. They wouldn't let up. He couldn't concentrate on much else and couldn't keep his mind from wandering back to the beginning of his depiction of Old Eben Flood. Rather than dwell on it, he decided to take Gail up on her offer to use the office whenever he wanted to, just as long as he was painting. Gail and Don gave him a curfew of 10:00, so he didn't think they would mind it so much if he got in a little time at the easel.

He pulled a smock from a bundle piled into a pink plastic clothing basket from the office closet. The paints were stashed away and he didn't want to mess up the recently neatened room so he only removed the orange and brown tubes from their slot in the desk drawer. He squirted a dab of each onto the canvas and returned the tubes to their resting places. Methodically, he separated each dab into two more globs and mixed two of them together, forming a third blend of orangey—brown.

While he spread it out to give some depth to his hill, he stole glances at Gail's paintings lining the floor along the wall. They were perfect teaching tools. Some of her paintings held more detail than others, each in various stages of completion. He felt particularly drawn to an image of a butterfly on a cornflower she had sketched out and begun to paint, using only the lightest yellows and oranges to gather up the outline of the insect and the surrounding background. Another picture used darker greens and blues within the leaves, and she had begun to add subtle details by dabbing with the brush, but had never finished.

Experimenting, he dabbed the tip of the brush the same way at the edge of the hill around Mr. Flood's feet, then scraped upward with a flick of his wrist. The paint dimpled along the canvas grains in an interesting effect. It pleased him.

His drawing teacher at Radcliffe had told the class about oil painting, about how the oils formed a rich blend of detail if done properly, much like the artist's pen, yet bolder and freer. There wasn't any money for paints at Radcliffe, so he'd never been able to experience anything like this. He knew he wasn't going to produce a new and perfect painting overnight, but patience was never a problem for him. He'd take all the time he needed. It surprised him how much he enjoyed working with the paints, focusing on the minute details projected from his mind's eye.

He chastised himself now for throwing away the drawings he had done for art class. He would have liked to have shown them to Gail, get her reaction, see what she thought of his work. Probably not the one of his mother, which would most likely open up a can of conversational worms he didn't want to swallow, but he could have shown her the older ones. He hoped she would have liked them.

Forget about it.

At least he'd have something new to show her. He liked the way she seemed impressed with his start of the painting. When she complimented him and touched him on the shoulder on seeing his initial work, it made him realize she saw something in him as well, something worthy of complimenting.

He told himself he wouldn't disappoint her. At least, not with painting, anyway.

CHAPTER 7

But the Past Can Often Haunt You

The day of the bonfire, Gary got out of bed with a bit more energy than the previous days. In the time he'd been with Don and Gail, his room had taken on a more 'lived in' look, so he straightened up before readying for school. He hadn't lost the cleanliness and orderliness instilled in him over the years, but Gail had purchased so many clothes for him, he didn't know what to do with them all.

The closet was too small to hold all of the hanging clothes along with the other storage they placed inside, including an old vacuum cleaner, several cardboard boxes marked 'kitchen' in black marker, and an old mahogany dresser that had been stripped and looked ready for a new staining. Other items lay jammed in the back behind the boxes, but it was too dark for Gary to go that far in, and he wasn't very curious to find out what they were. The entire room now serving as his bedroom must have been a convenient storage place for castaway items.

His dresser drawers jutted out from stuffing so many new clothes inside, most of them still in their plastic wrappers, along with underwear and socks galore. Most of the shirts were the same style as the one he wore the first day to school, and it gave him some cause for laughter. Gail had the strangest fashion sense, especially for someone his age, but if this was the only thing he had to complain about where she was concerned, he was glad.

He showered and dressed before eating a couple of bowls of corn flakes. When he was done, he gathered up his books, slung his bag over his shoulder, and headed for the bus stop to stand with the students he'd come to know as the 'Gloom Gang.' Not once had he caught a smile on any of their faces, except when two guys about a year older than he was went back and forth about some girl one of them had supposedly nailed the week before. It was nothing but posturing, completely obvious to him when he figured in the dork factor, but he ignored it like he always did with that sort of thing.

Zero hour whizzed by with Mr. Reynolds after he carted out several rows of badminton nets. The students had to set them up by spacing out the weighted poles and stretching the nets taut across them. When they were finished, each paired up with an opponent and played to ten points. The winner went to the next net up, and the loser went back one.

Gary fought all the way to second net and would have gone to the first if he hadn't lost a close game to a lanky yellow-haired guy. He didn't mind losing since the guy had a hell of a long reach.

And all the while he felt Mr. Reynolds' eyes on him, watching for something. This time, however, he didn't feel as uncomfortable as he did earlier in the week. It might be Mr. Reynolds was looking out for him, and he wasn't sure how to feel about it. No one ever looked out for him—except for his old roommate, Hector, but it wasn't the same thing. There was Mrs. Sanchez, but they never developed the rapport she fought for. And there was his mother. Now he had two people, Mr. Reynolds and Gail, three if you counted Don, and it produced a mixed bag of reassurance and anxiety. In time he'd grow used to it, maybe even like it. Who knew? It was too early to tell.

In English class, Stan slapped him on the shoulder before they headed in. Today, Stan wore a jean jacket with faded 'Korn' patches sewn prominently on the sleeves. His hair lay slicked back with a thick gel that should have been rubbed in a bit more, forcing sharp points into the strands.

"You ready for a little bonfirin' tonight? Gonna be a blast. Gettin' busy tonight!"

Gary nodded. "I'll be there."

"Oh yeah!" Stan cried, exuberant, but then he lowered his voice an octave. "I'll introduce you around."

Students held the bonfire near the Winsbury Forest Preserve every year around the same time. They called it, creatively enough, 'The Bonfire Pit' because some of the early town founders carved out a small section of the forest preserve near the parking lot for just such a thing. It wasn't a large area, but wide enough to accommodate a few hundred people if packed in resourcefully.

Gary threw on a light gray t-shirt and a blue jacket. He felt nervous. Walking into a crowd of strangers wasn't so hard, but talking and socializing was a different story.

Before he left, Don stopped him at the door. "Let's make sure you stay out of trouble tonight, all right?" His tone wasn't quite so stern this time.

Gail leaned against the wall behind Don. She winked over his shoulder, and Gary knew everything would be all right with his leaving for a while.

He ducked through the backyard and around the neighbor's fence before reaching the street. Above him, the streetlight glowed dourly against the darkening sky. It would be completely dark in a half hour or so. Perfect for a bonfire.

Ahead of him stretched a long baseball field, fronted by a diamond to the right. The dirt on the diamond had been kicked up around the base-runner paths which where pocked with deep ruts. The edge of the left field ended with a short, rusted metal fence serving as the beginning of a farmer's field. Low strands of green vegetation poked up just past the fence, but Gary couldn't tell what the farmer was growing.

Past right field, the ground sloped upward, leading to a pavilion surrounded by a dozen and a half picnic tables, some of them stacked against the steel girder legs supporting the fading orange top.

Gary headed through the field toward it, gliding his feet through the thick blades of grass, decapitating dandelions when he saw them. At the pavilion, he paused and leaned against one of the legs, took a deep breath of air. He stood surrounded by trees and fields with only a few houses huddled off to his right and a children's playground in front of him. The freshness of the town drew him in. The serenity of dusk absorbed him.

At that moment, he felt entirely at ease. He didn't feel the need to hurry to the bonfire. He still wanted to go, but the moment was so new and overwhelming, he could only revel in it. Giddiness pulsed through him. He planted himself on the nearest picnic bench, leaned his elbows back, and stretched his legs out in front of him. Night fell too quickly.

Over the trees, the half moon brightened a thin patch of hammer clouds. A porch light to his far right flickered briefly, brightened, then bled away into the darkness. Crickets hummed along the tree line.

It was good.

When it was almost dark, he left the bench, stretched his legs, and headed toward the trees until he found the trail that would lead him to the heart of the Forest Preserve. The trail began wide at the mouth and lay filled with water at the midsection. Dirt bike ruts, dug deep from spinning tires, led from the grass along the beginning of the trail.

The trees stood thin and scraggly at the base of the path, but thickened as he headed deeper into the woods. The night swarmed him, but far ahead, through the shadows, bits of light poked through like a kaleidoscope, making the leaves twinkle. The smell of the bonfire met him, and he knew he was close.

Finally, he found the end of the trail and exited into a squat length of grass that quickly thinned into a long patch of gravel. Ahead, several cars were parked and two others were entering the lot from the right. Around the bend, the flame of the bonfire flickered, sparkling orange and yellow in the distance.

It took him another five minutes to get there, and when he finally drew in close enough, he stood on the outskirts for a while, hands thrust into his pockets, staring at the flames. It stood up nearly three feet high, not the biggest fire, but just getting going.

Fifty or sixty students had already gathered around it, congregated in small groups of five or six, talking and laughing, drinking out of red plastic cups. Gary searched around for Stan but didn't see him yet. He didn't know anyone else, although it didn't bother him. He still liked to be alone, and being alone in a crowd was something he'd grown accustomed to long ago.

He did recognize the lanky yellow-haired guy from gym class. Their eyes met once when Gary first arrived, but the guy didn't acknowledge it, which suited Gary fine. He didn't seem the overly friendly type, and rarely made eye contact with anyone, which wasn't a surprise.

He circled the fire, weaving in and out of the groups of students. Sitting along the trees were several red and blue coolers, one of them marked 'Jungle Juice' with a black marker. Someone had attempted to cover it with a powder blue blanket, but didn't do a very good job of it.

Someone tapped his shoulder and he spun around to find Stan standing there, quirky smile broadened across his thin face, hair poking in all directions. Two guys stood behind him and they were even smaller than Stan. They looked to Gary like they could even be in eighth grade, but he doubted it. Stan clutched a can of beer in his right hand and waved it around as he spoke.

"Gary, hey! Glad you made it, man. Want a beer?"

He lifted the left side of his jacket to proudly reveal an interior pocket filled with cans of Miller Lite, like a seedy street corner salesman showing off stolen necklaces.

"No thanks," Gary said. He'd never actually had a beer before, but he had no desire to try it. He saw what it did to his father, and he didn't want to tick off Don and Gail.

Stan's face dipped with mild displeasure. "Come on, it's drugs. Everybody's doing it."

Gary scowled, and Stan slapped him on the shoulder. "I'm just kidding, man. I think they got Coke around here somewhere. How about that?"

Stan slammed the remainder of his beer and snatched another out of his jacket. The two students behind him stared at Gary with unblinking eyes.

"Coke is cool."

Stan led him toward the 'Jungle Juice' cooler, reached behind it, and came up with a can of Diet Sprite.

"Looks like this is all they got." He handed it to Gary.

Gary took it. Dirt grit rubbed into his hand. Stan ambled around a curve of trees and returned with a red cup.

"Here you go. Drink up."

Gary poured the drink into the cup and tossed the can behind the coolers.

"Not much of a drinker, huh?" Stan said.

Gary sipped from the cup and grimaced. It was warm and some of the dirt had fallen into it. The sandy grit rubbed along his front teeth. "I've only been here a week," he said. "I'm trying to stay out of trouble."

"Ah." Stan raised his beer in a mock salute. "Foster parents. Got to stay good for the Ps. FPs in your case, eh?"

Stan chuckled at his own wit, and Gary laughed along with him. If he were in Radcliffe, he didn't think he'd like a guy like Stan, always trying to sound and act like he was 'the Man,' trying to be cooler and funnier than he was. Gary could tell somehow that behind the front, Stan was a good guy.

"So do you live close?" Stan asked.

Gary motioned toward the path he'd taken to get here. "Not far. It's on Washington, that big white house with the white fence."

"Oh yeah. I've seen it, I think. It's down near the train tracks."

"Yeah, close."

Gary took another sip and watched the two younger students over the edge of his cup. They still stared at him with searching, diffident eyes.

"So what are your names?" Gary asked them.

The first one had a shock of Howdy Doody red hair and wore pop-bottle thick glasses. He cleared his throat and spoke up first. "I'm Richie," he said so quietly Gary had to cock his head to hear him.

The other student was squat with a round face and a terrible case of acne. "Pete."

"Gary." He shook their hands and they immediately poked their hands into their pockets afterward.

Gary figured them for freshmen, which didn't matter much to him. He understood how things were supposed to work in high school, even though this was his first experience with a real high school. He was a sophomore so he was only supposed to hang out with other sophomores, unless he hung around with juniors or seniors, in which case he'd be considered one of the 'in' crowd. But here was Stan, hanging out with freshmen, which he didn't think would help Stan's reputation any, and probably wouldn't even help the freshmen either, now that he thought about it.

But Gary didn't care much for high school politics or how things were 'supposed' to work. He'd had enough of social politics in Radcliffe. He wasn't going to worry about it anymore, or let cliques and clubs control him. At least, that was the plan.

They all walked around the fire, sipping their drinks, when Stan stopped and thrust his hand to his heart, clutching his chest.

"Holy shit!" he said.

Gary paused. "What?"

"Sally Kendrickson is here," he said. "Ooh! She's got friends."

The freshmen hemmed and hawed, rolling their voices in a terrible attempt to sound older than they were, but Gary could have sworn he saw the redheaded guy blush. He followed their line of sight to a tall blonde in the middle of a small entourage. From a distance, she looked close to six feet tall. She could easily have been a model, as could half her friends. A thin, white veil of a jacket draped around her and her blonde hair flowed down in thick curls along her shoulders.

"Man, I got a thing for her," Stan said. "A 'big' thing, if you know what I mean." He nudged Gary with his elbow.

Gary grinned. It was amusing, listening to Stan carry on. "What do you think you'd do with something like that?"

Stan nudged the chubby kid with his elbow and winked. "You see that? He's testing me. Good one!"

Gary laughed again and they continued around the fire to another cooler. Stan, with all the stealth of a cat hunting, snuck up to the cooler, reached in, and snatched out a bottle of Pete's Wicked Ale. He shoved it into his pocket and rejoined the group.

"I only brought a six pack," he said. "I have to keep the situation flowing."

Richie, seeing Stan's success, and probably wanting to be noticed like his older buddy, approached the same cooler. He looked around with an obvious awkwardness and popped open the lid. Stan nudged Gary and laughed.

"That kid's got to loosen up a little, don't you think?"

Gary watched on with interest. Richie reached in for a beer, but a wide Asian kid wearing sweatpants and bowling shoes came out of nowhere and slammed the cooler lid down.

"What the hell you looking for?"

Richie fumbled backwards and fell on his ass. He skittered up and ran toward them then, stumbling the whole way, looking like a refugee from Geek Television. The Asian kid didn't follow, which gave Gary a mild relief. He didn't want to deal with any confrontations here, or in Winsbury at all for that matter.

They hurried away anyway, though, just in case, and when they felt they were at a sufficiently safe distance, stopped to catch their breath.

"What the hell do you call that, Mr. Suave?" Stan said. "Real smooth, ass-wipe."

Richie shrugged and blushed some more, practically matching his red hair.

Gary leaned against a tree and took another sip of his Sprite. He wanted it to last. He gazed out across the fire and saw the girl who lived across the street from him. She stood just outside of the circle of light cast by the glow of the bonfire, off to the left of Sally Kendrickson and her beautiful following. She shifted uncomfortably and watched the fire, alone.

"Who's that?" Gary motioned to her with his chin.

"Who?"

"That girl over there," Gary said. "The one standing there alone with the dark hair."

Stan craned his neck, fighting to look past Sally Kendrickson. "Her? I don't know her name, but she's a little off, I think. I don't see her around much. She's pretty quiet. Off, though."

"Off?"

"Yeah, you know, *off.*"

Whatever that meant. Gary figured if someone was quiet and didn't really say much, it automatically made them 'off' in a place like Winsbury. Under those criteria, he'd be considered pretty 'off' in no time at all, then.

"Hey, tell me about Radcliffe," Stan said.

The two freshmen perked up with interest and Gary shifted his feet, uncomfortable. He didn't like the way they scrutinized him now, like he was so different from them, a bug on a pin.

"It wasn't a big deal." A blip of heat flared in Gary's chest. "Not really."

"Come on," Stan pressed. "Is everyone in there a bad ass, or what?"

Gary smirked. "Do I look like I'm some kind of bad ass?"

The question wasn't meant to be a real question, but Stan considered it carefully. "It's hard to tell with you. You're quiet, but so was Buford Pusser, you know, the 'Walking Tall' guy? Carry a big stick? Bruce Lee was quiet too, right?"

Gary shook his head and sipped his drink. He didn't understand the conversation.

"How about me? Do I look like a bad ass or what?" Stan flexed his arms and spun in a slow circle for inspection.

Gary didn't mean to, but he let a snort escape him. "I think we both need some work."

The freshmen chuckled. Stan grimaced. Gary felt bad. He didn't realize until that moment Stan was being serious with the whole 'bad ass' thing. He probably wanted to exude a tough guy image, especially in front of his friends, but Gary had a hard time playing that game, for himself or anyone else.

"I guess you look pretty tough," Gary corrected and Stan perked up. "Hey, I'm going to talk to that girl over there."

Stan squared off toward the girls and shook with excitement. "You're going to talk to Sally Kendrickson?"

"No, that one behind her." Gary rolled his eyes when Stan didn't seem to see her. "The *off* one."

"Oh her," Stan said. "That's cool. Hey, maybe she's not so off. What do I know?"

Gary left them there with their beers and headed in her direction. She hadn't moved in a long time, but stood gazing into the fire, flames dancing in her eyes, reflecting melancholy.

A small breeze drew up, and the girl tossed her head, flicking a wisp of hair from her eyes. Gary wondered what he might say to her, how he might strike up a conversation in a way that didn't make him look awkward. Strangely, though, he thought he would be more nervous than he was.

Half way to her, however, a bright light suddenly flashed through the group, coming from the edge of the Forest Preserve. Police cherries sprang to life and a mind numbing siren squawked through the darkness. It rattled Gary's bones.

A voice from a distant PA boomed: *"Party's over!"*

Students scattered like ashes thrown from the fire, many of them leaping into the forest, escaping into the darkness. The girl Gary approached sprang along with them, straight toward the trail he had taken here, finally disappearing in the rush.

Behind him, Stan's voice cried out an octave higher than Gary heard before. "Shit, man! They're early this time."

Then Stan and his two young buddies rushed off in the opposite direction, shedding beers as they went, tripping over their own feet.

Gary froze. His initial instinct was to sprint toward the trail along with the other students, but he saw some of the police running through the darkness toward them and he knew if they caught him running, it wouldn't look good for him. Besides, he wasn't drinking anything but Sprite, so he had nothing to worry about.

He started for the main road, nonchalant, hoping he was doing the right thing by not taking off with everyone else. From out of the darkness, one of the cops emerged like a dim wraith, tapping the walkie-talkie attached to his belt. When he saw Gary, he altered his path and headed straight for him.

Gary glanced at the man, then finally stopped when he knew a confrontation was inevitable.

"Where you going?" the cop said.

Gary faced him and took a sip from his cup. The cop wore a nametag that read Vedish. He was a robust man with a coarse, brutal face. His legs were too short for his body and his midsection a bit too puffy for his uniform. The gleam in his eye told Gary he enjoyed the business of busting up teenage parties.

"Just heading back home," Gary said.

Officer Vedish stopped a little too close for comfort, set his thumbs in his belt, and leered down at Gary's cup.

"What's in the cup?"

"Sprite."

"Sure it is." The cop held out his hand for Gary to hand over the drink.

"It is." He handed the cup over.

Officer Vedish sniffed it once then took it away from his nose. "There's booze in here."

Gary remained unfazed. "There's no booze in there. Sniff it again."

In a slow, overly dramatic movement, Officer Vedish turned the cup upside down, letting the warm Sprite spill onto the ground. When it was empty, he crumpled the plastic and dropped it to the ground. Not once did his eyes leave Gary's.

"I said there's booze in there."

Flames flared in Gary's chest, rising with the anger, but he was also afraid. He knew what the cop was doing. He wished he had run away with the others now.

"I said there was no booze."

"Are you calling me a liar?"

The heat in Gary's chest spread into his gut and threatened to pour through his fingers. It crawled up his throat and into his mouth, which was a big part of the reason he'd had so much trouble in Radcliffe.

"Hell, yeah," he said. "If there's another word for it, you can have that one, but I don't drink."

"What's your name?"

"Gary Sanderson."

Vedish snorted. "Ahh. I get it. I know who you are, kid. They told us you were coming. That's some pretty bad shit you did."

Gary's face flushed and some of the heat subsided, replaced by a new, more intense fear.

"This is a joke, right?"

Vedish continued. "Yeah, a Radcliffe boy. You Radcliffe boys think you're pretty rough and tumble. I think I might have to take you in."

Take you in. Those words rammed into Gary's brain like a hot poker and he immediately regretted the smart-ass remarks, everything he'd said, coming to the bonfire, the whole stupid, doomed-from-the-start evening. He could already picture Don's fingers wagging in disappointment, and Gail's eyes regarding him differently, the smoothness and pride drained completely away from her.

"Look," Gary began. "I'm not trying to cause any trouble. I was invited to this bonfire, and I swear there wasn't any liquor in the glass. I don't drink. Really. I didn't even know there was going to be booze."

Officer Vedish remained unmoved, and even crooked the corner of his mouth with contempt. "Just shut up and get in the car."

"Please," Gary started. "I can't get into any trouble. Please."

Vedish's mouth crooked a little more. "I said get in the car."

Gary drew his eyes away and knew there was nothing left he could do.

"I don't believe this." He headed toward the police car.

As Officer Vedish pulled away from the Forest Preserve, Gary decided he wasn't going to say anything. He would answer the cop's questions with the briefest of responses. Keep it short and simple, dull the impact of the blow. He might have argued with the cop, asked to be let go, but it wouldn't do any good. Even if he begged, it wouldn't do any good. He knew cops like this in Radcliffe. It never did any good to argue with them. They got off on it. They were the unreasonable types, and they loved to flex their authority like an extra pair of muscles. They practically wanted you to fight, in which case they could justify knocking you down a little, or sometimes they wanted you to break down, to make you cry a little maybe, in which case they called you a 'snatch' or a 'pussy' and proceeded to knock you down a little more.

"What's your name again?" the cop asked.

"I thought you said you knew me." He bit his tongue. Stupid move.

"Just give me the name."

"Gary Sanderson."

Officer Vedish tapped a key on his CB and it squawked to life. "Claudine," he said. "Can you send me some info on that new Radcliffe boy we got in town? The name is Gary Sanderson."

A few moments later, a tiny screen flickered to life and the cop pulled the car over to the side of the road. He read the screen and clicked his teeth. It sounded like a stone rattling in his mouth.

"Yeah, that's some pretty bad shit you did," he said. "You killed your daddy, huh? Damn."

Heat bubbled in Gary's chest again. He caught the unmistakable look of amusement in the cop's eyes reflected in the rearview mirror. They looked like Karge's eyes, or Big Ben's, an animal toying with its prey.

"So how did it feel, watching your daddy go down like that? What did he do?"

Gary attempted to swallow back fire and failed. *"Fuck you."*

Vedish slammed his elbow back into the mesh separating him from Gary.

"You got a serious attitude, kid." He bit back fire of his own. "You're lucky I got a soft spot. Where do you live?"

Gary gritted his teeth, bit his lip, tasted blood. His heart thrust itself against the front of his chest. "It's on Washington."

With that, the cop sped off toward town.

A block before the Morgans' driveway, Officer Vedish flipped on the cherries and slowed down, coasting up to the house. The man's eyes mocked him in the mirror, waiting for a reaction.

He knew what the man wanted. He wanted embarrassment. He wanted to watch the kid squirm a while before delivering him to his foster parents, to rub Gary's face in his past. He wanted the entire neighborhood to know Gary Sanderson was in trouble.

He stopped in front of the house at 9:30 p.m. and waited several minutes with the lights flashing, pretending to read the flickering computer screen, taking his time with his report. Soon, neighbors filtered onto their porches to investigate the commotion. The old lady next door emerged with curlers in her hair, the same burning embers in her eyes. A scowling woman from across the road crossed her arms with steadied defiance.

And finally, Don and Gail emerged from their own home, faces dual masks of concern and worry. Don waved Gail back and came into the center of the yard, as if approaching a sleeping bear. When he caught a glimpse of Gary's face in the back of the squad car, he shed the worry and shook his head with exasperated contempt.

Officer Vedish, mission accomplished, turned off the lights and unlocked the door. "Get out."

Gary hopped out and closed the door behind him.

"What happened?" Don asked, not even trying to mask his disappointment.

Officer Vedish sauntered around the car and leaned on the hood. "I found Gary here at the bonfire party. He had a cup with alcohol in it."

Don's gaze shifted from the cop to Gary now, eyes heavy with disappointment. "Get in the house."

Gary thrust his hands into his pockets. "Don, I wasn't drinking. I didn't even know there was going to be booze there. Why don't you tell this cop to let me take a breathalyzer?"

"Just shut up and get in the house. Now."

Gary bit his lip. Officer Vedish had won the battle. He hadn't taken Gary into the station, but he accomplished what he really wanted—to get him into some trouble.

Sure, teach me a lesson, Gary thought.

At the door, Gail started to say something to Gary but Don glared at her.

"Just let him go to his room," Don said, and Gail pulled her words back.

She stepped aside and let him go.

"Thank you, officer," Don said. "He won't be causing any more trouble tonight. We promise."

Through his window, Gary watched the cop head off down the street. The neighbors filtered back into their homes, domestic disturbance finally over.

From across the street, Gary saw the girl watching through her window. Her father stood behind her and he closed the curtain for the night.

Gary waited anxiously for Don or Gail to come up. He didn't know how long it would take for them to get there, but he felt the confrontation coming on. It was something he didn't want to happen, but knew was inevitable. It was his word against a cop's, and that was the problem. Even though the cop was a first-class Prick with a capital 'P,' his foster parents didn't know it. They weren't sitting in the back of the squad car with him, or standing in the field at the bonfire with him, watching him pour the evidence out all over the ground with a smug sneer on his face. And he was still a Juvie Boy as far as they were concerned, wasn't he, which knocked his credibility down to dirt level when it came to opposing a cop.

The feeling of a hot poker rose in his throat again just thinking about it, but he bit it back. How was he going to make Don and Gail believe him, when even in his own mind, he was nothing more than a screwed up kid from Radcliffe?

Soon, a set of heavy footsteps trudged up the stairs, and one loud knock thumped the outside of the door. Don came in then, nearly throwing the door open into the wall. Gary stood in the center of the room, waiting.

"Downstairs," Don demanded, his eyes bulging, his lips pressed firmly together like a man desperately trying to control his temper.

Gary followed him down to the living room where Gail waited on the gray loveseat. She held a hook rug in her lap though she wasn't working on it. A small box of rug thread in various colors sat beside her, along with a bright print of a canary hovering near a tree.

Don paced the floor. "What the hell was that about? We trusted you to go to that party, and look what happened."

Gary sat on the leather recliner near the window at the far edge of the seat. Behind him, the antique grandfather clock ticked in steady rhythm. Don's words bit him like a snake. It wasn't Don who had trusted him, allowed him to go to the party. It was Gail's decision, but that didn't make things any better.

"I know this looks bad, but I swear to God I wasn't drinking. I had a red cup, but it had Sprite in it. Really."

"That cop said he smelled alcohol in it," Don said. "Besides, if you knew there was booze at the party, you should have left immediately."

Gary paused. What Don said was true. If he'd known any better, and he did, he should have taken off at the first sign of liquor. He was an idiot for even staying. He side-glanced at Gail, searching for her reaction, but found none. She sat sullen, giving nothing away.

"I know," Gary said. "But that cop had it in for me, though. He said he knew I was a Radcliffe boy."

Don threw his hands up. "Jesus, here we go. Is this how we're going to start things off? We thought we'd give you an opportunity to change, but now I don't know if that's possible. If this is how it's going to be, you'll be back at Radcliff in no time, or worse."

The mention of returning to Radcliffe was like a slingshot to Gary's brain. He was a well of emotions now—anger, fear, despair. The cop screwed him good on this one, just like he'd intended, and Gary felt the urge to scream. Not at Gail and Don, but at the situation, hopeless as it was.

He chided himself for even being in the situation in the first place. *Things will be this way for a while,* he supposed. Cops and other adults would be looking for ways for him to screw up, all because of Radcliffe. He had to step wisely if he was going to stay out of trouble. He would have to work harder at it than most people. It was a tough place to be, but it was what it was.

"Can I ask you one question?" Gail said then.

Gary's eyes went to her, pleading, praying she wasn't overly upset with him.

"Are you telling the truth about the alcohol?" she asked. "You weren't drinking?"

Gary shook his head. "I swear."

"But you knew about it. You knew it was there."

He sighed. "Yes. I saw people drinking, but I didn't take any."

Gail paused for only a second then set her hook rug to the side. "Then I believe you. Why don't you go on upstairs."

He did. He felt the dark anger circling over Don like a cloud of black locusts, buzzing, buzzing, waiting to explode. This was something his foster parents were going to have to discuss alone, and it made him sick to come between them this way. He'd only been there a short time and look at the pain he'd caused already.

He wasn't even angry with the cop anymore. He was angry with himself.

Gary shut the door behind him. The pale glow from the streetlight cast just enough light through his window to illuminate the room with a soft haze. It was pleasant, like turning down the lights to watch a movie on television.

He wasn't ready for bed yet, but he was tired; tired in his bones, tired of bonfires and cops. Gail believed him, sure, but Don didn't, and that was a serious problem. He understood trust had to be earned over time, but what could he do against a cop who seemed to have it in for him? And for no apparent reason?

Downstairs, Don and Gail talked, their voices a low murmur. About him, no doubt. At least they weren't yelling, he didn't know if he could take fighting between them. It reminded him too much of his own parents.

It made his lungs burn, so he breathed in slowly, steadily, trying to relax, but it didn't help very much. If he cleared his mind and thought 'discipline' like Morpheus in *The Matrix*, maybe the burn might dwindle, but he found he wasn't very good at the whole Zen concentration thing. Actually, it seemed to make things worse.

With his eyes closed, he first visualized the mocking face of Officer Vedish hovering in the dark, laughing, his cruel mouth curled into a fetid smile. Then the face transformed into Don's, glaring through cold eyes, scowling, a mask of contempt and disappointment. Finally, it became his father's face, cocky and devastating. *"What are you going to do with that gun, you little shit?"*

"Forget this shit." He went to his sock drawer. He reached in, fished out Butchy, and set him on top of the dresser.

"What's going on, Butchy?" he asked the toy. "Why am I so freakin' ticked off? I can't stand this."

Raw anger flared, powerful, hormonal.

Butchy gawked at him. Gary spun him in his hands. The miniature gun scratched at his fingers.

"What am I going to do about Don? Do you think he'll ever trust me?"

He stared at the plastic cowboy figurine and didn't like what he saw. He saw himself rocking in his own bedroom when he was twelve, black eye searing with pain, listening to his parents screaming at each other through the floor vent. That day he saw Butchy sitting in front of him, asking him: *"What kind of cowboy do you want to be?"*

"But maybe you're right," he said. "A good cowboy would know he's got to tough it out, right?"

He buried Butchy back in his drawer and leaned against the window, the glass chilled his forehead. Things would be all right. Anything, even this, was better than a good day at Radcliffe.

Then, as if in response, he caught a glimpse of the girl. The light in her room flickered on, and her curtains lay parted. She sat at the small desk, looking toward him. Her hand came part way up to her chest in a stilted wave and Gary's heart leapt. He waved back. Then, shyly, she turned her head down and closed the curtains. Gary did the same.

He fell back onto his bed, unable to stop himself from smiling now. *Things are looking better already*, he thought. How quickly and easily a single smile from a girl could turn things around.

CHAPTER 8

Friends in Strange Places

At precisely 12:11 a.m., something terrible happened to Gary: hunger pains. He lay in bed asleep, dreaming of meatloaf - only in the dream, the meatloaf stood four feet tall and covered the entire length of the kitchen. Curls of steam licked the ceiling, onion and carrot bits, normally tiny, were the size of basketballs and poked out through the edges of the loaf. The smell was maddening. So maddening that as he gazed at it, sitting there in the dream world kitchen and practically calling his name, his stomach lurched with a massive growl that shook him awake.

He leaned up on his elbow, disoriented, until his stomach growled again, and he remembered the dream.

"Man!"

He remembered the tinfoil wrapped leftovers in the refrigerator, and wondered if meatloaf was as good cold as it was warm. He didn't mind sneaking down to grab some of it, but he didn't want to risk popping it into the microwave and waking either Don or Gail.

He slipped out of bed and crept down the stairs, the fabric of the carpet feeling rough between his toes. At the bottom, his stomach lurched and let out another resounding growl. He gripped it with both hands to stifle it, pressing his belly inward. It felt loud enough to wake the whole neighborhood. *"Shut up."*

When the last growl subsided, he slunk around the corner and into the kitchen, slipped open the refrigerator door, and retrieved that last piece of meatloaf. He started to unwrap it, but the crinkling of the foil made too much noise, so he cupped it in his hand and headed back toward the stairs.

As he passed Don and Gail's bedroom, their voices made him pause. He didn't like what he heard.

"Damn it, Gail," Don said. "I told you this was going to happen. We shouldn't have to put up with this shit."

"He said he wasn't drinking," Gail said. Her voice was calmer, reasoning.

"He knew there was booze there. He should have left."

"You're right, yes, but that makes me even more proud of him. There was alcohol all over the place, I'm sure, and he still didn't drink."

Don blared back. "The drinking isn't the point. It was his attitude. He had no respect for that cop."

"You're blowing this out of proportion."

Gary cocked his ear toward the door, realizing he shouldn't be there doing what he was doing, but unable to help it.

"You can't reform a kid like Gary," Don said. "He's too old now. Believe me, I know."

"You don't know anything about what he's gone through," Gail defended. "You have to give him a chance."

"What the hell do you know?" Don's voice was angry, derisive.

There came a long pause, but Gary waited. The conversation wasn't over yet, something remained. He felt it like electricity building up.

Finally, Gail spoke. "*Excuse me?* What do *I* know? How can you even ask me that question? You know exactly what I've been through. Damn it."

Don's voice was softer, after another long pause. "I'm sorry. I'm just worried about this. I know you want to help him, but I'm afraid of what will happen to you if it blows up in your face. In our faces, I mean."

"I'll be fine. We'll be fine. It's not going to blow up in anyone's face. I'll handle it. It would be nice to have a little help, though."

"I know," Don said. "I'm sorry. Seriously."

Gary slipped away from the door, but he didn't head to the stairs. Instead, he went back to the kitchen and returned the meatloaf to the middle shelf of the refrigerator. He wasn't hungry anymore, far from it, and there wasn't a single peep from his stomach the remainder of the night.

Gary shut the bedroom door behind him and went to the window. He doubted he'd see the girl across the street, but if he at least caught a glimpse of her, things might be better. He'd feel better if she would wave one more time, but there was nothing. Her room was dark and still.

The streetlight sputtered once and he looked up, but then it steadied again, casting an ever present glow. He didn't feel tired. No way he could sleep. The conversation downstairs rung in his ears. ... *You can't reform a kid like Gary ... He's too old now...*

Don might as well have said *"Gary doesn't have a snowball's chance in hell of starting a new life in Winsbury. He's a screwed up kid, and he'll always be a screwed up kid, bad things follow him around no matter where he goes."*

Gail defended him, but the conversation struck like a fist and anger rose in him again, but not like it did with the cop. With Officer Vedish, he wanted to scream at the top of his lungs until his throat gave out. Now, he didn't think he could manage a scream if he tried. He felt stifled and powerless. Inferior. Like someone had snuck up behind him and whacked him on the back of the head with a heavy rock.

He felt humiliated.

He didn't want to think about it anymore, so he started back for the bed when a soft tapping interrupted him. It came from the side window. He caught a dark figure sitting there on the garage roof, looking in. Adrenaline shot through him, piercing the tips of his fingers like needles. He froze in shock, frightened. *Who was it?*

Then he *did* think he could scream, until he recognized Stan's face, clearly amused at the fright. He wore the strangest grin. He tapped at the window with his index finger. Against his better judgment, Gary slid the window open.

"What are you doing here?" he whispered.

Stan squatted down and whispered back through the dirty screen. "Hey, what's going on?"

"How'd you get up here?" Gary asked.

"Didn't you know?" Stan said. "I'm Spiderman. That, and I climbed the garage. Your tree reaches right up."

And that was where Stan squatted, on top of the garage, one foot planted on each side of the sloping edges.

"How did you find me?"

"You said you lived in the white house on Washington, so I swung by after. I saw you in the window so I thought I'd climb up and say hello."

Gary caught a whiff of the beer Stan had been drinking. He was undoubtedly drunk. "You're going to get me in trouble," he lowered his voice even more.

"That's why I came by. I saw the cops take you out, man. I wanted to apologize."

"Yeah, I don't know what happened."

"Me either. They never really nail people and they don't even come most of the time. Something must have got a bug up their ass."

"Or someone."

Stan scoffed. "No way, man. You think they were looking for just you? I wouldn't worry about it. I mean, hey, you spent time in Radcliffe, right? No big deal. It isn't like you killed anyone or anything."

Gary leaned away, the blood draining from his face. He thanked the darkness for hiding his reaction.

Stan went on. "Seriously, I wouldn't worry about it. They probably just knew you were a bad-ass."

Gary laughed. "You've got a weird thing about bad-asses, don't you?"

Stan shifted his feet and groaned. "Birds of a feather, my friend. Ahh, my foot is falling asleep. Damn."

Gary started to close the window. "You better go, man, before you wake somebody up. I really can't get into any more trouble. It's already pretty bad right now."

"No problem. But hey, if you're not in too much trouble, maybe you can go to another party with me."

"Yeah, right." Gary leaned on the window ledge. He bumped his funny bone and cringed. "I doubt I'll be going anywhere for a while, especially a party."

"Keep your schedule open just in case. It's not a *party* party, but more of a gathering of friends. I'm not sure when it'll be yet, but I'll let you know."

Gary shook his head. "We'll see."

Stan stood up, paused for a moment, then leaned back down. His foot slipped and he almost fell down the side of the garage before regaining his footing. "Whoa! Close one. Hey, you never said what you were in Radcliffe for anyway."

Gary shifted his eyes, dug deep. "It was nothing. I... stole some stuff."

"What did you steal? Was it like TVs or something?"

"Something like that." Gary reached for the window.

"That's cool," Stan said. "Well, got to go."

Gary shut the window and watched Stan slip over the edge onto the tree branches. When his footing was finally steady, he raised his right hand, gave an emphatic salute with two fingers, and disappeared below the edge.

Gary shut the curtain and fell back onto the bed. A dull sleepiness crept over him. He drew his blanket up. A light blinked to life across the street.

It was the girl. She was hunched over her desk with a silvery nightlight behind her, writing. Occasionally, she turned her head upward and glanced out the window.

He wished he had a flashlight so he could signal her, get her attention, but he thought it might scare her. That was the last thing the girl needed, a stalker living across the street. He wondered what she was writing. Her pen moved furiously over the paper and every now and then she paused, peered into nowhere for a few seconds, then wrote furiously again. Was it a letter? A novel? Grocery list? *Sure, a late night grocery list.* What could have inspired her to get up so late?

He hoped she hadn't seen Stan. The thought made him nervous. Maybe it was what she was doing. Maybe she saw Stan and was writing a letter to Don and Gail, reporting on the strange nocturnal activities.

He shrugged it off. She didn't seem like that kind of girl to him. She seemed more shy and alone, and it made him want to know her even more. He didn't know why.

Her father entered the room and went to the window. Gary instinctively ducked out of sight, even though it was impossible to see him with the lights off. Her father drew the curtains closed, and a moment later, the silver nightlight faded away to nothing.

Gary climbed back into bed and fell asleep moments later.

"So what do you say to lunch with your foster mother?" Gail asked.

It was Saturday morning. The house felt cooler than usual. He rubbed his skin to quash the goose bumps. "It's cold in here." The hair on his arms stood on end and he shivered.

"I had the doors open for a little while. I like to air the place out every now and then. You know, clear things out. So? Lunch?"

"Sure! Where?"

"There's a little place off the main highway outside of town I love. Don doesn't like it very much, but now I have someone else to go with. I think he'll be relieved."

"Sounds great. I was going to do some homework but that's about it."

"Perfect." She did a little twirl. "Why don't you do that until about eleven-thirty and then we can go. Sound like a plan?"

"Sounds like a plan." He headed back to his room and studied, finding it difficult to concentrate. He finally gave up, showered, put on one of his new shirts, then went back to scrutinize his math book some more.

His nerves jangled and twinged. He didn't expect bad feelings to go away all by themselves, or so quickly, but he hoped a bit more time would have passed between the whole Officer Vedish incident and spending some quality time with Gail. She would want to talk about what happened, like any adult would, and that was something he didn't do so well. He didn't feel ready for a heart-to-heart.

At 11:30, she tapped on his door and they were off, zipping through town to the main highway. They drove past several parks, and in the distance a cemetery sat at the top of an otherwise bare green hill. A small crowd gathered there, the scene reminding him of his mother's funeral.

Before long, Gail pulled off the road and onto a gravel parking lot in front of a tiny shack of a place. A faded brown sign at the top of the front porch read *Shep's*.

Gary crinkled his nose.

"Don't worry," Gail said. "It's not as bad as it looks. If you like burgers, you're going to love this place."

It surprised him. Not that this place had great burgers, but that Gail would crave burgers at all, especially from a place like this. She didn't strike him as the burger type.

"Don wanted to stop here one time a few years ago," she explained. "I fought tooth and nail because, well, just look at it. But it turned out I loved it more than he did. Irony, huh?"

The interior surprised him even more, a rather stark distinction from the exterior. The room was all polished wood and bright, like the inside of an exotic vacation cabin. Waitresses in prim uniforms hopped between tables, in orderly fashion, like ants rushing around a hill. It made Rocky's look like a hole in the wall.

"Let's get a booth."

They took the far corner and a short, feather-haired waitress brought them water.

"Everything all right?" Gail asked.

He shrugged. "I'm okay."

She waited for more, but nothing came. "I mean are you all right, about last night?"

"I guess." He thought of telling her about the overheard conversation, but it might have looked bad from her perspective. *Meet Gary Sanderson, eavesdropping foster child.* Besides, the less said the better. Gary's Golden Rule for everything.

The waitress returned and Gail ordered a burger with everything on it. Gary did the same, minus onions.

"I don't want you to worry," she said. "We're going to run into problems. I expect that. We'll just have to work through them, that's all."

He wrung his hands together, cleared his throat. "I wasn't drinking at the party. I swear."

"I know. Really. I believe you."

He twirled his napkin with his fingers, tearing off tiny pieces.

"There's more to it than that, though," she said. "I'm not saying you were wrong. I'm just saying that we all have to be extra careful about what happens in our house. I realize this was out of your control, so I don't blame you. It's probably more my fault than yours. I didn't realize there would be trouble there, and I know it was a hard situation for you... foolish me, huh? I guess I've always been a little naïve."

Gary shrugged. "I don't think it's your fault."

She smiled. "Whatever the case, I want us all to be a little more careful in what we do, myself included. Having you with us is a special situation and we need to treat it that way. Sound good?"

What a relief, he thought. Apparently, that was it. End of discussion. Case closed.

The waitress brought two burgers. Gary's mouth began to water. "Sounds good," he said, and dug in.

"Not a good first week, I take it?" Counselor Ray said. His voice vacillated between mild amusement and dumfounded concern.

Gary sat in the same chair as last week, arms folded across his chest, lower lip jutted out in an uncharacteristic pout. He expected a lecture and felt one coming on, like a volcano rumbling the earth before it spouts off. *Isn't that what counselors are for, anyway?* They lecture you about what you are and aren't supposed to do. They dig around your brain, and then proceed to tell you why things shouldn't bother you. What if they didn't bother you in the first place? What if you *didn't* want to talk about it, to start?

"Busted by the cops the first weekend," Ray went on. "Ouch."

Gary waited. *Here it comes; he's about to tell me what a screw up I am and I better not say anything until he gets that off his counselor chest.*

It maddened him, the waiting. His face flushed at the thought of being lectured without having a chance to tell his side of the story. Ray wouldn't believe him anyway. Who would? Who would believe a juvie kid over a cop?

But the lecture didn't come. He looked up after a long, silent pause and found Ray sitting on the edge of the desk, sneakered feet crossed on the floor, waiting.

"Are you all right?" Ray asked.

Gary shifted in his chair. "I swear I wasn't drinking."

Ray's head bobbed up and down in thought. "I believe you. You don't look dumb enough to go drinking one week out of Radcliffe."

Ray's agreeableness took Gary by surprise. "You believe me?"

"Yeah. I do. You strike me as the kind of kid who can take care of himself, and I think it's pretty obvious you're doing your best to fit in. I'd say doing what they said you did isn't like you."

"Thanks."

"They probably just wanted to throw a little scare into you," Ray said. Then his voice lowered and he sported a bad John Wayne imitation. "You know, show you who's the boss in this here town, pilgrim."

Gary almost smiled. "Well, it threw a scare into my foster parents, that's what it did."

"I'm sure everything will be all right," Ray said. "Just do your best to stay out of trouble, which goes without saying. It's going to be harder for you to do that, you know, staying out of trouble. Everyone's watching you, and some of them are just waiting for you to make a mistake. I'd bet there are some people out there who are just itching to call you a screw up, no matter what you do."

Gary's thoughts flashed to Don's words from last night. They stung. "I know."

Ray rapped his knuckles on the desk. "Knock on wood for that one."

"Why do people knock on wood anyway? Is that supposed to help or something?"

"Oh, I suppose so." Ray sat up and went back around to his side of the desk. He took up his deck of cards, started shuffling. "It's an old superstition I picked up from my roommate in college. Long ago, some people believed spirits lived in the trees, and when you knocked on a tree, you were waking those spirits to help you. Weird huh?"

"Very," Gary said.

Ray finished shuffling, passed out a hand for Rummy. Gary swept up his cards and discovered two Aces, two Kings, two Queens, and a Jack. He picked first, and the first card he grabbed was another Ace. He smirked. He was on to Ray. No one has luck like that in cards.

"You know what I think?" Gary said.

"What's that?"

"I think you're dealing from the bottom of the deck."

Ray snickered. "What makes you think that?"

"Because every time we play I get a really good hand, and nobody gets it good like this all the time."

"You think so?" Ray still picked at his cards with nonchalance, arranging them in his hand. "I don't know. Maybe you're just very lucky?"

"No way. Not me."

"Why do you say that?"

Gary paused. Now he knew where this was really going. "Because I just don't get good cards like this, that's all."

It was Ray's turn to pause. He must have noticed Gary's reluctance to being drawn out, so he made light of the situation. "All right. I'm busted. That was another thing my roommate and I did. We liked to play cards a lot. Sometimes it helps to put some of the kids I work with at ease. No big shakes."

Yeah, you let them win a few games and they warm right up to you, is that how it is? Gary said nothing.

"Well, you're smarter than most," Ray said. "You caught me straight out. Not bad."

Gary gave his cards back and Ray reshuffled, dealt again. Gary watched this time and didn't notice any funny business, although he wasn't sure if he'd be able to see it anyway. This time, his cards were fairly random. He started the game.

"Remember what I said about those people that are just looking for a reason to call you trouble?" Ray said.

"Yeah."

"You know what you have to do?"

"What?" Gary said.

"Prove them wrong."

Gary picked up a card. Ray was right, and Gary knew it. He'd known all along, and that was exactly what he intended to do.

CHAPTER 9
Kindred Souls

Gary kept to himself and laid low for the next few weeks, pushing his efforts to stay on everyone's good side, redoubling his original intentions. His run-in with the law, while not forgotten, took a backseat to settling into his new life. He went to school and adjusted to his class schedule, although he still had a hard time with early morning gym class. Probably always would. He hung out with Stan by his locker and chatted things up, listening to Stan's stories of grandeur, most of it made up or greatly embellished in order to appear tougher than he really was.

Gary didn't mind listening to the stories. In fact, he found them amusing in an absurd sort of way. He wondered if Stan believed his own stories were true. They became a ritual between them, a shared lie they kept between themselves allowing them to grow closer to each other. Together, Stan was a tough bad-ass like he wanted to be, and Gary was a normal kid who had nothing whatsoever to do with Radcliffe and the death of his father. It was a pleasant lie.

He studied at night and caught up with the rest of his classes as best he could. He struggled with Math mostly, but discovered a real affinity for English. He received an A minus on his first paper, a two page analysis of *Mr. Flood's Party*, exploring the aspect of how changing times can cause loneliness in the poem. His teacher even wrote a big *Good Job!!!* in bright red ink.

He worked his few days a week at Rocky's Pizzeria, learning how to use the grill, how to run the kitchen a little better, how to serve the customers properly, and how to run the register. Rocky was a good enough guy, amiable, even though he drank too much. Gary ignored the last aspect of the man, since it didn't make him angry or violent. In fact, it made him friendlier and more talkative, and that wasn't so bad. Better than the alternative.

When he wasn't studying, he occasionally painted with Gail, and she taught him the best way to hold a brush for certain types of strokes; long sweeps that mimicked a shoreline, or quick dabs that splotched out the chaotic patterns of tree leaves. She was kind to him, and never mentioned the incident with Officer Vedish.

Don, on the other hand, remained a stolid figure and retreated further into the unyielding exterior he'd worn since Gary had known him, like a dark sea turtle. He said nothing of the incident either, at least not to Gary, and Gary hadn't heard any other late night conversations between Don and Gail about it, but it was obvious it still bothered Don. He hoped Don would eventually forget the whole thing because it *was* going to be an isolated incident, no matter whose fault it was, cop or no cop.

After a few weeks of stewing and brooding, though, Don finally spoke up.

Gary arrived home and set his book bag in his room, then readied to settle in to read his next English assignment. Don's truck was in the driveway, which wasn't unusual. He often came home early and worked in his wood shop in the basement. He busied himself with side jobs, restoring old furniture. But today, he wasn't in the basement, he was working on the backyard deck.

Gary closed his book and went down to see what was going on. A hammer thudded as Don pounded the railings out of one of the posts. He had just wrenched free one of the railings, and a hole around the side post was already dug out. The porch lay propped up on three cinderblocks, and when the last railing came away, the post leaned away from its former position.

Don saw Gary standing there and his face blinked from concentration on his work to an uncomfortable, creased disposition. He yanked at the leaning post but it resisted, hanging onto the hole like ornery tree roots. The base was partially rotted, though it was still strong enough to present some problems.

"Do you want any help?" Gary asked.

Don cocked his head. "All right."

Gary set a grip on the post. A new post lay on the ground on the other side of Don, and filled the air with the scent of fresh cedar.

"You got it?" Don said.

"Ready."

Together, they rocked it back and forth, gently at first, until the earth at the lower base loosened enough to come free. With a final tug, they yanked it up and out of the ground.

"There we go." Don tossed it to the center of the yard and picked up the new post.

Gary took up the shovel poking out from beneath the porch and stuck it into the small pile of dirt Don created, ready to fill in the hole.

"I'd like to apologize about the night when the cops brought you home," Don said.

The suddenness of the apology surprised Gary and he didn't know what to say. He could already tell by the pained expression on Don's face it wasn't easy for him to do, so he said nothing.

"I realize I should have given you a chance to speak your mind," Don went on after a short moment of silence. "I had to listen to the cop, but I should have let you talk too."

"That's all right. I understand."

Don set the new post in the hole and leaned a level on the side of it, watching the little bubble move up and down, then finally steady. Gary tossed in a few shovels full of dirt.

"I really wasn't drinking that night," Gary said. "I swear I didn't have anything."

Don's eyes remained fixed on the level. "Well, whatever the case, let's do our best to stay out of the police's hair. All right?"

And that was the end of the conversation. Gary filled the rest of the hole in silence. Don's eyes didn't once move from the level, and Gary knew he still didn't believe him. Probably never would. It was something he would have to either work on or get used to.

Thursday night at Rocky's turned out to be more crowded than Gary expected. The girls' junior varsity soccer team burst through the door in a whirlwind of giggles and ponytails after having won a match against Carol High, their longtime rivals.

Rocky's eyes lit up as they poured in, and he sent Gary back to handle the kitchen. Orders piled up. Gary felt comfortable in the kitchen already, not so much like he did in Radcliffe where he might have run the place with his eyes closed, but comfortable enough to work his way around. This was a fairly large group, though, and to top it off, four other groups of people came in within ten minutes of the soccer team. Gary hustled.

Pressure built.

He had the grill going at full capacity with eight burgers and six foot-long dogs sizzling. The hotdogs kept rolling off to the side and into the grease canals so he propped them in between the burgers to keep them in place. Four deep-dish pizzas bubbled in the oven.

Standing between the grill and the pizza ovens was like standing in a sauna. The heat swam around his body, leeching the sweat out of him, and the harder he worked, the hotter he got. Every five minutes he wiped the sweat out of his eyes with his shirtsleeve or with the bottom of his apron, which wasn't so white anymore. Now it was stained with a darkened mixture of pizza sauce, burger grease, and sweat. He hated to think of what his forehead looked like at the moment, and what effect it would all have on his threatening acne. On top of his head sat a white paper hat that already felt damp and itchy against his forehead. Rocky kept a large supply of them, which was a good thing because they didn't last more than a day or two. He thought he'd probably go through a dozen before the shift was over.

He flipped the burgers over one more time, rolled the hotdogs, then realized he had a large pizza with pineapple and olives waiting to be moved to the warmer for pickup.

"Damn!"

He dropped the spatula to the floor in an attempt to hurriedly set it down near the grill, then whacked his head on the corner of the oven as he went down to retrieve it. His sweat-soaked hat slipped off and soaked up a small puddle of grease he had accidentally made earlier in the evening. He kicked the hat under the oven and pulled out the pizza, grimacing. It was slightly burnt, but he hoped they wouldn't know the difference. If they did, he'd have to make a whole new one, and he didn't know what Rocky would have to say about it.

He reached to the side of the oven, whacked the bell, then hurried back to the burgers. He pulled eight burger buns and six hotdog buns, spread a knife's edge of butter on each, then set them on the grill to toast.

After retrieving a new spatula from the storage bin, he splashed a handful of water onto his face, then some onto the grill to watch it bubble. Steam billowed up toward the ceiling.

For safe measure, he flipped the burgers one more time, but in doing so, allowed one of the hotdogs to escape. Of course he saw the whole thing coming but didn't have hands enough to intervene. Instead of rolling into the grease canal, the hotdog slipped at an angle, away from the grease canal and straight toward the edge of the grill. He watched it roll to the edge and nearly panicked. He shot out with the spatula in his best attempt to save the runaway dog, but instead he missed and caught the grill with the back of his thumb. Pain seared through his hand. The hotdog dropped to the gritty floor with a bounce and a greasy splat.

"Damn!"

But Gary wouldn't give up. He dashed to the freezer, took out another hotdog, and threw it on the grill between the burgers to start cooking. The deep fryer dinged at him and he rushed back to remove the fries, shook them once, then set them into their straining bin. Sweat dripped into his eyes again. With a swoosh of his apron, he soaked up the sweat on his way down to retrieve the hotdog from the floor, when the hotdog strangely began to move of its own accord, heading halfway across the floor.

"What the...?" he started to say when he noticed the hotdog was not actually moving, but a large, beady eyed rat had taken hold of it.

"Jesus!" Gary yelled, and threw the spatula at the thing with all the instinct of a wild man.

He swept up a broom from the corner and proceeded to chase the rat through the kitchen, stomping with his feet when it tried to get past him, whacking with his broom, doing everything he could to get the renegade hotdog. Just as the rat disappeared through an insubstantial crack in the wall, hotdog and all, Rocky bustled through the doorway and whacked the dingy bell.

"Jeez, kid," he said. "Leave the pets alone. The burgers are burning."

With horrid realization, Gary dropped the broom where he stood and hurried back to save his burgers, along with the pizzas, which were starting to smell done.

An hour and a half later, a welcomed calm settled in. After the soccer team girls left, the only remaining customers were a young couple engaged in their third pitcher of beer. Gary had already scrubbed down the pizza oven, risking the chance someone might order another pizza. He doubted it, but you never knew.

It was part of his job to keep the kitchen clean, and he did a good job of it, if he *didn't* say so himself. The other worker at Rocky's Pizzeria, an older Mexican named Miguel, didn't clean the place half as well as Gary did. He constantly found dirty dishes waiting for him, doubling his work. Sometimes he found utensils hidden away for the obvious reason that Miguel didn't want to clean them. But Gary didn't complain. Work was work, and he enjoyed the kitchen.

Gary never met Miguel, but Rocky talked about him occasionally, mainly to complain. Gary asked Rocky once why he didn't just get rid of Miguel, but Rocky shrugged and said it was impossible to find good help in this town.

He especially enjoyed helping bring a new level of organization to the place. Not that it was all bad, but it certainly needed some work. Some storage bins were half empty while others overflowed. Inventory sheets were nonexistent. Cleaning procedures were haphazard. It would take a while, but Gary was up for the challenge. He'd clean the place up before long.

Rocky often helped him with the cleaning at the end of the evenings, which Gary appreciated. He didn't want to start coming home too late and risk jeopardizing his job by upsetting Don and Gail—especially Don—and he thought Rocky was sensitive to it.

Rocky swept the floor with the straw broom, compiling the dust and remnants of leftover meals into neat little piles. Every now and then he would pause, lean on his broom, and reach toward the shelf where he had a bottle of peppermint Schnapps hidden behind a can of jalapeno cheese. He would glance toward Gary through the corner of his eye, snatch the bottle, take a quick swig, then redeposit it in one quirky movement.

He wasn't getting anything by Gary, but his relationship with Rocky was like the relationship with Stan. Lies existed between them, but when ignored, they didn't present a problem and they got along great.

Rocky stopped sweeping and went to the closet for the dustpan. "We had a pretty good night tonight. You did pretty good."

"I burned a few pizzas." Gary scrubbed down the grill.

"I do it all the time. I think they like it better that way."

Rocky worked a pile onto the dustpan. He reached down and his shirtsleeve rose, revealing a faded tattoo. It was a dagger with a blue cross and greenish arrows.

"I like your tattoo," Gary said.

Rocky leaned up with a groan. His hand shot to his lower back to steady the pain. "Special forces. I was in the war."

"Was that World War II?"

Rocky spun toward him with a look of utter horror. "How the hell old do you think I am? It was Nam."

Gary laughed. "Oh, sorry."

Rocky grinned. "Damned kids, get your history all mixed up. You probably don't even know who's buried in Grant's tomb."

"Who?"

"Grant!" Rocky yelled. "See what I mean?"

They shared a laugh, and Gary continued to scrub down the grill. But slowly, his smile faded. The tattoo got him thinking. He wanted to ask Rocky a question, but he didn't know the best way to do it. It wasn't something you asked a person every day. He was afraid if he did ask the question, it might open up a whole new world of questions like it might have with Counselor Ray or his foster parents. He doubted Rocky was that kind of person. He seemed to be the kind of guy who would answer you squarely and wouldn't bother to search for ulterior motives behind it.

"Did you ever have to kill anyone?"

Rocky paused in the hunched over position he was in and didn't move for several moments. At first, Gary thought he'd offended him and immediately regretted asking. If he could have snatched the words from the air with his fingers, he would have, but then Rocky rose up and leaned on his broom, facing Gary. He took out his peppermint Schnapps and drank from the bottle in clear view.

"That's a pretty ballsy question."

"I'm sorry." Gary worked the grill harder, scrubbing as quickly as he could. Maybe he could scrub the air and forget it ever happened.

Rocky cleared his throat and hunkered onto his broom. His eyes glazed over as he contemplated.

"No, that's all right," he said. "You really want to know?"

The scrubbing stopped. Gary's face flushed with embarrassment, but he couldn't help himself. "I think so."

Rocky took an extra swig of booze, then another. "I don't like to talk about it much."

"So that means yes." Gary did his best not to sound disrespectful.

"Yes," Rocky said finally through a rush of escaped breath. "I suppose you're the kind of kid that wants to hear all the gory details about it, right? Like did I use a gun or a knife? Was there lots of blood and all that stuff? I know you've got a question. It's written all over your face. Why don't you just ask what you really want to know?"

"How do you live with yourself?"

Rocky fell silent. Gary's brain told him to take up the steel wool again and work the grill but his arm wouldn't listen to him. He remained fixated in Rocky's emotionless, scrutinizing stare, wondering what the man was thinking.

But he had to know. For an instant he thought he might tell Rocky about his mother, and about killing his father. He could say they had something very real in common, that they had both killed another human being, no matter what the reason, and he needed to know one thing now more than ever. The real question Gary wanted to ask but couldn't was "Will it ever get any better?"

A moment later, Rocky broke the silence. "I don't think anyone's ever asked me that before. The answer is 'I don't know.'

But it's a hard thing to live with, I suppose. Damned hard. I see his face sometimes, in my dreams. It's damned hard."

He finished the conversation by raising his bottle in a brief salute, downing the remainder of the Schnapps, then turning back to finish his sweeping.

CHAPTER 10
Beth

Gary trudged up Washington Street with all the urgency of a slug. His arms and legs felt like limp slabs of bacon after dealing with the night's rush. To accompany this, his t-shirt smelled of burnt hotdogs.

The night was calm, the sky dark and tinged purple at the horizon. In the distance, another train rounded a curve in the track and headed toward him, chugging and whistling.

Echoes of his conversation with Rocky swam through his head. *It's a hard thing to live with, I suppose. Damned hard.*

Gary knew. It was a damned hard thing to live with. People understood why he had done what he did; they told him so with their eyes, their heads cocked to the side as if considering a piece of modern art. The judge's eyes told him so when he sent Gary to Radcliffe instead of trying him as an adult. Some even told him flat out with words, usually in some effort to get him to talk about it, which never worked like they'd hoped.

So Gary understood why Rocky did what he did. The man was in a war, and that's what men do in war, isn't it? Men were trained by their governments to kill, then dropped in a foreign country with guns slung over their shoulders, and told to start fighting. He didn't know the specifics of Rocky's situation, but he imagined a few scenarios.

Maybe Rocky had been pinned down in a foxhole dug in the middle of a forest somewhere, and his team had been ambushed. Maybe it was like in the movies, with Rocky leaping out, spraying the jungle with automatic gunfire, holding the Vietnamese down while his buddies escaped. Or maybe Rocky had been captured by them and, in order to escape, he had to kill one of them. Maybe it was a difficult decision for him, the most difficult of his life, or maybe it was done in the heat of the moment. No matter what the reason, the fact remained, unequivocally, Rocky had killed a person. Maybe several people.

And after all these years, Rocky *still* said it was damned hard.

That was very depressing. All of this confused Gary to no end, the same arguments ran through his head over and over again like they had done the last four years, each year with more intensity as he grew older and understood other things more.

He remembered one time when he was ten years old, watching a movie on television called *Death Wish* with Charles Bronson. The main character's wife was killed and his daughter raped by a gang of thugs. They did it for fun, no other reason, then left on their merry way. The main character learned how to use a gun and started shooting robbers in subways. Halfway through the movie, when his mother heard the sounds of gunfire, she came into the living room and made him turn the channel.

When Gary asked why, she said "I don't think it's a good idea for you to see that sort of thing. People shouldn't kill people, not even in the movies."

"But why?" He found himself annoyed.

"Because the Bible says it's wrong. *'Thou shalt not kill.'*"

Weren't there reasons to kill, though? If a gang of thugs rapes your daughter and murders your wife, don't you have the right to kill them? If a terrorist group hijacks a couple of planes and knocks down the World Trade Center towers, mindlessly killing thousands, don't you have the right to kill them? If someone gets drunk and crushes your mother's skull with an ashtray you made, doesn't that person deserve to die, even if it is your own father?

No. His mother's voice echoed through his head. *Because it's wrong.* The Bible *says so. Straight and simple.*

His grandfather would have looked at him pointedly and answered with another question. *"What kind of cowboy do you want to be, Gary?"*

"Sure, what kind of cowboy," he mouthed.

The train drew close. The tracks were less than a block over. It arrived, passed on his left, rushing through the trees. The wind picked up in the massive machine's wake. The droning sound and the smell of axle grease warmed him until it finally passed.

He walked the final block and paused a moment when he saw, across the street from his house, the neighbor girl sitting on her stoop. She had her elbows draped lazily over her knees, head hung low.

He knew he smelled like bacon and burger grease, and he weighed that in his mind, coming to the conclusion if he didn't act now, he might not get another chance for a long while. It had already been weeks since he'd come to Winsbury, and he still hadn't met her. Who knew when he'd have another opportunity?

Nerves falling over themselves, he took a deep breath and went straight up to her, restaurant smells be damned.

She raised her head slightly, but didn't move away.

"Hi." He stopped at the edge of her yard. He didn't want to come too close, thinking he might scare her at such a late hour. "I'm Gary Sanderson."

"I'm Beth Carter." Her voice was soft, like a silk dress.

In the streetlight, her eyes were a gentle blue, but rippled with sadness. Every time he'd seen her she looked sad, and he wondered why. Her hair was long and brown, and lay in a limp ponytail down her back, taut with a green rubber band.

"I saw the cops take you away from the party that night," she said, quite matter-of-fact, like a reporter on television.

"Yeah, they thought I had booze in my cup. How about you? Did you get away clean?"

He saw her try to smile, but it was subdued somehow, as if she were wading through a river of molasses, exhausted. "They didn't even look twice at me. That was the first bonfire I've ever been to and it gets busted up so fast. I got lucky, I guess. My Dad didn't even know I was there."

Gary moved further into the yard, feeling more comfortable, and plopped down on a large rock.

"So you're from the boys' home?"

Gary shifted uncomfortably. "How did you know?"

"I heard my Dad talking about it to Mr. Morgan. It sounded pretty serious."

The discomfort rose further, like the red line in a thermometer. Tightness gripped his chest. "So you know why I was in there?"

"No, they didn't tell me."

What a relief.

"Oh, well it was no big deal." He changed the subject. "Why do you look so sad? I've seen you a few times and you always look sad."

Her response surprised him. "I should ask you the same question."

"Do I look sad?" He had no idea he might have looked sad to people. True, he felt sad, among other things some times, but he thought he hid it fairly well.

"Every time I see you."

He was about to respond when the front door opened and Beth's father huffed out. He was a rotund man with dark, thinning hair and a shiny silver watch tight around his wrist. Tufts of puffy dark hair sprang from his chest through his collared shirt, and even some from his ears. His back was probably covered with it.

"Beth, in the house now," he demanded through gritted teeth. "And you, get the hell out of here."

Beth rose obediently and headed straight through the door, not a notion of goodbye, nice to meet you, not a question asked.

Gary jumped up from the rock and gripped his apron. "We were just talking."

"I don't care. I don't want you in my yard, and I don't want you talking to my daughter."

Flames flickered in Gary's chest. "What's the big deal?"

"I know all about you," Mr. Carter said. "And I don't want you in my yard, so get out of here and stay away from Beth. You hear me?"

The flames in his chest flickered away and died off somewhere. It was too much right now to be angry. Wordlessly, he turned away, dejected, and headed home.

So who didn't know all about him?

He slept restlessly that night. He'd hoped by now he would have grown used to his new room and his new bed, but he hadn't entirely. And it wasn't just the room and the bed. It was everything around him. Just when he began to feel a little more comfortable, a little more at home in his surroundings, something barreled out of nowhere, knocking him backward, reminding him maybe he didn't quite belong.

Tonight it had been Beth's father. He hadn't expected the man to react the way he did. He said he knew all about Gary. What did that mean exactly? Did it mean he knew about Gary's father? Did it mean he knew Gary was one of those juvie Radcliffe boys? Everyone seemed to think they 'knew' what boys from Radcliffe were like, and not one of them seemed to have a good impression of him.

He tossed and turned for several hours. When he finally did sleep, his body ached and his dreams were uneasy, pitching up and down like a dinghy on a tumultuous sea. A kaleidoscope of images twisted in his mind, of faces hovering in great circles, drifting from the sky then zipping toward him through the darkness, speaking.

"What kind of cowboy do you want to be?" Only it wasn't his grandfather. It was Butchy, the cowboy toy, polishing his gun, leaning against the alarm clock on the dresser. His plastic, hand-painted eyes glowed like red coals, burning the dark away.

"It's a damned hard thing to live with," Butchy said, only it was Rocky's voice, stolen directly out of the man, then Rocky's face blurred from the tip of the sky and fell on him.

Gary turned away to protect himself from the oncoming rush, but instead came face to face with his father standing twenty feet tall, looming over him like Jack's Giant, holding the ashtray he'd used to kill his mother.

"What are you doing with my gun, Gary?" his father said. *"What do you think you're going to do with that, you little shit? You a killer, Gary? You think you got what it takes?"*

Gary realized he had the same gun he'd used to kill his father so long ago.

"You're not real." Gary's voice emerged a limp and pathetic little thing, easily torn away by the wind.

His father chuckled cruelly under his breath and his eyes lit dully orange like Butchy's on the dresser. *"You know what I'm going to do with this ashtray? I'm going to kill your mother with it."*

Gary quivered. His legs were tubes of jelly beneath him. He nearly reeled. The gun lay cold in his hand as he watched his arm rise up, aiming the gun toward the sky, toward his father's chest.

"What do you think you're doing?" his father asked. *"Give me the gun. Now."*

Gary's hand tightened on the trigger. In his dream, he began to cry. He'd never felt more like crying in his life and he couldn't stop it from happening. The dam holding his emotions in check finally broke and the tears rushed through him.

"You're not a killer, are you Gary?" His eyes glowed smugly and his teeth flashed in the night. He smiled. *"You can't do it again, son, because you ain't got it in you. You're not a killer."*

Gary saw the ashtray and his eyes thinned. A clump of strawberry blonde hair and dried blood caked the corner. His mother was dead and it was too late again. His father laughed and the sound of it echoed in his ears.

At the last moment, Gary's body stiffened with renewed resolve and he pulled the trigger. His father dropped to the earth, like he had done once before.

"I guess I am a killer." Gary fell to the ground, blinded by tears.

He awoke to the sound of gunfire in his ears and sulfur in his nostrils, then realized with tremendous relief he was in his bedroom, alone. The smell disappeared along with the residue of the dream until all that remained was the soft glow of the streetlight bleeding through the window. He glanced at the dresser to be sure Butchy wasn't there. Nothing.

He rubbed his eyes. They were wet with tears. He chided himself for that.

"Stupid crying," he breathed, and wiped his face with the flower print comforter Gail had yet to replace. "Stupid dreams."

When sleep finally overtook him again, the dreams were gone, and all that remained were a few wet tears soaked into his pillow. By morning, those would be gone as well.

Excitement flooded through Gary the next Friday night. Not only because it was the end of the school week, but he had plans to go fishing with Stan the next morning, sometime. He'd never gone fishing before and looked forward to trying it out.

He also didn't have to work, which was always a plus on Fridays. Fridays were the worst days to work because every family in Winsbury it seemed, packed up the kids, and all their neighbors' kids, and God-knew-who-else's kids, and took them out to Rocky's Pizzeria. Great for Rocky, bad for Gary.

The last crazy Thursday was a hectic day, but Friday's were actually much worse in comparison.

But tonight he had something to look forward to, although he wouldn't admit it to Stan. Tonight, he was going to help Gail prepare dinner. His mother used to let him help her in the kitchen from time to time, and he'd always enjoyed that, stirring mixtures of food in glass bowls with wooden spoons like a mad scientist concocting a secret recipe. He enjoyed taking all of the pieces of the formula, throwing it all together, and watching what came out of the oven when they were finished.

And tonight, Gail was going to show him how to roast a chicken.

He was already good at flipping burgers and chicken breasts on the grill, and even mixing up the sauce for the pizzas at Rocky's, but roasting a whole chicken was a different thing entirely. You had to learn a different technique to make it taste just right. It wasn't like you could just rip it out of its packaging and throw it onto a grill, although trying it out did appeal to Gary. Nope, you had to clean it out and bake it for a while with the heat up good and high, or at least that was what the cookbook said when he glanced through it.

When it was time to start the dinner, Gail called him down from his room. She led him to the kitchen where she had a medium sized chicken thawed and waiting for them on the stove in a deep green and white flecked cast iron pot. She had already set the table with gleaming porcelain plates and set silverware. A white apron fit snugly around her waist, cleanly starched and pressed, perfect.

"Are you ready to help me with the chicken?" Her prim lips pursed into a smile.

"I'm ready."

"Good," she said. "The first thing we have to do is wash our hands, and then clean out the chicken."

She moved the pot to the counter beside the sink and stepped away. Gary followed, washed his hands thoroughly with the industrial strength soap, then blotted them on a towel. Gail put his hands on the thawed, floppy bird.

"Just reach inside and remove the guts," she said.

He hesitated a moment before reaching his hand into it. It was cold from the refrigerator, but also damp and slimy inside. It reminded him of a movie he'd once seen called *The Blob* about a jelly like creature from outer space that consumed its victims whole. He toyed with the idea that the chicken was a Blob in disguise, masquerading as raw poultry, waiting for some hapless victim to come along and stick his fingers in.

When his fingers were in up to the knuckles, he felt what he had gone in for. The guts were bundled neatly in a small wrap of thin paper, which he easily removed and set in the sink.

"It's a lot more difficult to remove them when the chicken is frozen." Gail turned on the water to rinse the meat. "That's why it's a good idea to thaw out the bird early on. Some people eat the gizzards, but I don't recommend it. Yuck."

She rinsed the sink and tossed the neat little package into the garbage.

"Next is the seasoning." She brought the bird back to the oven. She removed a tray of spices from the cabinet above her head and surveyed them all. Easily a dozen canisters lined the tray.

"Any ideas?" she asked.

Gary wasn't so sure on spices, but he chose garlic and basil from the collection, two of the main ingredient spices in Rocky's pizza sauce.

"Nice," Gail said. "Italian style chicken. Very nice."

Together they added the seasoning to the inside and outside of the bird with a few shakes of salt and pepper for good measure. When they finished, she brought the stuffing out from the refrigerator and instructed him how to stuff the bird.

"This is going to taste great," Gary said.

"And the last step is to place it in the oven."

Gary set the lid on the pot, opened the stove, and slid it onto the wire rack. Gail turned up the heat to 400 degrees and closed the door.

"That should do it," she said. "Good job."

"Thanks."

"I can handle it from here, unless you want to help me make the mashed potatoes."

"I'd like to."

"Great, but that won't be for another hour or so."

He helped her clean off the countertop and empty the dishes into the sink. She washed and he dried. She dipped her hands into the scalding water and he winced for her. How could she put her hands into such hot water? When she dipped her hands in again, a joke popped into his head, something about asbestos hands, but the scars on Gail's wrists tore the words from his mouth before he could utter them.

There was no mistaking where they had come from. Some time in her past, Gail had tried to kill herself by slitting her wrists. They were faint things, small lines of pale skin raised along the length of the wrists, still noticeable but long since healed over.

Gary backed away, suddenly flushed with embarrassment, for discovering something he thought should have been kept a better secret. He bumped against the table. In doing so, he accidentally knocked one of the table settings out of place.

Gail spun around, shocked. "Be careful!"

Gary froze as Gail hurried to right the table setting, hands dried on her apron and moving the setting back into its rightful place.

"I'm sorry." Gary fumbled his way toward the kitchen door, feeling horrible for what he had just done but not entirely understanding what it was. "I... I didn't mean to move the plate."

"Gary, wait." Gail's eyes pleading with him. Before she said another word, she leaned back against the sink and breathed deeply. "I'm the one that needs to say I'm sorry. I didn't mean to snap at you like that. You didn't do anything wrong."

He didn't move from his position near the door. His eyes wanted to go to her wrists, but he fought the urge. He felt like a mannequin glued in place that might shatter if he shifted this way or that. As always, Gail's smile disarmed him, but things were different somehow. He had displeased her, and it tainted things.

"I'm sorry," Gary repeated.

She came away from the sink and held her arms out, waiting for him in the center of the room, but still he didn't move. He couldn't move, and he didn't know if he wanted to, or if he should. When he didn't go to her, she went to him and wrapped her arms about his back, squeezed him gently into her, and laid her head on his right shoulder.

He didn't hug back. It felt foreign to him, like something out of kilter with the world. He knew he shouldn't feel such a way, but he did, and his body stiffened like a board.

She backed away, but kept her hands on his shoulders. "I really am sorry."

He cocked his head and grinned as best he could. "It's no big deal. I'm sorry too."

"It's just that I want everything to be perfect." She released her hands and leaned back on the sink, wringing her hands into her apron. "That's all. I... didn't mean to startle you."

"I know." Gary's feet finally loosened from the invisible glue in the floor. He picked up a crumb from the counter he suddenly noticed.

"You know," Gail said. "We're glad you came to stay with us. Things really are a lot better with you here."

"Thank you." He tipped his hand and the crumb fell into the garbage can. "I'm happy too." He couldn't help but wonder how things were before he came along for her to say such a thing, and how long ago in her past she had hurt herself.

"You just wait and see." She spun back to the sink, a new excitement rolling in her voice. "Everything is going to be perfect."

He watched her and hoped she was right, even though her shoulders remained tense as a rabbit in a den of wolves.

"You can't even tell me you've never gone fishing before." Stan pierced a fat, writhing earthworm with his fishhook and coiled it around twice for good measure. "My friend, you have lived a life of serious deprivation."

Stan's Saturday fishing hole was a small pond just outside the edge of the Winsbury forest preserve property, so it was legal to toss a line in every now and then. The pond was just a little bit longer than it was wide and it was kept stocked with bluegills and sunfish each year. It started at the edge of a copse of trees where it met a dry creek bed, and ended with a dirt trail and a ramp where guys on their mini-bikes liked to jump the shallow edge.

The sky was bright blue, and the sun bled through a stretch of bulbous clouds. When Gary inhaled, the sharp smell of pine needles and vegetation poking up through the water's surface filled his nose.

"There's nothing better than fishing." Stan drew his pole back, threw the line, released. It was a perfect cast, landing halfway across the water with a 'spelunk.'

"Is this where you break out into your 'Fishing is Life' speech?" Gary drew his own pole back, attempted to throw the line, but when he released, the weight fell straight down to his feet. His earthworm fell off the hook and lay twisting dully in the dirt.

"Nice one. Here, do it like this." Stan mocked the casting motion with a fluid wrist jerk. "It's all in the wrist."

Gary reset the worm and tried again, this time casting it out nearly as far as Stan's.

"Not too bad," Gary said proudly. "So where'd you learn how to fish?"

Stan reeled his line in a few feet, slowly, teasing the fish, making subtle jerking motions on the pole. "My Dad taught me when I was younger. The key is to use real worms, not those lame rubber flies or that smelly gunk shit. Sometimes shrimp works, but where the hell do you get live shrimp around here? Didn't your Dad ever teach you how to fish?"

"He didn't fish much."

He reeled in the line, recast it, hitting near the center of the pond again. He was starting to enjoy the casting more than anything.

"There you go," Stan said. "That was a good one."

At the edge of the pond, something splashed in the water. Stan immediately drew in his line and cast in that direction. "So they're hanging out over there today."

Gary chewed his lip. "Do you do a lot with your Dad?" he asked.

Stan snorted. "Not anymore. We don't really get along."

"Why not?"

"I don't know." Stan continued to reel in slowly, dragging the worm along, clicking his tongue. "He's always giving me shit about something. I don't like to talk to him anymore. What about you? What happened to your Dad that you have to live in a foster home?"

"He died in a car accident." He'd prepared this answer long ago in Radcliffe when the subject came up. It sounded natural enough, and it worked.

"I'm sorry, man." Stan finished dragging the line, recast toward the center again. "That's got to be pretty rough."

"Not the slightest bit." Gary's jaw creased with tension.

"What's that?"

"Nothing."

Stan bounced up on the balls of his feet. "So where do you go on Mondays after school? I didn't see you heading to the buses."

"I have to meet with a counselor after my last class. Counselor Ray."

"Aww, man!" Stan giggled. *Rubbin' Ray!* Has he tried anything on you yet?"

"What?"

"Yeah, they call him Rubbin' Ray. He's always rubbing people's shoulders. Mostly the guys."

The thought made Gary a bit queasy, set him on the defensive. "He's all right. He hasn't done anything like that. Believe me, he's a lot better than my counselor from Radcliffe."

"You better grow eyes in the back of your head, man." Stan laughed. "Rubbin' Ray will be coming for you!"

Gary blew it off. Yet another instance of Stan trying to get under his skin. It was all in fun, but it was starting to annoy him. He changed the subject. "Ever catch anything in here?"

Stan shook his head and tried reeling the line in small, jerking motions. "I caught a sunfish in here once, but I mostly get bluegill. And they're always dinky."

On cue, Gary's line pulled and he gripped the pole with both hands.

"Hey, you got one."

"What do I do?"

Stan dropped his pole. "Just reel it in, baby, slowly. Don't let it get away."

Gary righted his feet and pulled up on the pole, reeling the line toward him. The fish jumped once before he pulled it all the way out, and when he did, he saw it was indeed a dinky little fish, only about five or six inches long and bony thin.

"What do I do with it now?" Gary asked. He was filled with curiosity and exuberance. It was the first fish he'd ever caught.

Stan crossed his arms, laughing. "Well, you got to take it off the hook."

"All right." Gary's face scrunched into a grimace.

Its skin glistened in the sun and the mouth moved in furious pulling motions, fighting for oxygen.

Stan laughed even harder at Gary's expression. "It's not that bad. Come on, you can do it, tough guy."

Gary took the fish in his hand, and it was worse than the inside of the chicken from last night's dinner, cold and slimy but *alive*. It wriggled for a moment before finally lying calm in his hand as he worked the hook free. The hook eventually came out with a snap, the tiny fish started to wriggle wildly again.

"Now what?" he asked. "Do we eat it or something?"

Stan took the fish from him and set it gently back in the water. It darted quickly away. "Man, twenty of these things wouldn't even make a lunch. Besides, you wouldn't want to eat anything out of this place."

"Thanks." Gary recast his line with a new worm, hoping to catch another fish.

Several hours later, the single bluegill was the only fish either of them had to show for the afternoon, but it was good enough for

Gary. He caught his first fish, and it was something he'd always remember. At one point, Stan thought he had something huge wriggling at the end of his line, but after a five minute struggle with the pond beast, it turned out to be a submerged log that had snagged his hook.

They joked about it, inventing a mysterious pond creature hiding below the water by day and stalking the unwitting citizens of Winsbury, Illinois by night. It waited in darkness to leap out and first dine on their eyeballs, moving on to suck out their entire supply of bodily fluids, then finish up by using their bones as toothpicks. Strangely no one had encountered the dried out remnants of those victims—they joked—the empty skins of unsuspecting fishermen. The creature looked like a cross between the *Creature from the Black Lagoon* and Barney the Dinosaur, they imagined, only it was bright orange with red tinged hair, not that lame purple. Stan added the detail that it was cross-eyed, and that half the time it missed its mark, so if you suddenly heard a startling 'splat' of a wet, soggy monster landing behind you, you shouldn't think. Just run.

That one had them rolling for several minutes.

Gary was happy to be hanging out with Stan away from school and bonfires. He was a different person outside of school, less of an impostor, less a caricature of a kid from a B-movie trying to act tough to fit some unspoken script. When he smiled that afternoon, it was a genuine smile, self-reflective and unassuming, and his stance was easy, unguarded. Even his clothes were different. Instead of the shell of a leather jacket that locked him inside of himself, he wore plain old blue jeans and a faded 'Joe Cartoon' t-shirt, his appropriate 'fishing attire' he said, with the Frog in a Blender calling out 'Wuss.' In short, he was simply Stan, the real kid he'd met in English class those weeks ago.

By 2:00, they talked of fishing again soon before parting ways. Gary said he would love that, and took the long path through the forest preserve home. He'd come to love the path with its winding trail and tall grasses lining the edge like fur. He told himself one night he'd come out when he didn't have to work or do anything else and just enjoy the trail, the quiet serenity of it, maybe drag up a rock and breathe in some nature.

When he arrived home, he set his shoes in the corner and went about his weekly chores. Don had mentioned Gary taking on chores several weeks ago, even though Gail said she didn't think Gary needed to do anything other than study and do well at his job. But Gary agreed with Don.

"I'd like to help around the house," he said, and Gail acquiesced.

It wasn't much to do, in reality. Every Saturday his job was to vacuum the carpet, including the stairs, which took him, from top to bottom, the entire length of ten minutes. He suspected Gail, in her obsession for cleanliness, re-vacuumed during the week while he was at school. When he did vacuum, hardly any dirt came up.

His second chore was to take out the garbage, but he checked the bag and it wasn't full. Garbage day was Thursday, so he didn't have to do anything there.

His final chore, and by far the most difficult, was the upstairs bathroom. Gail and Don used the downstairs bathroom mostly. Gary was the only one to make any mess in the one upstairs. After a couple of times cleaning it, he couldn't believe how much mess a single person could make. How many stray hairs could a single body drop in one week? How much gunk could splatter and stick to the inside of a toilet bowl? It didn't take long for him to get into the habit of wiping down the bowl after each use, rinsing the sink, and toweling down the mirror when he accidentally splashed it with water or toothpaste. When Saturday finally did roll around, his bathroom was already fairly clean by most standards, but he still spent a good hour in there anyway because his new home didn't have ordinary standards.

As he cleaned the bathroom, he invariably asked himself how Gail would clean it if she were in his place. A fleck of toilet paper that might have gone unnoticed in the corner of the room was now an eyesore standing out like an ink spot on a silk blouse. A dark eyelash in the tub might as well have been a dead and blackened tree branch.

Of course Gail never said anything to him about such things, but he knew how she felt. She kept everything in the house in perfect condition, from the placement of the shoes by the door, to the flawless table settings, to the spotless porch. Even the painting room, a veritable opportunity for mess and chaos, sat clean and organized. The paints were always tucked into their appropriate drawers and the unused canvases stacked primly in the closet behind closed doors.

Gary wondered how a person could come to be so obsessed with perfection. Was it normal? Was that how people were in small towns like Winsbury? Was there some unwritten law saying if you wanted to live in a pleasant suburbia you had to obsess about your lawn and the cleanliness of your home?

His mother had never been this way, but then again, he didn't grow up in a pleasant suburbia. His was a town of wild, unkempt lawns and shouting neighbors. It was a dark, brooding place where you had to be careful when you left your block.

Things were better now, or at least they were going to be.

With his chores finished, he settled into the kitchen with Gail and they paged through her favorite cookbook, searching for recipes they might make later on. Anything with a ground beef or ground turkey base would do.

Gary thought spaghetti would be nice, but Gail shook her head, saying that would be too simple. In the end, they narrowed the choices down to turkey tacos or chili, and figured they'd wait for Don to get home to make the final decision.

Gail closed the recipe book and looked at Gary. Her eyes narrowed in thought, as if mulling a decision.

Finally, she spoke. "I think we should go out to dinner tonight, what do you think?"

Gary nodded. Dinner out was always good. "Sure."

"Good, because there's something I'd like to talk to you about. I think it's about that time."

Gary swallowed nervously. "All right."

Gail smiled and patted his hand with reassurance. "Don't worry. We'll have a nice time."

CHAPTER 11
Risks Worth Taking

Choosing a restaurant proved much easier than choosing a recipe. Gary said he didn't mind going anywhere, even Rocky's if it was where they wanted to go, although he secretly he hoped they wouldn't go there. Since working at Rocky's, he'd received his fill of pizza and hotdogs.

Gail chose a little place called Estrella's, a Mexican restaurant with white cedar walls and black shutters. The sign out front read *Estrella's—the Star of Winsbury*, and she explained that *estrella* in Spanish translated to "star" in English, which Gary found rather creative.

The restaurant was deceptively small on the outside, looking like someone had plucked a house out of one of the many Winsbury neighborhoods and plopped it down in the business section of town. Inside, the dining area was surprisingly spacious, with dozens of wood backed chairs and tables covered in white cloth. A fireplace stretched up to the ceiling with a warm, inviting fire. The place was a little more than half full.

"Nice place, huh?" Gail nudged him.

A young Mexican hostess with a pink flower in her hair led them to a booth against the far wall. From his seat, Gary could see through the window into the parking lot and down the street. Scattered headlights buzzed by. His reflection peered back at him, menu propped up in his hands.

Gail and Don sat together across from him, and Don tapped his hands on the tabletop. "So how is everything going for you?"

"Pretty good, I guess," Gary replied, which was true. Things had been going good for him lately overall, and he was happy for it.

"Glad to hear it. School work going all right? Work isn't getting in the way?"

"Not yet. I guess math is pretty hard, but I'm doing well on the quizzes, and Rocky said he didn't mind it if I needed to cut back on hours. I don't think I'll need to. Not yet anyways."

Don leaned forward on the table, shaking his head, lips pursed. "Good, good. I guess a lot can be said for hard work and keeping your nose to the grindstone."

Gary thought Don was searching for a reaction, and he looked down at his menu. When the waitress came around, Don and Gail each ordered the enchilada special, but he had his eyes set on the big beef burrito. The menu description read: *Burritos as Big as Your Head*, and it was far too enticing a description to pass up.

She took his order and winked before heading for the kitchen, returning a few moments later with drinks, setting glasses of water and a pitcher of diet Coke in front of Gail and Gary. In front of Don, she set a bottle of beer. The beer made Gary nervous. It conjured images of his drunken father staggering around the house, smashing pictures and windows and whatever else he could get his hands on that would break into little pieces.

Gail watched him, then glanced at Don and smiled that smile, the one that always made everything all right. She raised her glass of water.

Gary lifted his own glass and they clinked them together over the center of the table.

"Well, I'm glad we're here tonight," Gail said as she set her glass down. "Because there is something I've been meaning to talk to Gary about, and I think this is the perfect place for it."

Don's smile withered and his fingers tightened around the neck of his beer bottle. It looked to Gary like a landslide of words waited at the inside of his lips, but he bit them back and swallowed them down with another swig of beer.

"Is everything okay?" Gary asked. His heart shuddered against the inside of his chest once, then stopped, frozen. Blood swelled into his face and images of Radcliffe flashed in his head. He was going back soon, to Radcliffe. This is what she brought him here to say.

"Oh, God yes." Gail placed her hand over Gary's. "I didn't mean to scare you. Really, everything is all right. I'll tell you a little later. Our food is coming."

A long sigh of relief escaped Gary as his heart blipped and started again. The waitress set his burrito in front of him, along with a healthy scooping of beans and sour cream. His eyes widened at the size of the thing that was supposed to be a burrito lying on his plate. He'd never seen a piece of food so large in his entire life, and Gail laughed at the shock on his face. Even Don managed to look surprised through his souring mood.

"It's as big as my thigh." Gary put both hands around it and struggled to lift it. The end of it flopped down and began to leak. He took a bite and savored it, Mexican spices bursting in his mouth. *Delicious.*

Don cleared his throat from the other side of the table. He shifted a bit uncomfortably, but steadied himself. "Have you made some friends?"

"Yeah, Stan," Gary said. "He's the guy I went fishing with today. He's all right. I met Beth across the street, but—"

"What?" Don interrupted.

"Her father came out and told me to leave," Gary went on. "He said he knew all about me. I think most of the neighbors don't like me."

He searched Don's face for a reaction, found nothing. Don picked at his enchilada and took another drink of beer.

"How do you feel you've been adjusting though?" Gail crossed her hands together and leaned forward on her elbows. It reminded Gary of Mrs. Sanchez in Radcliffe, the way she spoke to him, always leaning forward, always crossing her fingers when she asked him questions. "I'm curious because you never talk to us about what happened with your father and mother."

The few bites of burrito he'd had lurched in his stomach. This was clearly what Gail had wanted to talk with him about.

"I don't really like to talk about it, I guess." Gary shifted his eyes away from them uneasily.

"I know what you're going through," she said, "and when I say that, I mean that I really know."

Gary set his burrito down and it lay there like an old tire, leaking out beef and beans and sauce, decompressing.

"I was abused when I was a little girl," Gail went on. "By my mother. She used to put out cigarettes on my back and my legs for not cleaning the house properly, and for not being 'her little angel,' she used to say."

Gail waited, but he said nothing. He continued to stare into his burrito, concentrating on the nooks and crannies of the beef, watching the liquid fat soak into the limp shell. He felt he would vomit all over his plate at any moment.

"That's part of the reason we chose you to come live with us," Gail said.

Don scowled and side-glanced at his wife, then shifted in his seat as if something had bitten him on the ankle.

Gail went on. "It was hard for me to deal with at the time, and I think things would have been a lot easier if I knew someone who understood me, somebody I could talk to."

And then the flames reared in Gary's chest, the same ones that had stung his insides for so long. This time, he wondered how much she really did understand him.

"Did you hurt her?" Gary was surprised at how suddenly the question fell out of him, like it did with Rocky.

"No," Gail said. "She drank herself to death when I was sixteen though, and my sister and I went to live with relatives. It took a long time for me to heal."

He glanced at her wrists and his gaze lingered on the scars. *A long time indeed.* Gail suddenly moved her hands into her lap, out of view.

Gary nodded. He attempted to pick up his burrito again, but it squashed like a wet noodle. His appetite was gone now, petered out like the burrito.

"I want you to know that you have someone you can talk to about it," she said. "It's very important to me that you know that. Whenever you're ready. Believe me, it helps to let something like that out. You can't keep it all bottled up like you're doing. I know. I hate to see things tearing you up inside when I know I can help you."

Gary cringed and a bubble of emotion floated up from within him. He couldn't tell what the emotion was. Anger? Sadness? He bit it back and swallowed it. "All right."

He gave up on the burrito, pushed it toward the center of the table and waited for Don and Gail to finish their dinners.

The ride home from the restaurant was quiet and somber. The tension was thick as tar. The burrito in Gary's stomach felt like a piece of hardened lava. He didn't want it to be this way. He also didn't want to be a source of tension between Gail and Don. He didn't understand the animosity Don held toward him, but he supposed he understood why the man had clammed up like he did.

He felt the same way. Who wants to talk about that stuff anyway? *Why do people have to bring crap out into the open when it only serves to make you feel worse?* Don didn't like to talk about things, that was clear, but Gail needed to for some reason. In a way, Gary understood that as well. The fact that he understood them both confused him. He didn't want to deal with it—nor with any of his past—but some part of him, some part in the unfathomed abyss he didn't truly understand, called out to him. And called out to Gail. That part wanted to talk about it. It was a small part, but he felt it growing, and it troubled him to no end. He didn't understand what was happening to him or why, and God knew where it would take him.

When they arrived home, Don made the excuse of needing to get a few things done in the basement and slipped away almost immediately. Gail slumped into a seat at the kitchen table with a glass of iced tea, setting her chin in her palm, staring blankly at the wall.

Gary started up the stairs but thought twice about it and went back into the kitchen for a moment. He felt like one big awkward mannequin masquerading as a human, all sticks and metal joints, barely able to walk. Gail's powdered face was a bit paler than usual and slightly puffy, but the rims of her darkened eyes were dry. Tears wanted to get out, and it made Gary's knees feel like tubes of jelly again.

"Can I have some tea?" he asked.

Gail jumped. "Oh, I thought you went up to your room."

"No," he fumbled, reaching for something to say. "I guess I was thirsty."

"Here, I'll get you something." She rose, took a glass from the cabinet and poured him some iced tea. "Would you like some lemon with it?"

"Sure."

She retrieved a lemon from the refrigerator and sliced it up into eight pieces, then dropped a wedge into his drink. All indications she might cry disappeared at that moment, and it occurred to Gary that busying herself like this cleared her mind a little bit. Maybe it was why she kept herself busy all the time. Maybe it distracted her from some of her own issues. He couldn't be sure, but if that was the case, he thought he understood it.

He took the tea and sat at the table across from her, nervous to the point of trembling, sipping from his drink. It was cold and sweet. The ice clinked against his teeth.

"I'm sorry if I upset you."

It was difficult for him, speaking to someone openly when he felt upset. It made him feel vulnerable, like he was twelve again. "I didn't mean to—"

"It's not your fault," she interrupted him. Her hand fell onto his for a moment, then darted back to her chest. "It's just... a hard thing for Don to deal with. That's all."

Gary didn't know what to say. She smiled, but it wasn't the usual smile, the strong smile of a woman in control of her life, in control of her happiness. It was subdued, a mask put on for Gary's benefit.

"He tries to be strong, but it's not what we need. He doesn't understand what it's like to be one of us, you know, children of abuse. He thinks it's better to just not talk about things, that our problems will go away on their own. I used to feel that way until a few years ago when I started therapy. I think I'm better now, and that was why I wanted to help you. I think people like us need each other sometimes."

Gary was rife with conflict. Again he sat between Don and Gail. He didn't know enough about himself to bring out the part that Gail was talking about, the abused little boy she wanted so desperately to help. He didn't want that part of him to come out. It was the part of him that killed his father, the beast he needed to keep chained in the dungeons of his mind. Gail didn't understand him like she thought she did. If she did, wouldn't she know he couldn't let that part of him out? Didn't she know some cowboys do things that are bad and some do things that are right, like an English knight? Hadn't he already proven he wasn't like the latter, the kind that would do no wrong?

Watching Gail in such pain gnawed at his flesh and bones, cancerous, picking at his brain. What could he do? Should he let that thing in him out? He couldn't do it. It would only make things worse. He knew it for sure.

Gail's hand came away from her chest, more slowly, more gently this time, and fell down onto his. Her emerald eyes found his and shone with an understanding Gary knew wasn't exactly right, but he decided to say nothing about it. At least he would give her that much.

"You can go," she said. "I'm all right. Really."

He hesitated, wondering if she truly meant it, but when she took her hand away and turned, he understood she wanted to be alone. He went up to his room and closed the door behind him. *Not a good night. Not in the slightest.*

He leaned his head on the window and stared into the yard. Across the street, Beth's light flickered so he dimmed his own, letting himself see better. She sat at her desk, hunched over the top, lit only by the silvery nightlight that sat in front of her, scribbling furiously into a notebook. Her hair fell down onto the paper occasionally, and she'd brush it away with a subtle movement, only to scribble away again.

She stopped suddenly and cocked her head toward the ceiling, then waited for several moments.

She must be thinking. I wonder what she's writing?

He was fascinated, mesmerized by Beth and he didn't know why. She was quiet in a subdued sort of way, and the way she moved her hands and her shoulders and her body suggested sadness to him, so maybe that was the reason. It might have been her looks with her freckled face, brown hair, and tiny bones that nearly made her look too young for high school. But mostly it was her eyes. The day they spoke in her yard, he had caught a glimpse of something in them, something hidden among the blue that swallowed him up, a beckoning thing touching places in him never touched before.

So this was another secret he was going to have to keep. He would speak with Beth again, there was no question of it, even if Don wouldn't like it. Gail might not have a problem with it, but he wouldn't tell her just in case. He wasn't sure how or the best way for him to talk to Beth, but he'd find a way.

He thought about Radcliffe. He certainly didn't want to go back to that place, not in a million years. He told himself he wouldn't get caught if he just talked to Beth once in a while. Why, was it so bad if he just happened to see her at school and happened to stop and talk to her for a little while before class? He wouldn't tell if she didn't. He wasn't even sure if she'd want to talk to him anymore... but he had the feeling she would, and someday they might become friends. He felt it in his bones.

Before he closed the curtains, Beth paused once more from her scribbling and reached into her desk. She removed a small brown bottle, unscrewed the cap, and tipped it into her hand. From the distance, Gary couldn't tell for sure what it was, but it looked like a pill bottle. She popped the contents into her mouth and threw her head back to swallow.

Maybe she's sick... I hope there's nothing going around. He closed the curtains and headed to bed.

Sunday morning, Gary hopped out of bed and went straight to the window. He might have dreamt about Beth during the night, but already his dreams had begun to slip away into the muddy recesses of his brain. He knew he wouldn't see her, but he had to look anyway. It had become a reflex for him to look out the window to see if she was there, hoping to find her looking back. But he found nothing.

He took a long shower and spent the remainder of the morning with Gail and Don over breakfast. Gail prepared French toast with cinnamon and showed Gary a trick or two in preparing the batter.

"Just a squirt of syrup in the egg and milk helps the bread brown in the pan better."

Gary tucked the bit of information into his mental notes file. Pretty soon he'd make breakfast for them, and he wanted it to be right.

Don buried his nose in the newspaper, peeking up every now and then, his gray eyes meeting Gary's across the table. Don gave him the guy nod when their eyes met and averted his eyes back to whatever story he had been reading.

He still feels uncomfortable. Gary left it alone.

Gail was happy as ever going about her business, making the table perfect, and carving up wedges of cantaloupe to garnish their plates.

Gary had formed a habit of waiting until she had everything completed, including the dirty dishes set neatly in the sink waiting to be washed, before starting to eat. She could have run her own restaurant and would have been the best in the business the way she made such a nice presentation of everything, especially food. A meal wasn't just a meal to her, but like one of her paintings, a work of art with the table as her canvas. Waiting was the least he could do to let her get a short glimpse of the completed work before digging in. Don had the same attitude, scouring his paper until Gail finally took her seat with them.

"That was great, honey," Don said when his plate was cleaned. It was so clean, in fact, it looked almost like they could have set it straight back into the cupboard.

"Was it?" Gail asked.

"Absolutely. Best ever."

Her smile was back and even a little playful on her lips. "Glad you liked it."

Whatever remnant of anxiety Gary felt eased off. They were okay; the tension that crept between them the night before had worked itself out overnight.

"I've got a few things I need to take care of down at the shop this afternoon, so I'll be back later on," Don said.

Gail kissed Don at the door and watched him pull out of the driveway. Gary helped clean the kitchen while he was gone. Gail finished up with the dishes in the sink while Gary dried. He wondered if he should say something to her about last night, but thought it best to keep silent. She was already happy, and if something isn't broken, you sure don't need to fix it, like his grandfather used to say.

When the last plate was back in its cupboard, Gail grabbed a towel and leaned on the counter. "I'm going to do some painting today." She dried her hands in slight, wringing motions. "Want to help?"

"Maybe later, if that's all right," Gary said. "I think I'm going to hang around outside for a while. Maybe go to the park, if that's okay with you."

"Sure." She tossed him the towel. "Good job with the drying." She disappeared up the stairs.

Gary headed to the front yard and sat on the porch. He watched Beth's window through the corner of his eye but saw nothing. Her father emerged from the house, hopped into his car—a brown Oldsmobile—and backed out of the driveway. Gary hid behind one of the porch pillars, not wanting to be seen. When her father was gone, he looked back at their house and saw Beth in the backyard.

His nerves began to twitch. He wanted to talk to her again, and this was the perfect opportunity, finally. But what if her father came home suddenly? What if her mother looked out the window? He'd never seen her mother, but he assumed she had one. What if Gail came looking for him?

In the end, he decided a couple of minutes were worth the risk, especially since Don was down at his shop for a while. It wouldn't be for too long anyway. *Just a minute*, he told himself. He hopped up off the porch and headed down a small trail that led between the two houses, across the street and down to the train tracks. A line of maple trees blocked the view of the tracks, but did nothing to dull the thunderous sound of the trains when they barreled through town.

At the end of the trail, he doubled back through the trees and stopped at the edge of Beth's yard. Her yard had no fence but lay surrounded by another, smaller line of maples serving the same purpose. She sat on a dried tree stump, hunched over a notebook like he'd seen her do the night before. Although no one was around, she wrapped her left arm over the edge of the notebook and arched her back so her chest and head covered any possibility of anyone viewing her writing.

Gary almost didn't want to say anything for fear she might think he was spying on her, but when he saw it was unlikely to catch her in a break, he cleared his throat and signaled her.

"Psst."

Nothing.

"Psst. Hey!"

Beth's head shot up, and she immediately drew her notebook closer to her chest. Her thin hair lay tight in a ponytail, but several clumps toward the front had fallen out and covered her cheeks. When she saw it was Gary, she quickly closed the journal and moved to the center of the yard where she could talk to him.

"What are you doing here?"

"Your dad's not around, is he?" Gary asked.

"No," she said. "He has a bowling league on Sundays. I'm... sorry about the other day." She moved closer to him, still clutching the notebook to her chest.

"That's all right," Gary said. "It wasn't your fault."

"Make sure he doesn't catch you again." Her eyes twitched toward the street, wary. "He can get pretty pissed off."

"No problem." Gary gathered up his nerve. He felt his cheeks flush from within. "I know I'm not supposed to talk to you, but, uh... I thought maybe you'd want to go out and get a coke or something sometime with me."

She lowered her head and flushed a little herself. "I don't know."

"Not right now or anything," Gary countered, embarrassed, feeling like a clunky mannequin again. "Just sometime, if you want. I work at Rocky's Pizzeria downtown. Maybe you could stop in. Free soda."

He caught a faint smile growing, partially hidden by her hair, and his heart warmed. He thought she might turn away, but she finally looked up at him.

"Fine. Maybe."

"That's great," Gary said. "I guess I'll... see you there sometime."

They stood together, both of them awkward, both of them eyeing the street and the back of her house.

"So what are you writing?" he asked.

Her grip on the notebook grew tighter. He could almost see her knuckles turn white. "It's nothing. Just some journal stuff."

"Oh, a journal. I thought about keeping a journal once, but I didn't think I'd have anything to really say."

"You could write about Radcliffe," she said.

That made him feel a bit uncomfortable, but not as much as last time to his surprise. "That's true."

He was about to ask her where he might meet her in school sometime, but her mother poked her head through the back door and called to her.

Gary darted behind the trees. His heart froze and he chided himself for getting caught already, but her mother went on as if he weren't there.

"Can you help me for a minute?" The words were slurred and lazy.

"Sure, Mom," Beth said dully.

With a quick glance back to Gary, she went to her backdoor and headed inside. Gary slipped back through the trees and walked down to the train tracks.

Gary sat on the track rail and tossed rocks against the building, listening to the stony pings they made when they bounced off. The air was quiet, save for a small breeze that brushed against his skin, carrying the coppery smell of the dirt and wood from the tracks to his nose.

He secretly hoped he would see Beth coming down the trail but he knew it wouldn't be happening any time soon. Not yet, at least. He got a good feeling from their brief conversation. He liked her already. Watching her made him feel giddy in the strangest way, like a bizarre drug floated through his system.

He felt the tracks vibrate before he saw the train coming. It was such a massive thing to him, rounding the corner in the distance. The heat it generated distorted the air around it, making it look like a traveling oasis. At first it felt like it would never arrive; it grew slowly, chugging along until its low rumble crept into his ears like a swarm of locusts. Exhilaration rushed through him. Adrenaline stabbed through his veins, his skin.

Superman beat a train? No way.

It was huge, a mythic colossus bearing down on him. The wind drew still, as if everything around the train had been sucked into it like a gargantuan vortex, or a massive black hole. He waited, allowing the awe of the thing to fill him, then stood and stepped off the tracks to watch it pass. He could have waited longer, but he didn't want to cause any commotion with the engineer, and what was the point? He'd already achieved the feeling he wanted, the thrill of it.

As it passed, it seemed to draw the tree line toward it as if the laws of physics were bent to its will. When it had finally gone by, he flopped back onto the track and watched it disappear over the far horizon. He couldn't help but smile.

He hoped he would see Beth again soon.

Gary deeply admired Gail's paintings. She'd gone to lie in the backyard hammock, preferring to lounge in the early evening while she had the chance, she told him, leaving him to fend for himself in the art room. She had set her latest piece on the floor and added the painting of Old Eben Flood to the easel for Gary to work on, but right now he was more interested in viewing her work.

It was different from what he had seen from her before, unlike the bridges and the dams and the barns and the lighthouses lining the walls along the floor, cluttering up the corners. This one didn't use the various shades of browns and greens and oranges, the dark earth tones Gary came to associate with her work. The painting closest to the easel was a whirl of various shades of blue, a swirling vortex of ocean colors leading from the center outwards in a clockwise motion to the edges of the canvas.

The outline of a woman lay suspended in the center of it, her head and left arm reaching up toward something distant above her, as if about ready to pluck something from out of thin air. Her right knee was raised and crossed over her other leg, like a nimble dancer. Her thighs and her midsection were dappled in dark blues and blacks, yet stood in easy contrast to the tinged background. A single shaft of yellow illuminated her back, like the sun breaking behind her.

Gary stood in awe of the painting, captivated by the colors and the woman in the center. He wondered what she might be reaching for, and where she stood, if she stood in any kind of a real place at all. He was sure Gail wasn't finished with it yet, but he admired it just the same, and the creativity of it stirred something in his own mind.

He pulled a new canvas from the closet, unrolled and stretched it onto a frame, then tacked it onto the easel. The paints had already been laid out for him and he selected three tubes: French Ultramarine, Viridian Hue, and Titanium White.

The French Ultramarine was a deep blue color that reminded him of the sky at the horizon after the sun goes down, just before it gives way to blackness. The Viridian Hue was a dark green, the color of the thickest Amazon jungle. With the Titanium White, he'd be able to mix up any shade of either color he wanted, and even make a few interesting ones by mixing the blues and greens.

With the paints, he swirled together six dimples of color and set to outlining his thoughts. In his mind he saw Beth sitting on the stump from her backyard, but in his scene she and the stump were down along the train track, looking toward the horizon. He would make her smiling, and he would make her eyes bright and round and shining like he knew they could be.

He began with the outline of her body and the stump beneath her, then dabbed in the tree line behind her with a round, flat brush. He used a thin piece of charcoal to draw in the beginnings of the tracks, careful to make his lines straight, leading to a point in the upper right of the canvas. He'd never been much for straight lines, but these were fine for now.

Before long, the canvas came alive with color and the beginning image of Beth. Of course he didn't think he'd be able to finish it. If Don saw he was painting Beth, he'd become upset with him and he didn't want that. He didn't want to cause any more trouble, for himself or for Don and Gail. He decided the painting wouldn't be the way he wanted it to be, but it would be close enough. He wouldn't paint her face. He'd leave it a dark blur, something that wouldn't give away who she was, but he would know, and maybe someday she would know.

In just over two hours, his outlines were completed and he began to fill them with his blended shades of blues. He used a brush with long, thin sable hair to add a crosshatching pattern around the center figure, attempting to add some dimensional depth to the work like Gail's painting had, but it was slow going. He realized it would take him more than a few hours to achieve the desired result, but that was all right. If it took him all year, he'd do it.

"How's it coming along?"

Gail surprised him by popping through the door and he jumped, nearly smearing his current stroke half way across the canvas.

She came fully into the room and stopped, realizing she had frightened him. "I'm sorry. I should have knocked."

"That's all right," Gary said. "I guess I was just concentrating a little too hard on this."

She swung around to his side and set her chin in her hand the way she did when she looked at her own paintings. Her eyes narrowed and her lips pursed in consideration.

"Where's the other painting you were working on?" she asked.

"It's underneath," Gary said. "I saw the one you were working on and I thought of this."

She pondered his work a bit longer, cocked her head to the side. "I see the color similarities, but it is definitely different. In a good way. Very good, very artistic."

"Do you really think so?"

"Oh, absolutely. I like how you've started the trees back there with the flat brush. Very innovative."

His heart swelled. "Can you tell what it is yet? I know I just started."

"Sure," she said. "It's a woman sitting on something down by a set of train tracks. It looks like a log she's sitting on. Is that right?"

"Yep."

"Keep it up, kid, and you'll be the next Picasso. Seriously."

"I hope I can get as good as you."

She tousled his hair and it tickled him. "Get out of town. You're such a little schmoozer."

She regarded the canvas once more, and her eyes swept across it from top to bottom, falling finally onto the figure in the center. Gary watched her from the corner of his eye and noted the expression that came into her face. What was it? Concern? Fear? He didn't have time to ponder it for long. She shook it off and brought back her smile, denying her own thoughts it seemed to Gary.

"Keep up the good work." She headed back into the hallway.

He watched her go and wondered if she knew it was Beth in his painting. Could it be so obvious to her? Do women just know these things? No, he concluded. There wasn't much to tell from a single painting, and such a simple one at that.

CHAPTER 12
The Mousetrap

It was Gary's turn for the Sunday night shift at Rocky's, so he ate an early dinner and headed out.

Gail had whipped up a quick meat and potato pie by stuffing leftover taco meat and some boiled potatoes into a pocket of dough and baking it. "It's a pseudo pastry." She pulled it out of the oven with her rose print oven mitt. "Miners' wives back in the twenties used to make these for their husbands to take down into the mines for their lunches because they stayed nice and warm for them. Only they didn't use taco meat, of course. I wonder if they even had tacos back then? Hmmm."

Gary eyed the dough pouch with suspicion. It looked like a huge pizza pocket, but with meat and potatoes?

Gail caught his expression and chuckled. "Don't worry. It's good. Just try it. Besides, what are you worried about anyway? You seem to eat anything."

"That's true," Gary said. "Anything you make."

"Good, now eat."

And it *was* delicious. Who knew meat and potatoes could taste so good? He couldn't tell what, but there were some other spices she added aside from the taco seasoning that gave it a nice kick, making his tongue tingle. It didn't take him long to finish the whole thing.

"Now that wasn't so bad, was it?" she said with a proud smirk. "Maybe that will help you resist the temptation of all those burgers and hotdogs at Rocky's."

Gary dropped his fork onto the plate with a small 'chink.' He would probably have a hotdog with mustard later on, maybe a little cheese, but he didn't tell her this. He loved the hotdogs there.

Gail offered him a ride, but he opted to walk, preferring the fifteen minute trip down Washington Street where he could stare at the multicolored houses and the various people in their yards and feel a part of it all. Sometimes he turned left at Allen Street and cut over to Lincoln Avenue where the Catholic Church was.

The houses were different there from the ones on Washington, older and earthier, much more statuesque than the rest of town with dark shutters and angled, pointy roofs. He never saw people in their yards on Lincoln Avenue and wondered what kinds of people lived in such houses. Were they rich? Old? Were they real?

When he had the time, he liked to cross through all the side streets and take a roundabout way toward Main Street, moving like a mouse through a maze. Winsbury still fascinated him, and he reveled in the fact that he was here, living in a town like this, away from that other place that still made him cringe with a single thought. It was almost like a dream.

Finally he reached Main Street, passed the drug store at the corner and popped into Rocky's, ready to work. Two customers sat in the corner, an elderly couple with matching sets of silver hair waiting for menus. When Gary passed through the door, their eyes perked up at him, and the old man craned his neck, waiting for someone to attend to them.

"Has anyone helped you yet?" Gary asked.

The old man wrapped his knuckles on the table. "Not yet."

He retrieved two menus from their slot by the register and brought them to the table. "I'll be right back with some water."

He took their drink order, brought it to the table, and let them alone to look at the menu. In the backroom, Rocky leaned out the back door, smoking a cigarette and blowing the smoke into the alley.

"There are some customers out there," Gary said.

Rocky flicked his cigarette butt out into the alley. "Did you get them?"

"Yeah. I got their drinks and they're looking at the menu."

"Thanks."

Gary took his apron from the rack, slipped it around his neck and waist, then proceeded to scrape off the top of the grill. Hardened pieces of ground beef and hotdog flecks lay scattered over the top like crumbly stones. From the corner of his eye, he saw Rocky slip his hand behind the cheese containers, take a nip from his poorly hidden bottle of schnapps, and slip it back again.

Gary figured he was drunk already, which wasn't uncommon on Sundays. It wasn't uncommon any day, as a matter of fact, but Sundays were particularly bad because it was one of the slowest days. It didn't bother Gary, nothing could bother him tonight. Thoughts of Beth danced through his mind, and it gave everything a new perspective.

"What are you so smiley about tonight?" Rocky positioned himself in the center of the kitchen and propped his hands onto his hips, almost mocking himself. "You meet a girl or something?"

Gary blushed. "Well, actually..."

"There it goes!" Rocky squealed before Gary had a chance to finish. A grin spread over his face and he slapped his thigh with the flat of his hand. His white paper hat tipped over the edge of his forehead. "It's all over now. Let me give you one word of caution. Beware of women! They'll steer you down some of the darnedest paths you'd never dare go if you had any sense in your brain. Every path but the right path. Believe you me."

Gary laughed and scraped a large piece of white gunk off the grill. "Did a woman steer you down the wrong path, Rocky?"

Rocky's eyes glazed over, and he stared up toward the ceiling as if recalling a pleasant memory. "I've been steered wrong so many times by women I can't tell if I'm coming or going."

They both laughed and Rocky headed to the dining area to take the elderly couple's order. When he returned, he slapped the order down on the counter. Scrawled on the tiny green slip of paper was "1 small cheese pizza."

"Slim pickin's," Rocky said.

Gary yanked up a small wad of dough from the dough bin and began the preparation.

"So what the hell is that?" Rocky asked.

"What?" Gary looked up and brushed the lock of hair away from his eyes to see Rocky staring at the contraption he'd made the last time he worked.

"Oh, that," Gary said. "That's my better mousetrap." It was a simple thing, really, consisting of a coffee can propped up on a stick with a can of jalapeno cheese sitting on top of it. "Thanks for reminding me."

He took a Dixie cup from the cupboard, added a spoonful of jalapeno cheese from the cooler, and set it beneath the coffee can.

"You think mice like spicy stuff?" Rocky said with a smirk in his voice.

"Why wouldn't they?"

"What are you going to do if you catch it? You gonna kill it?"

"I don't know. I hadn't thought of it. I guess I have to catch it first."

What would he do with it? It surprised him that he hadn't considered what he might do. He could kill it, or he could just let it go in the alley, but then it might come back.

Rocky slipped over to the schnapps shelf and took another nip. "You know, killing is some rough business. Even with rats."

The phrase came at Gary like a clamp on his chest. *Killing is some rough business.* How well he knew, unfortunately.

"Yeah, I guess so." He let the hair fall down over his eyes this time. He made the pretense of mixing up the pizza sauce, but it was already done.

"Back in Vietnam I had my own little mousetrap," Rocky said. "Did I ever tell you that? Except it wasn't for rats."

His words were starting to slur now, and Gary figured he must have been drinking all day, since early this morning. Still, he couldn't help but be captivated by the man, by the memories he had. He saw so much of himself, of his own future, in Rocky.

"It was just a hole we dug and covered up with leaves," Rocky's gaze glazed over again, as much with the booze as with reminiscing. "And one day we caught us something."

Gary's throat was dry. Part of him didn't want to hear the rest of what he knew was coming, but he couldn't help it. Another part did want to hear it all.

"It was a young guy," Rocky said. "Probably not much older than you are now. He didn't have a gun and he was yelling something in Vietnamese."

"What did he say?"

"I have no idea. To this day I have no idea, but the guys behind me were yelling too. They kept yelling '*Kill that sum bitch! Kill that sum bitch!*'"

Rocky's voice bellowed, and for a brief moment, Gary thought of the elderly couple in the dining room, but then quickly forgot about them. Rocky took his schnapps from the shelf and drank it openly now. He wiped his hands on his sleeve. His eyes reddened, perhaps on the verge of tears.

They were silent. Gary slipped the pizza into the oven and closed the oven door with a clang. Hearing Rocky behind him, the sniffles and the shuffling feet, he already knew the ending to the story. Again, he was torn. Part of him didn't want to hear it, any of it, but he would hear it, *had* to hear it. From the day he asked Rocky about killing anyone, it had become inevitable.

"So what did you do?" Gary asked when he felt the silence had to be broken.

Rocky straightened the cap on his head and drew up his glassy eyes. "So I killed him."

And simple as that, that was what had happened. Wasn't it the way of it with his father? Hadn't he stood there, a twelve-year-old boy before his father, holding the gun he'd stolen from the drawer only minutes earlier, deciding whether or not the man should live or die? Only Gary didn't have anyone screaming in his ears, screaming out for him to take a life. He had made that horrible decision on his own. He'd always known it.

"Why did you do it?" The words weighed heavy in his jaw like a piece of brick.

"Because it was what I was supposed to do." Rocky threw back another drink. "It was war back then. I thought I'd forgotten about it, but you got me thinking about it again the other day."

"I'm sorry, I didn't mean to..."

"No, no, that's all right. It was a long time ago. Long time. It changed who I am."

Rocky's eyes burned into his own, and Gary had to look away. The mousetrap sat propped against the wall, a tiny rust spot forming on the outer lip of the can.

"Do you think he would have killed you if he had the chance?" Gary asked.

"I don't doubt it for a minute."

The questions fell out of Gary like water through a gushing faucet. He couldn't stop them if he'd tried. "But do you feel bad about what you did?"

Rocky paused this time. "You know what? I'd have to say I do, Gary. I feel like shit about it."

He punctuated the thought by downing the remainder of his schnapps, then staggered to the back door. He opened it up, tossed his bottle into the alley, and lit up another cigarette.

"Can you take care of the customers the rest of the night?" His voice grew wispy, melancholy. He didn't even look at Gary.

"No problem." Gary went into the dining room. He felt deeply sorry for Rocky, but he didn't want to be around him anymore that night. It stirred up too many questions about himself.

Gary felt like the walking dead the next day at school, a stiff, mindless zombie. His bones ached and his head throbbed. He felt like Rocky looked last night. He wondered if hangovers were contagious or something. It wasn't that he was tired from overwork or lack of sleep the night before. It was from Rocky.

After their conversation in the backroom, Rocky proceeded to get even drunker and practically passed out behind the cheese shelf, the remnants of their conversation buzzing in the air like a cloud of gnats.

All the talk of death and killing simultaneously repulsed and drew Gary in, only he didn't consider himself one of those rubber-neckers on the highway craning to see the bloody pulp of an accident on the side of the road. He was one of the participants in the accident, the single cause and reason for the collision that took a life. He had a right to look, even though he didn't want to.

The most disturbing part of Rocky's story was not so much the story itself—which was horrible enough—but in the way he told it. It was disturbing the way his eyes widened and grew blank while he searched for the details, the way they darkened, as if haunted by the past. At that moment Gary saw the disgust, the self-loathing, in the man; it was so much like himself, a futuristic, twisted version of his own face that looked back at him from the mirror every morning. It was the same expression, the same face, only with thirty-some odd more years of pain and guilt.

He did his best that morning to pretend nothing was wrong for Gail's benefit. He didn't want her to know he was upset. That might lead to a discussion of why he was upset, which he'd done his best so far to avoid since he'd been in their home. He sensed she knew something was wrong anyway, but hoped she would attribute it to getting up on the wrong side of the bed. Luckily, she left him alone.

School was no different. Mr. Reynolds wasn't in a particularly good mood and had the entire gym class performing calisthenics most of the morning. Gary didn't mind the exercise so much. Busying his body distracted his mind, but it all flooded back when gym class was over.

In the hallway before his next class, he shuffled through the locker he only visited three times during a normal day. His classes lay scattered at all ends of the school and most of the time it wasn't feasible to head all the way back to his locker so he did his best by loading down his book bag. He closed the locker door. Stan stood there grinning, practically swimming in his leather jacket. He'd slicked his hair back over his skull, amazing Gary at how much gel a person could goop in their hair before reaching a saturation point.

"Hey, Stan."

Stan reached into his pocket and leaned on the row of gray lockers. He crossed his sneakers and they squeaked over the gleaming, newly polished floor. Gary thought for a moment Stan was going to pull out a pack of cigarettes, but instead his hand emerged with a pencil. He tapped the eraser on his palm as if it were a Lucky Strike, as if he were packing it.

"Guess what?" Stan said. "It's party time, my friend. Tomorrow night, you and me. I've got the place. Can you make it?"

Stan continued to tap the pencil over his palm slowly, coolly, with the steady rhythm of a metronome. He cocked his head forward so that when he looked at Gary, his gray eyes looked upward past his brow ridge, which made him look all the more devious, and Gary all the more nervous.

"I don't think so," Gary said. "I had some serious trouble the last time, and I don't think they'll let me go. Besides, I have to work again."

Stan's pencil stopped, and he straightened up from the locker, pouting. "Aww, man. I was really counting on you being there. I told a bunch of guys you were going."

Gary shouldered his book bag. It felt heavier today. "I'm sorry."

"Well, can't you just stop by before work?" Stan's face brightened with the possibility. "For like an hour maybe?"

Gary softened. "I don't know. Maybe. Where's it at?"

"It's close to you. On Lincoln Avenue."

Lincoln Avenue? That in itself intrigued Gary, the street where the massive, shuttered houses loomed. "It can't be for long. I'll try to stop by before work."

"Sweet." Stan reached into his pocket again and pulled out a piece of paper. He scribbled on it with the pencil and shoved it into Gary's fist. "There's the address. I'll be there pretty much after school so just show up on your way to work. That's cool."

"All right, man."

They smacked fists and headed in opposite directions.

Gary said nothing to Gail or Don about the 'party' he was stopping in on for a couple of reasons. One, he didn't want to cause any trouble with his foster parents and two, he didn't think of it as going to a 'party.' Maybe some of the people would be partying there, but since he was only stopping in for an hour or so before work, he didn't see any harm in it. Besides, Stan really wanted him to and he didn't want to disappoint his friend.

He left early for Rocky's after eating a quick dinner and waving goodbye to Gail. She made no remarks about his leaving and seemed to suspect nothing, which gave him a twinge of guilt that he swallowed down hard.

He crossed over to Lincoln Avenue and headed to the address Stan had written down for him. It was an enormous house; a two-story, dark brick home with a black wrought iron fence around the perimeter of the yard. The grass was short and neatly groomed. Rows of squat bushes and trees lined the front of the place. The fence gate sat partially open and a light flickered from somewhere within.

He slipped through the gate and headed toward the door, suddenly self-conscious about his clothes. He was dressed for work in his worst t-shirt. It had grease stains at the bottom and along the edges of his sleeves from Rocky's grill. He wasn't far from home and he was half-way to deciding whether or not to go back and change when the front door flung open and a flat nosed guy with straw-like, sandy hair poked his head out. He'd never seen the guy before and figured he must be a senior.

"What's up?" he said.

"I was invited by Stan."

"Stan? You mean Stanley?"

"Uh, yeah."

The guy smirked and cleared himself of the doorway so Gary could pass through. The inside foyer lay dark within. On the wall in front of him hung a gold encrusted mirror that confirmed the grease stains on his shirt. The interior walls were dark yellow and brown stone, and his shoes thudded against polished wooden floors. A white carpeted stairwell led up into the house, but the flat nosed senior shut the door and headed through the lower hallway, so Gary followed.

Down a set of stairs and through the kitchen brought them to the basement, where the room opened into a large group of perhaps fifteen or twenty guys surrounding a keg of beer. A stereo sat on the far ledge beside a curtained window, blasting out club music with a heavy bass. Someone had turned the bass on the stereo all the way up to get the effect. The basement stretched along the entire length of the house and looked large enough to be an entire home, complete with television and stereo, its own bathroom and shower, a pool table, a pullout bed, and a stocked bar. No parents around. He wondered where they were this evening.

He didn't recognize anyone immediately, except for a few of the guys he'd passed in the halls of Winsbury High, nothing more than faces and blurs to him. They were all seniors, he knew for sure, which gave him some level of discomfort. Seniors and juniors usually didn't mix well, at least from his own experience in Radcliffe, but things would be different here. Stan was here, after all.

Stan, clad in his leather jacket, hovered in the center of one of the groups at the outskirts of the keg, sipping beer from a green plastic cup. When he saw Gary, his eyes lit up for the briefest moment, revealing his true excitement, but he quickly slipped into his cool-headed Stan persona. His eyes narrowed and he sauntered over.

"Yo, Gary," he said. "Glad you could make it."

"Sure." They smacked knuckles, their standard greeting.

"Want a beer?"

"No thanks. I have to be at work in an hour."

"You sure?"

"Yeah, thanks."

"No problem," Stan said with some mild disappointment. "Come on over and I'll introduce you to some of the guys."

As they wound through the crowd, the odd sensation of eyes on him crawled up Gary's back, which didn't surprise him, though it disturbed him. It was this way in Radcliffe all the time. Groups of guys congregated like mini gangs, always wary, always watchful. Gary didn't like to be reminded of Radcliffe so strongly.

When they arrived at Stan's group, he finally recognized two of the guys from his first day of school. They were the idiots who practically bowled him over and commented on his shirt, the greasy pony-tailed guy and the one with the long mustache.

Ponytail wore a sleeveless muscle shirt that revealed his fairly large biceps. His shoulders and forearms weren't quite so toned, but were certainly bulky, and Gary figured this guy was strong as hell. He wouldn't want to run into him in Radcliffe. When he'd first run into him in the school hallway that morning, he had thought the guy might be Spanish or Greek, but now, in the light of the basement, he saw that neither was true. He was just a white guy with an incredible tan. When the guy laughed, his voice boomed through the basement, even over the bass of the stereo.

Mustache stood next to him, not quite so bulky but large in his own right, looking pasty next to his tanned friend. His forehead angled quickly back from his nose to the crown of his head, giving the impression of a Neanderthal. He wore a jet black shirt with black jeans and black cowboy boots, reminding Gary of his initial impression of an evil Wyatt Earp.

Mustache was in the middle of them all, laughing about something Ponytail was saying when Stan and Gary approached. The group of eyes drew to Gary, but both Mustache and Ponytail took their time before paying any attention.

"Hey, guys," Stan started when they didn't acknowledge them, his voice raising an octave. "This is Gary, the guy I was telling you about."

Ponytail finished his story, something about jamming his guitar and strumming the rhythms, then set his stone-like eyes on Gary's frame. His upper lip curled with disappointment, and something in his eyes revealed recognition.

"So you're the bad boy from Radcliffe?"

Gary disliked the guys immediately. It wasn't just from his first encounter with them in school, which certainly held a part in it. Mostly it was from the personalities they exuded, the strained, tired looks they gave him, as if interrupted by someone's annoying child. Their eyes told Gary how they felt about him, and about everyone else in the room: that they were better than all of them, that they tolerated the mediocrity around them by choice, and that everyone would do well to know that from the get-go and perhaps bow down and kiss their feet for it. Gary might have left immediately if it weren't for Stan.

"No, it's just Gary."

Mustache and Ponytail smirked in unison. Apparently Gary didn't know the rules. Stan shifted on his heels from the obvious tension.

"Are you sure you don't want one beer, bro?" Stan asked.

"No, thanks. Really."

Ponytail's hand snapped up and thwacked the back of Stan's head. Stan winced but he laughed nervously, overdoing it a bit in the process, pretending the slap was the funniest thing in the world.

"What about me, Stanley?" Ponytail said. "Don't you want to get me a beer?"

"No problem." Stan took Ponytail's cup before heading to the keg.

Gary didn't move. A familiar heat flared in his chest. Here was a side of Stan he'd never seen before, and a side he didn't like much now that he'd seen it. This was the groveling Stan, the one eager to please the older students, the one that allowed them to slap him in the back of the head for a joke.

His thoughts flashed back to Willie, Karge, and Big Ben at Radcliffe, the ones who attacked him in the kitchen before he left. They were bullies in a place where bullies ruled, and that wasn't too different from Ponytail and Mustache, but at least the Radcliffe bullies had set out to do what they tried to do, commanded at least some respect. They inspired fear, whereas the bulky seniors before him inspired nothing but contempt in Gary. He figured they'd never even been in a fight before, and ruled over their little group through sheer attitude and size. He hated that.

Stan returned with the beers and handed one to Ponytail. "So, Gary. This is Brubaker, this is his house." Then Stan pointed to Mustache. "And this is Dorn." Mustache-Dorn smirked and delivered a peevish nod.

"Thanks for the beer." The pony-tailed Brubaker tapped Stan on the back of the head again. "Stan's like our little pet around here. That's why we keep him around. He's a good little dog."

Gary's eyes thinned. "Is that right?"

"That's right," Brubaker said. "Isn't that right, Stanley?"

Stan laughed again. It was hollow but forceful, his obvious attempt to ingratiate himself to the group.

"So what's the deal with Radcliffe?" Dorn asked, contempt etched into his face mixed with only a mild interest. "How'd you get stuck there? Did you rape your sister or something?"

The group of guys in front of Gary bubbled a collective laugh with Brubaker the loudest. Stan laughed nervously and watched Gary for a reaction. It was obvious to Gary how Stan felt at that moment, that it was important to him for Gary to fit into this group of 'friends,' but Gary couldn't do it. He'd seen enough of this sort of thing in Radcliffe and there was no way he'd get sucked into what he used to call the idiot crowd.

He righted himself and glared into Dorn's eyes. "I thought that was your sister."

The mild grin shrunk from Dorn's face and Brubaker released a belly laugh.

"Oh, slam! The boy's got a tongue. I don't think he's going to be a good dog... what do you think, Stanley?" With that, Brubaker delivered another slap to the back of Stan's head.

The heat flared in Gary's chest. If he would have been in Radcliffe at the moment, he knew he would have been all over this guy, but he calmed himself, clenched his fists in his pockets. "What's the problem, man?"

The group started to laugh again, but Brubaker's eyes grew wary. "Problem? There's no problem."

Gary took a step back and faced Stan, ignoring the group in front of him. "Why do you let him slap you like that? I don't think it's very funny. It's actually kind of stupid."

Stan shrugged and took a swig of beer. His face creased with uncertainty. "It's just a joke, Gary."

A new kind of smile spread onto Brubaker's lips and Gary could see what was coming. The guy reminded him of the type that liked to torture animals as a kid.

"What, you don't like it when I do this?" He landed another slap to the back of Stan's head. To top it off, Dorn slipped around the back of Brubaker and delivered a slap of his own.

Gary locked eyes with Brubaker for a good thirty seconds before turning back to Stan. It was an intense few moments, where anything possible could have happened.

They could jump me anytime here. Gary almost expected it.

"I have to go. I'll talk to you later."

He turned and eyed the room, surveying his surroundings. He didn't know what might happen and he didn't like the situation. He knew no one here but Stan, and that wouldn't help him. Everyone here was a friend of the host, the tanned and stupid Brubaker, and Gary basically just called the guy a jerk without actually saying the word. If any situation were ripe for getting his ass kicked, this would be it.

He saw a fireplace along the wall with a poker leaning against it. Above the fireplace, lined along the mantle, were five bowling trophies of various sizes. All potential weapons. If someone decided to jump him, he'd grab one of those and start swinging. He didn't want to do it, but if he had to, he'd defend himself. He'd leave a few guys with bruises or broken bones.

He listened for the rush of air or the shuffle of feet that comes before a sudden attack from behind, but none came. When he reached the stairs, he realized he would be all right. No one was going to touch him. He paused there before heading up and turned once to look at Stan. Stan still stood with the crowd, watching him with the others. For a moment, Gary hoped Stan might detach himself from the group, from Brubaker and Dorn. Stan's foot began to shuffle forward and Gary saw the silent yearning in his face, but a moment later, it was gone. Stan wouldn't be going anywhere. He was caught in the trap that was Brubaker and Dorn.

Gary turned away, headed up and out, to the edge of Lincoln Avenue, ready for work. He had a new impression of Lincoln Avenue, and it wasn't a good one. He was worried, not so much for himself, but for Stan. He could understand someone like Stan wanting to please his friends. He'd known people like that, a lot of people, but it didn't have to be this way. It was clear to him Stan wanted to be the 'bad ass' guy that he so often rambled on about, but this wasn't the way to make it happen.

He wished Stan hadn't said anything to them about Radcliffe. He didn't want that going around anymore than it already had been. He couldn't control the rumors that went with things like this, but any information guys like Brubaker and Dorn got could be used against him, just another thing to use as leverage and get under his skin. He somehow knew this wasn't the last he'd see of the two of them. He just hoped it wouldn't be the last he'd see of Stan.

CHAPTER 13
Secret Places

Luckily for Gary, it was another quiet evening at Rocky's Pizzeria. After his encounter with Stan's buddies, he wasn't in the mood to deal with the general public. There hadn't been more than two customers in the first couple of hours, so Rocky slipped up beside him and instructed him to shut down the grill.

"Why don't you head on home, kiddo." The faint scent of schnapps drifted down to Gary's nose.

"Are you sure? Do you want me to clean the grill?"

"The grill?" Rocky said. "I'll take care of it. You just go on and have a good night."

"No problem. Thanks."

Gary headed up Washington in the still silence of the early evening. The sun hung lazily on the horizon, ready to dip down across the other side of the earth. He took no side streets this time, avoiding Lincoln altogether now. The sidewalk beneath him stretched toward the top of the hill, cracks running like dark veins bleeding into the grass. He stepped around the cracks, avoiding touching them with his feet.

When he reached the top of the hill, his heart leapt at the sight of Beth making her way carefully around the side of her house. Gary waved to her, but she didn't see him. She stepped through the trees and paused at the edge of the trail leading down to the railroad tracks, surveyed the area for a brief moment, then disappeared down the path.

Her father's car wasn't in the driveway, so he took the opportunity to follow her, passing between the two houses in long strides, careful not to hurt the pristine grass. He reached the tracks, about a football field's length from her. She shuffled slowly down the dirt path, completely unaware of anyone following, kicking at random rocks, her ever-present journal tucked beneath her arm.

Gary hurried, but not too quickly. He didn't want to startle her. When he got within ten feet of her and she still hadn't heard him coming, he stopped and cleared his throat.

"Hi, Beth."

Her head snapped to the side so quickly Gary thought she might have gotten whiplash. When she saw it was Gary, she relaxed some.

"Whoa," Gary said. "I didn't mean to scare you like that. I almost snuck up on you, but I figured I'd give you a heart attack or something. Looks like I almost did anyway."

She turned to face him, bringing the journal up to cover the Winsbury High School emblem on her sweatshirt. "That's all right."

Her hair was collected in a ponytail again with several stray strands poking out like a haggard washwoman. Her skin was pale and thin, her eyes grim with weariness. Gary found her beautiful nonetheless.

"I hope you don't mind I followed you," Gary stammered. "I mean, I'm not following you, but I saw you coming down here. I mean..."

"Really, it's all right. I like to walk down here sometimes. It's quiet."

Gary smiled. "Train tracks are quiet?"

She smiled back and it warmed him. "When there's no train on them they are."

"That's true." He approached her and nudged a stone with his foot. "So were you going to write some more journal stuff tonight?"

Her eyes fell to the journal and she let it fall down to waist level. She didn't open it.

"I thought about it. I usually like to write when the inspiration strikes me. Sometimes it happens down here."

"So you're a writer?" Gary asked, impressed. "What kind of stuff do you like to write?"

"Poetry mostly." Her eyes dipped away from him and the journal rose again to protect her.

Images of *Mr. Flood's Party* flashed in Gary's mind. "That's great. I really like poetry."

Her fingers slipped along the edges of the journal, fumbling with loose flaps of paper. Her eyes came up again, shining, emboldened. "You like poetry?"

"Well, I'd like to like poetry. I've only read a few things in school, but I like what I've read so far. We didn't study much of it in Radcliffe."

Their gazes came together for a long moment, and the air between them drew calm and silent. Nothing else existed in that moment. Beth's fingers ran faster along the edge of the journal. For an instant, Gary thought she might open it and read something to him, but in the end, her gaze broke away and the world rushed back around them.

"Maybe you could show me some of yours sometime so I can see what I'm missing." Gary did his best to recapture the fleeting moment.

He was happy when she relaxed again and smiled. "Maybe."

Far down the tracks, the distant train broke the new silence with a soft whistle. Beth spun toward it and her chest rose and fell more quickly. Her eyes grew wide with what he thought was a mixture of awe and fear. The train somehow galvanized her.

"There goes the neighborhood," he said. "Are you okay?"

"It scares me sometimes, the train. That's all. Just look at it. It's so huge. It's like the devil coming after you."

Gary squinted down the track at the glowing ball of light heading toward them. "I never thought of it that way. I can see why you're a poet." He stepped onto the tracks and balanced on one foot. "You don't have to be afraid of trains. It won't get you. All you have to do is step off the tracks."

She glowered at the coming train, her hands tightened over the journal in front of her. "Sometimes it's not that easy."

Gary dropped between the rails and held his arms out, facing the train. It was getting rather close now and they could hear the rhythmic chugs getting louder.

"Sure it is. Watch."

He closed his eyes and held his arms outward, reaching toward the trees and the sky. He imagined God reaching down to him and plucking him up from the tracks for an early evening sky ride. He glanced at Beth through the corner of his eye. She scurried away from the tracks and into the bushes for cover, eyes wide, afraid and fascinated. But she didn't leave.

"You're crazy." Her former hint of a smile was a full—blown grin.

"Here it comes!" Gary cried and clenched his eyes closed. He stood in the early darkness, listening. He could hear it, the gigantic beast rampaging down the steel tracks toward him, desperate, hungry to swallow him whole.

The engineer laid on a quick blast of the horn, and Gary squinted forward, making sure he had enough time to move away. He glanced once more at Beth, catching her futile attempts to cover her eyes from the event that obviously captured her total attention. He loved it when the smile crept more fully onto her lips. With just enough time by his calculation, he spun in a half circle, placing his back to the train. He waved once at Beth then took a deep bow.

"Gary!" she cried out, though the word was torn away by another blast of the horn.

He finally stepped off the tracks. A moment later, the train whizzed by, kicking dust up onto his pants and the back of his shirt. The cool breeze blasted him and it felt good. At the edge of the trees, Beth hung back, protected by a thicket of bushes, laughing heartily in amazement.

"That's crazy!"

"See?" Gary said. "All you have to do is step off."

When the train passed, Beth reemerged from her hiding spot and they watched the train go together until it finally disappeared into the horizon. Before long, her smile slipped away and her face transformed once again to the leaden, pensive expression Gary was used to.

"Is everything all right?"

She thumbed her journal but didn't open it. "Yeah. I guess so. I should go."

"Okay. I'll wait for you to head up before I go. Just in case."

She smiled thankfully and climbed up the trail through the trees, her ponytail dangling behind her. At the top, she turned once and smiled, giving him a quick wave. Her eyes glinted in the growing darkness, and then she was gone.

Gary supposed this was it. His heart raged inside him and every fiber of his body throbbed with heat. He didn't know for sure, but he guessed this might be the beginnings of love.

Once again, inspiration struck him. He headed straight for the painting room and went to work on his image of Beth. He'd been able to work on it a few nights since he'd started it, but the more he worked on it, the further away from finishing it he felt. Each stroke called for another, every detail begged for something new. The blues had taken shape nicely, blending in unexpected shades and gradients into the nooks of the canvas, the light blues curling like smoke over the darker, midnight blues of the work.

He needed a better view now. He turned the easel around to face the window, then cracked the curtains open so he could see Beth's house across the street. The view wasn't as good as the one from his room, but it was good enough. He could see the light on in her room, and he could partly see her sitting at her desk hunched over her journal, scribbling away. He could only imagine what she wrote and he wondered if any of it might be about him.

On the canvas, he added detail to her hair. The brush fluttered over the oils, spreading a gentle line of light brown, forming the strands like gold around her head. It was the only color besides the shades of blues he'd started with and the contrast was beautiful to him, like an angel's halo, but still, in the center of the canvas, the face was blank.

How desperately he wanted to paint her eyes while they were fresh in his mind. He'd never been able to stare into them before like he did tonight, mixing himself up like a giddy child, the blue swirls of them turning, glowing like the moon. He knew exactly how he would paint them if he could.

He smiled. They'd had a moment down there by the tracks that evening, hadn't they? He couldn't ignore the way the entire world melted away, ceased to exist when their eyes locked together.

It could have been pouring rain and he wouldn't have noticed. There could have been another train barreling down on him and it would have never touched him.

He wondered if Beth felt the same. Could she? His hands shook at the thought, at the possibility she didn't feel anything for him, that it was all imagined, a product of his overeager mind. But he recalled the curl of her lips and the dip of her eyelids as she stood at the edge of the trail, and the way her eyes flashed at that moment. It calmed him, steadied his hand.

He had a new idea. He took the unfinished painting of Beth and leaned it against the desk, then took up a new canvas. He began with blue. If he couldn't paint her eyes into his portrait, then he would paint only her eyes. Wasn't it the only way he could give them justice anyway? The only way he could give them the detail they deserved?

Before long, the canvas came alive with swirls of blues and dark greens, the colors of midnight hues meshed with the eyes of the girl he was falling in love with.

Night seeped in and a pair of headlights moved up the hill, hovering over the blacktopped street. Beth's father pulled into the driveway, skulked into the house, and let the door fall closed behind him. Shortly after, he was in Beth's room, talking to her. Her head turned to him briefly then back to her desk, but not before she reached into her desk and took the pills from the dark brown bottle she held there. Before long, her father pulled down the shade, and the light went out.

Without even thinking, Gary painted a doorway behind Beth's eyes, and within the doorway, a dark, shadowed figure.

"Who's that in the doorway?"

He spun, shocked, to find Gail leaning against the doorjamb, watching him. With the canvas turned, he wouldn't have seen anyone coming. He wondered how long she'd been standing there.

"It's nobody, I guess," he said. "Just a new idea I had."

He returned to the painting, his heart still racing slightly. Gail lingered behind him a moment longer, perhaps waiting for him to continue, but he couldn't. It felt like his hands were clenched in a vice.

"Sorry to bother you," she said and disappeared.

Gary set down the brush and stared through the window at the street. Beth's window remained dark the remainder of the evening.

Thursday night, Gary hurried down Washington with a crust of toast in his grip, late for work. He'd lost track of time while brushing up on his history reading, since he hadn't done so well on the last quiz. Not bad, just not the best he could have done. Don told him work would be the first thing to go if his grades weren't up to par, and he didn't want to lose the job. Last week Gail had helped him open up a savings account and he had close to $400.00 socked away. Another couple of months of work and he'd be able to start thinking about a car, although he hadn't broached the subject with Don or Gail yet.

On his way out, Gail caught him at the door and insisted he eat something before he left, and when he said he didn't have time, she thrust the piece of toast at him.

"Eat this then," she said. "I'll make myself another."

He took it gladly, and it made him laugh all the way down the block. A piece of toast wasn't going to do a whole lot to fill the ravenous hunger he felt so often these days, but he knew she didn't like the fact that he ate so many burgers and hotdogs and slices of pizza down at Rocky's.

"It just isn't what a growing boy should be eating," she told him on several occasions, and even though he told her every time he didn't eat the food there, she never believed him. She was right on that account.

He burst through the front door and winked at 'Moosey' the moose head, who perpetually guarded the place. Rocky was taking an order from a younger couple. He followed him into the back and put on his apron and paper hat.

"Sorry I'm late."

Rocky dismissed it with a wave of his hand. "No problem. It's slow again."

"Yeah, how do you stay in business?"

"Ahh, we make up for the slow nights during the lunch rush and weekends," Rocky said. "You're lucky I don't make you work on Saturday nights."

Gary took the young couple's order from Rocky and dropped two frozen burger patties on the grill before adding a batch of fries to the deep fryer. Hot grease bubbled up and crackled, as Rocky disappeared into the back returning with, a case of plastic cups on a dolly. Suddenly he slipped and lost his balance, nearly toppling over the dolly. Gary dropped his spatula and hurried to him, grabbed him by the sleeve to steady him.

"Are you all right?"

"Whoa," Rocky said. "Thanks, kid. Balance ain't what it used to be."

He shook it off, dipped his hand into his hiding spot behind the wall of cheese cans, and took a nip from his bottle. Gary considered saying something to him about the drinking, but decided against it. He didn't think he had the right to tell Rocky what to do or how to live his life, and he didn't want to upset him either. Hell, the guy had obviously been drinking for years, and his business was still running. The customers apparently didn't mind, and he could take care of himself, so what more was there?

He couldn't help but feel concerned for Rocky though. He didn't want to see anything bad happen to the man. Through the constant drunkenness and the aprons stained with pizza sauce, Gary saw a good man, a man he had come to like and respect.

He finished up the burgers, dropped them onto toasted buns with lettuce and sliced tomato, and brought them out to the waiting customers.

"Can I bring you anything else?" he asked.

The young guy, a black haired Italian with a nose the shape of a walnut, shook his head. The girl, a frumpy blonde with puffy cheeks smiled up at him, reminding him of a young Ethel Mertz. "No, thank you."

"Enjoy your meal." Gary turned and noticed Beth through the window standing on the sidewalk, looking in.

He rushed to the door and flung it open, his blood instantly pumped full of adrenaline and grins. He couldn't believe she was here, and he couldn't believe how happy it made him to see her.

"You came!" he cried. "I can't believe it. You finally get to see the world famous Rocky's Pizzeria."

Beth picked nervously at the sleeves of her dark blue sweatshirt. She wore a Chicago Cubs baseball cap with her hair poking out through the back and the bill hung low to partially cover her face. Her skin was as white as a soft sheet at the base of her neck.

"I actually can't stay," she said. "My mom is waiting for a prescription next door at the pharmacy, so I thought I'd stop by, see if you were working." She glanced up from under her cap and her eyes shone brightly through the shadow formed by the bill.

Gary's heart sank, but he was still glad she stopped by in the first place. "Can't you come in for a coke or anything? I've got extra pizza in the back. Maybe a burger? I'm sure Rocky wouldn't mind if I made an extra one."

He heard his own voice and the way it pleaded with her, but he couldn't stop himself.

"No, I really can't. My mom will be waiting for me."

"Cheese fries?" Gary tried desperately, flashing his most winning smile. "I make a mean cheese fry. Extra peppers?"

She cracked a smile. "No thanks."

"All right." Gary gave in. "But don't be afraid to call on me if you ever have any burnt pizza or burger needs. I'm always available. Twenty-four seven."

She laughed softly, almost under her breath, but Gary heard it. It was like music.

She shot a long glance toward the pharmacy and clenched her hands again, and Gary understood. She didn't want her mother to catch her talking to him.

"Well, I have to go," she said. "I'll see you later."

"No problem."

She hurried off down the street toward the pharmacy. He could have sworn she was skipping. How maddening it was to see her in such tiny snatches of time. *Soon,* he thought. *Soon.* He'd be able to see more of her soon.

He saw Beth two more times over the weekend, each time in five minute stints by the train tracks. She didn't know, but he'd gone down there several times on both days, hoping he might find her there, hoping it would look like a coincidence or a chance meeting. He felt nervous each time he saw her, and a little giddy when she smiled at him after appearing through the trees at the trail's edge. No trains passed through during their conversations, and Beth looked more and more at ease with every passing minute, her gaze lingering more, and her smile appearing more quickly.

They spoke of poetry and of school but of nothing substantial. Gary had the immediate sense Beth was as silent and protective of the work in her journal as he was of his time in Radcliffe. He held the deepest respect for that, so he pressed nothing toward it.

Each meeting left hope for the next, and on Sunday afternoon, he felt their friendship move to the next level. They walked slowly along the tracks, not going too far as they knew they had to turn around soon, their feet forming smudged trails in the dirt. Beth let her journal fall away from her chest, and now it dangled easily beneath her right arm, swaying in steady rhythm. The bill of her Chicago Cubs baseball cap pointed upward toward the sky instead of obscuring her eyes and the upper part of her face. Her hair lay neatly in its ponytail through the back.

Gary had been talking about work, about how he was helping Rocky to straighten up the kitchen the last few months, when Beth's left hand slipped toward him and reached into his own. He looked down at it. The pale white of her skin settled gently into his like a dove nesting there, so soft and warm that he instantly wanted to wrap up his entire body in that hand forever.

He made no reaction, however, except to squeeze it firmly, accepting it, not wanting to let it slip away. He didn't want to frighten her either, so they walked hand in hand a bit further down the track as he continued his conversation about the kitchen without skipping a beat.

At a moment when he was practically finished talking about Rocky's, she paused and faced him.

"I'd like to show you a place," she said. Again, the demureness, but not so distant as usual. "It's a place I like to go when I want to be alone. Can I show you?"

"I'd like to see it."

"Tomorrow?" she asked, her eyes pleading now, nervous. "Is tomorrow all right? My father usually works late on Mondays."

"Tomorrow it is then. I have to see my counselor, though, first."

"Counselor?"

"Yeah, it's Counselor Ray at school. Have you heard of him? He's that skinny guy with the big gym shoes."

"Oh yeah, I've seen him, I think. Don't they call him Rubbin' Ray or something like that?"

"Yeah, I don't get that. They make me see him once a week. You know, to just talk about how I'm adjusting and all that."

She squeezed his hand gently. "How are you adjusting?"

He squeezed back and smiled. "Very good, I think."

She let their hands slip away from each other and started up the trail through the trees alone. "I'll see you tomorrow then? After your meeting?"

"I'll be here."

And she was gone.

The next day, on his way to Counselor Ray's office, he walked through the dark hallways without a care, his mind racing with thoughts of Beth. She was going to show him *a place*, she said. His overzealous curiosity leapt at the thought of it, of spending time with her. She liked him, that was certain now. *She* had been the one to take *his* hand, not the other way around, and she had made the daunting effort to invite him to her secret place, the place she liked to go to when she wanted to be alone. And she would be alone with him this time.

Above, the dying fluorescent light blinked at him, making his shadow bounce along the corrugated lockers. He'd always hated the hallway, the oppression it exuded, but today it didn't bother him one bit.

Counselor Ray's door stood ajar in anticipation of his visit, as usual. He wrapped his knuckles on the doorjamb and adjusted the book bag on his shoulder. Ray sat with his legs draped over the desk, his massive sneakers partially blocking Gary's view of him.

"Come on in, Gary."

He flopped into the chair waiting for him. Ray adjusted his position, shifted his feet to the side part of the desk so they could see each other. The bottoms of his shoes were heavily worn, and the crisscross patterns were barely more than faded rubber grooves.

"What are you so happy about today?" Ray asked him.

Gary crossed his left foot onto his right knee. "What do you mean?"

"That smile on your face. What's that about, Mr. Smiling Gary?"

"Am I smiling?" He felt the skin around his chin and cheeks with his fingers. He didn't realize he had been. "Nothing, I guess."

Counselor Ray's feet came off the desk now and he leaned forward, pulled his worn deck of cards from the nearest drawer. "It's good to see you smiling. I can't say I've seen much of that since we've been meeting together."

Gary nodded. "Yeah, I guess not."

"So what does it all mean, all that smiling? Would you say things are looking up for you in Winsbury? Is life treating you right?"

It was a pleasant thought, Gary supposed, and perhaps it was even true. "That's a good way to put it. Life is treating me right."

"Good. I'm glad. Really."

"It's sort of nice. Different, but sort of nice, I guess."

Ray's amused expression changed, becoming more pensive and inquisitive. Gary knew what was coming. His elation slipped away. His defensive walls slammed up around him.

"Why don't you ever want to talk about what happened with your mother and father?"

The smile was gone now, completely. He said nothing.

"I know it's hard," Ray went on, "but you need to tell someone about it. Don't you think?"

"No."

"You haven't talked about it with anyone. Even your counselor at Radcliffe said she had to drag things out of you."

Gary shifted in his chair. The air in his lungs felt like steam in his chest. "You said we didn't have to talk about anything I didn't want to talk about."

The cards flew back and forth in Ray's hands, flickering effortlessly from finger to finger. "I know I did, but you're going to have to say something to somebody eventually. That's really the point of our meetings, you know. You may not want to let it out, but you can't hold something like that in forever, as much as you want to right now. It's going to find its way out of you one way or another, and if it finds its own way out, it probably won't be very good for you, if you know what I mean."

Gary glared at the man. Maybe he was right, but it didn't matter at that moment. If he was going to talk to anyone about it, it certainly wouldn't be him.

The cards stopped shuffling in Counselor Ray's hand.

"It's your deal." Gary scooted up to the desk.

Counselor Ray rolled his eyes and let a heavy sigh fizzle out through his nose. "Fine."

Gary let him win every hand to at least make him a little happy. The same thought kept skipping through his mind. Beth. Beth.

"So where's this place you want to show me?" Gary asked.

He stood at the base of the tracks with one foot up on the rail, hands thrust deep into his pockets. It had rained earlier in the afternoon, and the air was thick, humid and smelled of earth and sharp metal. His unkempt hair flopped over his left eye and fought its way back there with each attempt to brush it away.

Beth stood away from the tracks at the base of the grass near the long limb of a tree that seemed to reach for her. She wore no cap today. Her hair fell down over her thin, scrunched shoulders and curled inward at the ends. The humidity gave it a fullness it hadn't had before, and Gary imagined her at age thirty looking exactly as she looked to him now. She even wore makeup over her eyes, a light dusting of blue eye shadow that almost went unnoticed.

"It's not far," she said.

Gary followed her down a length of the track, past the industrial buildings looming on the left and far past the subdivisions dotting the right. The trees thickened. The curve of the track stretched as far away as ever.

Ten minutes down from their trail opening, Beth turned left over the tracks and entered a practically invisible path. Gary would have missed it if he had not been looking for it, and he wondered how long she had been coming to this place. The path eventually widened, and the greenery thickened even more, covering their heads, giving Gary the impression of walking into a cave.

"We're almost there," Beth said.

Finally, they approached an entrance of sorts, an opening in the trees that led to a small field. The sun shone off to the west, and the moon had begun to rise, barely visible. An extremely large tree loomed before them, looking to Gary like the shape of a gigantic mushroom. The wispy branches stretched outward and hung low to the ground, covering the trunk of the tree, making it barely visible. In the winter, it might look like a massive, skeletal thing, something out of a nightmare flick, but now he understood why Beth chose this place. It was perfectly hidden away from everything.

"Come on." She parted the branches with her arms and slipped inside with Gary behind her.

He surveyed the ground. A large rock with a smooth, flat top sat several feet from the base of the enormous tree trunk, perfect for sitting. A faded brown plastic lawn chair leaned against it, its back cracked and chipped from years of wear. Toward the center, Beth had stacked a long board up on two egg crates, forming a makeshift table where she set her journal down.

"This is it. This is my secret place."

He wished he could have had a place like this of his own growing up. "Not bad. I'd say it's a pretty secretive secret place."

Her eyes followed his. "You won't tell anyone, will you? Not my father?"

"I won't tell anyone. I promise. Especially not your father. He'd kill me anyway."

"Good."

She dragged the brown lawn chair away from the rock and sat, facing it. Gary took the cue and hopped up onto the rock, crossing his ankles in front of him. The rock had a sharp edge around the smooth top.

"I like to come here sometimes and write," she said. "I made this table for my desk and I have a chair and everything."

Gary reached his foot out and ran it along the edge of the board. "This is a great desk. A person could do plenty of thinking behind a desk like this."

He hopped off the rock and walked around the base of the tree, brushing against the branches with his fingertips. Beth followed him, watching.

"Does it always look like this?" he asked.

"No. In the winter you wouldn't even know it was a hideout, but once it hits spring it grows in pretty fast."

Gary turned and she was there, so close to him he could hardly believe it. He smelled the faint scent of the soap she used on her face. It was better than perfume; more real, more her. The impulse to kiss her was overwhelming and grew.

Awkwardly, he leaned down to kiss her, his nerves nearly shattered from the moment. For an instant, she seemed ready to reciprocate, but when their lips were ready to touch, she pulled away.

Gary's face immediately glowed a fine hue of red and spurred his self-consciousness. "I'm sorry."

"It's not your fault," Beth said. "It's just that I..." She paused and her face grew long and wispy, like he'd seen Rocky do several times before.

"What?"

"Nothing. I just... nothing."

He watched her, waiting for her to continue, to say anything, observing the pain etched into her face like acid washing a stone. The urge to press her for information felt like a stack of bricks crushing his chest and shoulders, but he suppressed it. He respected the need for privacy and silence.

She reached into her pocket, pulled out a little white pill pinched between her thumb and forefinger, and popped it into her mouth.

"What was that?"

"Nothing. Just valium."

"Valium, huh?"

"It's a prescription. It keeps me calm."

Gary eyed her face, wondering if the pill would have any observable effect, if it would start to work quickly. Nothing so far.

"I thought only strung out people took that kind of stuff."

She ran her fingers through her hair, half turned away. "I'm not strung out. You don't have to watch me, you know." She changed the subject. "So why were you in Radcliffe?"

Now Gary's discomfort rose, though not nearly as much as it would have with anyone else. After a moment, the discomfort disappeared and he found himself staring into Beth's upturned face, into her freckled eyes. A calmness settled over him. He imagined telling her everything he'd done, everything about Radcliffe and about his childhood, about his mother and his father, and it didn't bother him. In fact, he found himself wanting to tell her. The words and emotions were like flames in his chest roiling around a gigantic sun, desperate to burst out of him.

He cleared his throat and clamped his hands together, fingers intertwined like braids of steel. "I've been telling people it was for stealing, but actually it was for something a lot worse."

He studied her face, wondering what she might think.

"What was it?"

And now he didn't want to tell her, but it was too late. Maybe Gail and his slew of counselors were right all along. He had to tell someone, had to dig himself out from beneath the rubble of crumbling pain, but what would she do and what would she say?

"Part of me doesn't want to tell you because I think you might hate me for it, but part of me wants you to know. I've never told anybody else."

"You can tell me," Beth said. "I won't tell anyone. I won't judge you if you promise to never judge me for things that I've done."

Gary nodded. "I killed my father."

Finally, her face changed. Her eyes, normally disengaged and sullen, glistened softly and gave way to something fuller, something more real to him. A dull pink patted her cheeks and her lower lip fell the slightest bit. She began to cry.

"Oh my God."

"I was pretty young," he went on, needing to rid himself of it all. "He beat me up that day really bad, and he was beating my mother. I kept thinking I was tired of him beating up on my mother like that. All the time, all the time. And I knew he had a gun in his bedroom."

Beth covered her mouth with a pale, tiny hand. Gary went on, tears coming into his eyes for the first time since he was a boy. One rolled down his cheek—a strange, foreign thing—so he controlled it as best he could. Quickly, the tears subsided, sucked into the back of his head where he wanted them.

"So I took the gun and I went downstairs and I watched him around the corner. He hit my mother with this yellow ashtray I made at school, and I heard her just crack. He just... broke her, like she was a porcelain doll or something. So then I shot him with the gun."

"I'm so sorry." She touched his hand.

Gary wiped the tear away from his face. "She died in the hospital later on. That's when I had to go to Radcliffe."

"Didn't you have any relatives or anyone that could have taken you in?"

"Nobody wanted me, I guess. I can't really blame them. Do you hate me now?"

She took his hand.

They stood there in the silence, the dull air thick like a fog. He felt like someone punched him in the chest, and it felt strangely *good*. Beth let her journal fall away from her. She opened it up to her last entry and handed it to him to read.

> *The sky is an ocean of beauty*
> *alive with the sun and the stars*
> *but some of us fall upon the waves*
> *and some of us break upon the shores*
> *where light cannot shine*
> *where beauty cannot find.*

He thought of *Mr. Flood's Party* and Old Eben Flood and how that poem made him feel. He liked Beth's poem much better. "It's very beautiful."

"Do you really like it?" Her voice was modest now, uncertain.

"I really do."

She tore it out of the book, folded it four times into a small square, and handed it to him. "You can have it, then."

He clutched it tightly in his fist, wanting it, wishing he could devour it whole, but instead he attempted to hand it back to her. "I can't take this. You made it."

"Please. I want you to have it. It... would mean a lot to me."

Resigned, he set it neatly into his pants pocket. "Actually, in a few days, I'll have a surprise for you. I hope you don't mind waiting for it."

"What kind of surprise?" Her face came alive and it warmed him.

"Yeah, right. Like I'd tell you. I can't ruin it."

"Fine," she teased, and though she still smiled, her eyes and her face drooped with exhaustion.

It must have been the pill she'd taken. Maybe that was why she always looked so tired and sad to him, so pale with those dark circles under her eyes.

"I should go," she said.

Together they headed through the clearing and toward the tracks.

"Wait. When can I see you again?" he asked.

"I don't know..."

"Soon, I hope. I'd really like to see you."

The dullness in her eye leaked away for a moment, and something almost twinkled there.

"How about Saturday?"

His heart leapt. "Here?"

"Sure. Maybe I'll have a surprise for you, too."

His heart leapt double-time, and his throat was instantly sapped of its moisture. "I can't wait."

He waited his standard five minutes after Beth had gone before heading up the trail. With nonchalance, he slipped behind his house and squatted down to his knees, his back balancing against the edge of the deck.

He pulled Beth's poem from his pocket, unfolded it, and read it silently to himself, mouthing the words without sound, rolling them over his tongue. He liked it immensely and thought Beth was a very good poet. This was much different than the poetry he'd read in English class. He struggled with understanding, with a way to describe the difference to himself. To him, it was so much more self-directed, like the poem wasn't really a poem at all but a coded diary entry, speaking volumes about Beth if someone could only read between the lines.

She wrote *some of us fall upon the waves* and *break upon the shores*, and to Gary it didn't sound like the words of a happy person. Not that poetry had to be happy. Old Eben Flood didn't seem all that happy while he was talking to the moon, and that was a good poem. It was clear to him she was depressed, and the poetry was just another indication of it, maybe her way of dealing with it.

He ached for her. Not necessarily to touch her, but to help her. How alike they were, bearing such strange sadness in them like loads of heavy steel crossing their shoulders. He'd already unloaded some of it tonight with her, told her his secret, the thing he'd done to deserve such self-condemnation, and it felt good to let it out. It was a relief, more so than he'd expected. He suspected, soon, that it would be her turn to unload some of that steel. Giving him the poem, something she had been so keen to protect all along, was the first step. He could tell.

And he knew he could help her. He knew it in his blood he could. *Soon.* He folded the poem and slipped it back into his pocket, feeling the smoothness of the paper slip along his fingertips. It was only moments since Beth left and already he missed her.

He would see her on Saturday. He told her he couldn't wait, and he really couldn't.

CHAPTER 14

On The Verge of Change

Gary's brush whipped feverishly over the canvas that evening as he fought to finish up his work before Saturday. It was the painting of Beth, and he hoped he would be able to give it to her at their upcoming rendezvous. He spun the easel around and faced the window, peering through the slightly parted blinds, hoping to see her across the street, to serve him a moment's inspiration.

His mind rifled through the events of the day, and he wasn't sure if his brain could process it all. He couldn't believe he'd told Beth about his father. That was something he'd sworn he'd never talk about unless he had to, a secret that would die with him.

Mostly he couldn't believe he was going to see her again. He imagined her face and how she might smile when he gave her the painting he'd created for her, how she might lay her hand on his shoulder and lean into him, perhaps even kiss him. They might even make love together, something he'd thought about quite often, but doubted would happen any time soon. He'd never made love before and wondered what it was like, especially with Beth, but he didn't want to pressure her into anything she didn't want to do.

There was love between them, he was sure. It was almost painful to think about, considering her unmatched mixture of overwhelming smiles and dull, lifeless eyes. He felt something between them, something powerful developing even a boy of his age could understand. He also sensed a rift of some kind, an unrelenting obstacle directly opposing that powerful feeling, something he couldn't fully discern. He only knew it all had to do with her.

Like he had hid his past, she was hiding something from him. He knew that as he knew they were so alike, so sad looking and melancholy, bearing the weight of something heavy and tiresome that, even if they wanted to, they couldn't pretend it wasn't there. It wasn't difficult to notice something weighed down on each of them, though it would never be entirely obvious what that *something* was.

And again, as with his own terrible secret, he would have to wait to hear it directly from her. He hoped she would be able to open up to him someday, like he did with her.

He dipped into his dark blue mixture and ran thin, uneven lines around the figure of Beth on the canvas, outlining her frame in a faint glow. He'd noticed the effect on Gail's blue painting and admired it, and even though his didn't come out exactly as Gail's had, he was surprised at how much he liked his own. He was about to accentuate the new lines with a lighter shade of feathered blue when he heard Don clear his throat behind him.

"You haven't been seeing that girl across the street, have you?" Don asked pointedly.

An ice pick stabbed his heart. "No, not at all."

Don came fully into the room, filling the doorway with his large frame. He glanced at the painting and tapped his foot. "Mr. Carter across the street said he caught you talking to her in his yard."

The temperature in Gary's chest rose a notch and it made him nervous. "I don't know why he says he 'caught' me. That was a while ago. How was I supposed to know he doesn't like us idiot juvie boys?"

He immediately regretted the last statement, especially the combative tone, but it bothered him that Don told Beth's father about his past. What difference would it make?

"That's not the point." Don crossed his arms, curling his lips down, assuming his role of authoritarian. "He asked you to leave his daughter alone, so that's what you'll do. You have to respect his wishes. He's her father."

Gary tried to bite back his tongue but didn't bite back fast enough. "Sometimes fathers don't know what's right for people."

He said it halfheartedly, and the words felt cold, like ice water dripping from his mouth, but he meant them. He always felt nervous around Don, and he hated that, especially after all this time.

"What did you say?"

"Nothing." Gary gripped his paintbrush between his thumb and forefinger, massaging the sable hair to dull the blue. "I'm not seeing her. I just... didn't like what her father said to me, that's all. I'm sorry."

Don studied him for a moment, and then took a step backward. "All right. I believe you. It's just that... I want you to respect what other people want. Got it?"

"Yeah, I got it."

"No problems with that?" Don pressed.

"No problems."

"Good then." Don smiled, but it didn't hide the doubt on his face. "I'll talk to you later."

"Okay."

Gary laid the final touches onto the canvas. He did so mechanically, unable to grab those feelings he had earlier, before Don entered the room. It didn't matter, though, he had done enough, and after he treated the canvas, he would roll it up and give it to her at their meeting, even if she had to hide it.

His stomach lurched now. *What made Don suspicious? Could it have been the painting?* Had he been spying on Gary, watching him closely? It didn't matter. Don probably knew nothing and wanted an excuse to see what was going on with him. He liked to be in control and was testing him. That had to be it.

Gary certainly didn't want to go back to Radcliffe, and he wasn't going to rock the boat around his new home, but he would still see Beth, had to see her. She was a drug in his system, filling his blood, and he needed her now. He promised himself he'd be more careful from now on. *Even worse than going back to Radcliffe*, he decided, *would be to not see Beth anymore.*

Friday evening, Rocky's Pizzeria wasn't quite hopping yet, but the dining room was nearly half full for the early bird specials, mostly families who liked to congregate together with young children strapped into their chairs. Gary figured families like these had a collective understanding that screaming children can really bother folks in public restaurants, so they grouped together for moral support. He counted four families at a glance as he moved toward the register, accumulated peanut shells crunching beneath his feet. Half way across the room he propped his paper hat up onto his head, crushing it down over his floppy blonde hair, and it crinkled in his ears. He'd need a new one soon.

'Moosey' watched him from his perch on the wall.

"Excuse me," a man from the corner called. He was a dark skinned fellow, Greek perhaps, with the beginnings of a thin, handlebar mustache. His wife was a plump redhead with long, dangling earrings. A chubby kid sat between them.

"Can I help you sir?"

"We ordered a pizza a half hour ago, and we haven't seen that other guy since." He tapped his fingers with irritation.

"Oh, I'm sorry about that," Gary said, freezing for a moment, a kernel of concern percolating for Rocky now. "Let me check to see what's going on. What did you order?"

"Medium garbage pizza. And we can use some drinks here, too."

Before going to the back, he brought them a pitcher of coke and took the orders from the three other tables, all pizzas this time, one with pineapple and bacon, one of his favorites. While taking the orders, he kept one ear toward the kitchen doorway, listening for Rocky to come barreling out with the garbage pizza, or at least for some movement back there. *Nothing.*

"I'll be right back, sir." Gary headed through the back door.

The kitchen was a tad smoky and redolent of burnt cheese. He yanked down the pizza oven door and grabbed the oven mitt from the counter to pull out the offending pizza. It was the garbage pizza, which meant Rocky had been here not so long ago. The pizza wasn't as bad as he expected it to be, but the edges had begun to turn a dark shade of brown. Some of the cheese had melted off and started to burn, causing the smell, which can happen when you put on too much cheese. That wasn't like Rocky.

"Rocky?" Gary set the pizza onto a serving tray. "You back here?"

The back door stood ajar. He could be out smoking, but for half an hour?

"Rocky?"

No answer.

He carried out the pizza, filled a few more drink orders, and turned back to the kitchen. The floor gleamed up at him, reflecting the fluorescent lights from the ceiling in dim granular patterns. He prided himself on how much he'd helped to clean up the kitchen. It had taken him a while, but he'd done it. Even Miguel, the fulltime help, seemed to be cooperating with some of the organization Gary had slowly imposed on the place. He'd never seen it look cleaner.

"Yo, Rocky," Gary called, trying to keep it light.

He passed the shelf with the cans of jalapeno cheese and glanced behind the row where Rocky kept his bottle of schnapps. *Nothing. Not a good sign.*

He peeked through the crack in the back door and saw the strewn grit of the back alley. A faded, rusty green dumpster sat just outside the door. It was such an ugly place out there, with the discolored bricks of the building next door, jagged and crooked with concrete muck between them jutting out like frozen ooze.

"Rocky, you out there?" His voice betrayed his worry.

"Uhnn..." It was a soft, pained moan from the alley, like the weak groan of a wounded animal.

Gary rushed to the door and stepped one foot out. There, propped against the wall to his right, lay Rocky. He held his head in his left hand, making quick circular motions along his forehead, rubbing, rubbing. His bottle of schnapps lay shattered in the center of the alley, the contents of it soaked into the gravel.

"What happened?" Gary bent down and took Rocky's bicep in his hands, attempting to pull his boss up into a better sitting position.

Rocky groaned a bit louder and looked at Gary, his eyes unfocused. "Nothing," he stammered, "I... I tripped on something and fell. Damn it, I think I whacked my head against the dumpster."

Gary propped him backward and inspected the head wound. A sizable bump grew to about the size of a golf ball. A small cut sat in the middle of the bump and had begun to seep blood, but the line of blood only made it an inch or so before stopping.

"Do you want me to call a doctor?" Gary asked.

"No." As if remembering something important, Rocky bolted upright. "Where's my bottle?"

Gary pointed to the middle of the alley with his thumb. "Casualty of war."

Rocky slumped again. "Oh, well."

"Are you sure you don't want me to call a doctor? I think you've been out here a while. It doesn't look so good."

"No, I'll be all right." Rocky climbed to his feet.

For a moment, Gary thought he would stumble over, the way he wavered and clung to the wall for support, but half a minute later, he steadied himself, although he still rubbed his lump with the palm of his hand.

"Shit, did you get the pizza in there?"

"I got it," Gary said. "It only burned a little. They didn't say anything."

"Didn't I tell you I think they like it better that way?"

Gary took Rocky by the arm and led him into the kitchen where he propped him onto a stool and leaned him against the wall.

"Really, I'm all right." Rocky didn't fight him. "Thanks for all your help around here. You're a good kid."

His breath reeked of peppermint schnapps, and Gary knew that even though his bottle had broken, there was plenty more to be found hidden around the kitchen. If he hadn't had so much of the stuff, he probably wouldn't have fallen and whacked himself so hard, or at least he would have had the presence to catch himself. Gary considered saying something this time, perhaps telling Rocky he should try to cut down on the drinking. Maybe he'd mention how much his father drank and how bad it fucked up the family.

But he couldn't do that. It wasn't his place to tell an adult what to do, especially someone like Rocky.

He dampened a cloth and wiped the blood away from Rocky's forehead, dabbing it softly, trying not to exacerbate the wound or make Rocky cringe. When he was done, he yanked a packet of frozen hamburger patties from the freezer and pressed it to the lump.

"This will help," he said.

Rocky held onto the burgers and glanced at Gary, his eyes dull and glassy, the rims red and swollen.

"Thanks a lot, kid," he said. "For taking care of me. I owe you one."

"No problem," Gary said. "If you're sure you don't want me to call a doctor or anything...."

"I'm sure. Seriously. Why don't you just go out to the dining room and make sure everyone is all right. I think I'll just relax for a minute. I think the whack on the noggin took a little more out of me than I thought, but really, I'll be fine. I've seen worse than this."

Gary searched Rocky's face and saw the truth there. He would be all right. The booze, ironically, probably helped him as much as it hurt him, like a drunk in a car accident can whack into a tree and walk away with a few bumps and bruises.

"No problem." He headed to the dining room to get the restaurant rolling again.

Why do I feel so uneasy?. Because I've never seen Rocky this drunk before, not enough to hurt himself. What's going on with him? There must be something going around.

He thought of Beth and the pills she took and wondered if she was walking the same road Rocky was walking, the same road his father had been on. His father was the worst of the lot, and let the drinking turn him into a thing Gary couldn't call human. Rocky wasn't the violent type, but his road didn't look like a good one to travel. *Who* wants *to fall down drunk in alleys and nearly kill yourself by slamming your forehead into a rusty old dumpster?*

He wondered about Beth. He would see her tomorrow, and perhaps then he'd learn more about it, but for now, he didn't want to speculate. Maybe there was a reason for the pills, something necessary in them. He would get to know her better, and then maybe he could better assess the direction she was going. He didn't want to unfairly compare her to his father or to Rocky.

But what of his own road? His wasn't anything to brag about, it was a winding, twisting path that stretched out all to hell, and he didn't have any room to look down on anybody else's.

But it was clearing up, wasn't it... his life was leveling out. The fog was thinning and soon, he hoped, he'd be able to look ahead to something without so many curves, something worth moving toward. So far he knew he would see Beth there when that road grew more calm.

Early Saturday, Gary rolled up his portrait of Beth and tied it with a bit of string. Before he left the house, he dropped it out the side window where he could pick it up on his way out. He realized it was dishonest of him, but he didn't want Gail to see him carrying it out the front door and begin to wonder what he would be doing with it. He didn't think she would believe he was going to show it to Stan while fishing.

Gail probably wouldn't care if something developed between him and Beth. She might have even supported it if it weren't for Beth's unreasonable father. He hoped things would change in the future, and counted on it. Hell, he was still a relative newbie in the neighborhood and still considered the *Radcliffe Boy*, and would probably carry around the onus for quite some time. Best to lay low until people realized he wasn't so bad.

The morning was warm and the sky a light shade of blue that made him think of the ocean—he'd never seen the ocean except in movies, but he pictured it being that color. He reached the tracks and let the rolled up-painting dangle freely in his hands, no longer feeling the need to conceal it.

Beth was already there, waiting for him, wearing the same loose, worn jeans that flared out around her ankles and a gray-blue sweatshirt. When she saw him, she half smiled and waved with her right hand. He noticed she didn't have her journal with her.

"What's that?" she asked, looking at his rolled up painting.

"Oh, nothing."

She rolled her eyes and clicked her tongue. "Nothing, huh? Well, then I don't have a surprise for you either."

Gary cocked his head and studied her face, still partially obscured by her hair. She truly did have beautiful eyes. "So we're going to play it that way, eh? We'll see who has the most willpower."

He folded his arms, holding the painting beneath his left armpit, waiting to see what she would do. She only stood there, staring at him, not making a single gesture or sound, the hint of an amused smile coming into her lips. Gary didn't last very long.

"Okay, you win. Here is your surprise." He handed the painting to her and she took it, stroking the edge of the string between her thumb and forefinger.

"What is it?"

"You'll have to open it to see."

She peeked through the end and crinkled her nose. She started to undo the string, but stopped and smiled, this time with a bit of deviousness.

"I actually do have a surprise for you," she said. "I think I should take you there and open it up when we get there."

"Where?"

"You'll see."

They headed off the tracks toward Beth's secret place under the tree, but to Gary's surprise, they passed it and continued through the high grass toward a cornfield in the distance. The leaves reached for his legs and arms with deceptively sharp edges, like soft knives ready to slice him open. Tufts of thin grass and dry dirt brushed away with his shoes.

"Where are we going?" he asked.

"We're getting close."

Her sweatshirt flapped on her back from the wind. He visualized touching her hair, but he didn't want to startle her. He didn't understand it, but he desperately wanted to take her hair in his hand and let it slip softly between his fingers like silk. Every now and then she would glance back and he would catch her profile, the hint of a smile.

"What are you looking at?"

"Just shut up and follow me," she said, the smile growing bigger.

Gary loved when she smiled.

He guessed their destination when a small barn rose into view over a hill. It was a dark gray, wooden thing with missing boards on the side facing them, abandoned. No road led to it, but the cornfield thinned around it, as if it were poisoned.

"Is that where we're going?" he asked.

"Just follow me."

Before long, they slipped inside. He half-thought they would find bails of hay or large, gleaming machines and farm equipment, but it was empty save for dust and rotting wood. The floor was divided into four separate areas by short walls without doors, and Gary didn't know enough about farming to guess what the rooms could be used for.

Maybe they kept cows in there, or horses or something, way back when they built this thing.

Beth motioned to him and he followed as she climbed up a ladder to the hayloft. The ladder was fraught with slivers, but sturdy as a tent pole. At the top were ancient piles of hay, dried and soft.

"So what do you think?" she asked.

"It's nice. It's a barn."

She laughed softly. "This is my other secret place. I don't come here too often but I like to sometimes, when I want to get away. I keep thinking they're going to tear it down someday, but every time I show up, it's still here."

"It's a nice place to go, I guess."

She fell back and sat comfortably in the hay, then fumbled with the string on the painting. She pulled and it came away easily, and she unrolled the painting. For a moment, Gary's heart sank because there was no expression to her, no reaction to let him know how she felt about the gift. She turned her face up to him and her eyes softened.

"It's so beautiful." Her voice was like honey. "Is it me?"

He nodded. "I wanted to paint your face, but I didn't want us to get in trouble. I guess your father talked to Don and Gail about me talking to you."

"Yeah. He doesn't like me talking to you at all."

The hardness came back into her eyes. At least he'd had that little moment.

"I wish I could keep this," she said. "It really is the most beautiful thing I've seen in a long time, but if I get caught with it...."

"I know," he said. "I didn't really expect you to take it home, I guess. I just thought... I don't know what I was thinking."

Which was true. *What in hell made me think she could take the stupid thing home, when I had to sneak it out of the damned house just to give it to her?* What a ridiculous, idiotic, stupid fool he'd been to even consider....

"I can keep it here," she said, and Gary's heart lightened.

"Here?"

"Yeah, I can keep it on the wall. Right here."

She set it against the wall, straightening it out against its will. "How would it look?"

"I think it would look perfect."

"Good," she said. "The next time we come here I'll have to see if I can bring some tacks or something like that."

She set it down and let it roll up back into its original position, then flopped back into the hay.

Gary followed suit, leaning back and facing her. "So you really like it?"

Her face betrayed almost nothing, but he could see a new softness in her that hadn't been there before. "I really do."

"I'm glad you like your surprise," he said. "I really like my surprise too."

"Really?" she asked. "That's funny, because I haven't even given it to you yet."

"Oh, I thought this was it, I mean, I thought the barn and your secret place and...."

Her hand slipped into her pocket and when it came out, she held a small wrapper.

"What's that?"

"It's a condom."

His chest flushed with a new heat he'd never felt before. His throat felt like he'd swallowed a melon. He'd never seen a condom, having achieved puberty in Radcliffe. He'd never been with a girl, although he'd wondered like hell about it. Hector had talked about sex all the time, and even though Gary knew it was mostly a bunch of bullshit, he believed Hector had sex before and knew a hell of a lot more than he did.

"Do you want to use it?" Beth asked matter-of-factly.

She didn't look nervous to him, but he still couldn't be sure what might be going on behind her eyes. She was such a quiet person, strong, never giving away what she might be feeling. She was a lot like him, he supposed, but not at this particular moment. At this moment, he figured even a blind man would be able to see what was on his mind.

Of course he wanted to use the condom, but could he? Moving any closer to her made his entire body quiver like Jell-o. Molten lava seared in his chest. Its heat streamed into his skull, burning away at the skin from the inside. There was no more moisture in him. He was a statue.

It didn't seem to bother Beth, she only watched him with observing eyes, the eyes of a woman far beyond her years. "You don't have to be nervous. It's okay if it's your first time."

The initial thing that came to mind was a lie, but he couldn't, especially not to her.

He looked at her, doing his damnedest to keep his eyes raised and locked with hers. He'd never been more embarrassed in his life.

"I've never done it before," he said weakly.

"Come here." She took his hand. She pulled him to her and kissed him, her lips warm and yielding against his own. The tip of her tongue darted in and brushed along his teeth. He retracted his own, awkward and unsure of what to do until she sought it out and they touched. It warmed his entire body.

She pulled back after a while, then pulled off her shirt. Her white lace bra covered the roundness of her small breasts. "You can touch me."

She was soft as a pillow, softer. When he touched her, all thoughts of Skater and of Radcliffe dispelled immediately, and there was nothing but Beth. Not even Winsbury, not even the world. There was only Beth.

They kissed again. She pulled off his shirt and drew him toward her. She lay warm against him, the heat of her body circulating through her, and through him. His body flushed with embarrassment when his erection brushed against her thigh.

"I'm sorry...." he started to say, but she hushed him.

"It's all right. Really."

She stood and removed the remainder of her clothing, then lay back into the hay watching him, waiting for him to come to her. He stood and removed his own clothing, watching her. A part of him observed that, strangely, Beth behaved almost like a robot with practically no expression. She had never shown much expression before, but at a time like this? The way she moved, the way she looked at him, and the way she waited for him as if she'd done this a thousand times before, mechanically going through the motions, unaffected.

Jesus, Gary, she wants to have sex with you so just shut the hell up and do it.

He went to her, praying to God he wouldn't screw up what he was about to do, finding those prayers answered in her. When her hands fell onto him, he relaxed, and she guided him toward her. She hesitated and held up the condom.

"Can you put this on?" she asked, and helped him do it.

The condom was lubricated and smelled like cleaning chemicals. He hadn't expected it, but he slipped right into her, perfectly. His stomach brushed against hers. His face flushed and all the hair on his body reached out, prickling his skin.

"Are you all right?" he asked.

"Mm hmm."

Her hand sought his thigh and pulled him inward, deeper. He made love to her slowly, afraid he might hurt her in some way if he pushed too hard. She didn't make a sound. He didn't breathe. She only stared into his eyes the whole time, like a woman scrutinizing a painting, without expression.

He did everything he could to keep his eyes entwined with hers. This was their first time, his first time ever, and looking away might be disrespectful to her. But he couldn't help it when the avalanche of an orgasm thundered into him and his eyes clenched closed with all the force of a slamming vault.

"I'm sorry." His body released itself and he fell limp against her. "I'm sorry...."

"Shhh. It's all right."

When they were done, he lay next to her. Her warm, slow breath caressed his shoulder. For a moment he felt he might be able to say the words to her, *'I love you, Beth.'* They climbed the morass of his lungs when she shuddered delicately against him. Her hot tears dripped against his skin.

"Beth, are you all right? Did I hurt you?"

She shook her head, unable to speak. More tears.

"Did I do anything wrong?" he asked, almost desperate.

"No. It's not you. It's me."

He thought of her pills.

"Why won't you tell me?"

She continued to cry, clasping him close to her as if clinging for her life.

He tightened his arm around her, as tightly as his muscles would let him. "Whatever it is, I'll do anything to make it better. Anything, all right? You just tell me when you're ready to talk."

Her tears disappeared finally, replaced by the emotionless stare he'd grown accustomed to. Her eyes lay dull in their sockets, her face lax.

They stood again at the edge of the train tracks, near the path heading up toward Beth's yard. Humidity pressed Gary's hair to his forehead. He thrust his hands into his pockets, wondering what to say in such an awkward silence, especially after what they had just done together. Did she even want him to say anything? Did she expect him to say anything? To do anything? Was there something boys were supposed to do in this situation?

He was at a loss, but the awkwardness came only partially from their act of love. It also came from Beth's stony silence, her nonchalant way of staring out into nowhere as if nothing happened, as if she hadn't broken down into tears after they made love, hadn't lost herself into her quiet nowhere after that, barely speaking to him, telling him nothing.

She put her hands on his shoulders and kissed him on the cheek before heading up the pathway toward home. Her eyes were still dim and wet at the corners, the rims red from her earlier tears.

She turned. "I'll see you soon."

"When?" he asked.

"Soon. Maybe in a few days. We can meet at the tree. You remember where it is, right?"

"I'll never forget." He kicked a clog of dirt into the trees. "Beth, I... want to help you. Will you let me do that?"

She shrugged, and he saw the whiteness of her shoulder, her neck.

"Is it me? Are you sure I didn't do anything wrong?" he begged.

"It isn't you."

"Just tell me what's wrong then. Tell me what I can do to make it better."

Her eyes came up to his and they were soft, pleading, as if the words she wanted to speak lay chained behind them. "Soon. Maybe I'll tell you soon."

An hour later, he trudged through the forest preserve, heading toward the fishing hole where Stan would be waiting for him. He normally enjoyed the green, wiry trails, but today he couldn't bring himself to look any further than his own thoughts.

Beth and I made love. It was so completely unexpected, yet it was so wonderful and strange and both everything and nothing like he'd expected his first time to be. Physically, of course, it was everything he'd hoped for, like wrapping his entire body up in a warm blanket and wrenching every bit of sheer pleasure from him.

But there was something wrong with his heart. It was the best way he could explain it to himself. Not only his heart, but *her* heart, the heart they formed together, or the one you'd expect to form when two people make love. There wasn't the romance he'd thought there would be, no intertwining of limbs and bodies becoming one and all that like a chick flick. When it was over and the physical pleasure left him, he realized perhaps to Beth it was only an act they performed. At least it was the impression she gave him.

It was the look in her eyes that disturbed him the most—the dull, blank stare of a store window mannequin looking through him when the act was over, when she finished crying for reasons she wouldn't say. He'd always expected his first time to be something shared between two people, not something someone would simply 'do' for him, like a favor or an act of kindness.

But still, he had made love finally, hadn't he? That in itself was mostly enough to allay his disturbance. That, and the tenderness that crept into Beth's eyes on their way home from the barn. There was real tenderness in her buried somewhere beneath the meek exterior, and he saw it and loved her for it.

He stepped out through the trail edge into the clearing near the fishing pond, still half way engrossed in his own thoughts. Stan was already there, staring stolidly out over the water, fishing pole bobbing up and down in his hands.

"Sorry I'm late," Gary said.

Stan reeled in his line, checked the lead sinker, and tossed it out again. "Oh, don't worry about it."

He seemed distracted, his forehead folded up in concentration, staring toward the other edge of the pond. He pursed his lips in thought and shrugged in his leather jacket.

Gary, distracted with his own concerns, didn't mention anything about it. He trudged over to Stan's pile of gear and sifted through it, nudging the bright orange tackle box with the toe of his shoe to see if another fishing pole lay behind it. Nothing.

"Hey, where's my pole?" he asked.

"I guess I forgot it." Stan's eyes never left the water. His lips were still pursed.

"No big deal. I'm not much of a fisherman anyway."

He flopped onto the ground near Stan and crossed his legs. "I saw Beth earlier today."

"Oh yeah?" Stan said, his voice bland as flour.

"You're not going to believe this, but I guess I'm in love with her."

"Are you serious?" A little more reaction from Stan, but not much.

"I know," Gary said. "It's... weird, I guess. I don't really know what to do about it. Her father hates me and my foster father doesn't even want me to see her. End of story for him."

He considered telling Stan about what actually happened this afternoon, but he didn't entirely trust Stan to keep his mouth shut about that sort of thing and a rumor, whether true or false, was the last thing he needed right now.

Stan reeled in his line once more, changed the pink rubber worm to a green rubber worm and recast the line. It sailed easily to the center of the pond and dipped below the water's surface.

"Are you all right?"

Stan nodded, but his shoulders were tenser than a stretched rubber band. "Yeah, I'm all right. I've just got a lot on my mind today. It's no big deal."

"No problem." Gary picked up a handful of stones, stood up, and threw them one by one across the pond, landing most of them on a small dirt pile. "If you ever want to talk about it, just let me know. Seems to be a lot of that crap going around."

"What do you mean?"

"Nothing." Gary tossed another rock. "One time, when I was maybe eight or nine years old, I got busted for throwing rocks. I was with a friend of mine trying to play fast pitch at the school when we got this great idea to see who could bust out the principal's window with a rock first. I don't even remember which one of us got it first, but we both got caught by the cops. They fingerprinted us and everything, and my Dad kicked the shit out of me that night. I'll bet that stuff is still on my record."

Stan grunted. "You must have a pretty long record."

Since Gary had been there, Stan hadn't once looked at him and Gary figured he could take the hint.

"Well, I should head out of here. Got some stuff to do."

"See you later."

Gary paused, let out a deep breath he didn't realize he'd been holding. The last time he saw Stan was at Brubaker's house at the party, and it hadn't gone over very well. He supposed Stan was still sore about the whole incident, torn between the group of bullies that smacked him in the head and the new kid from Radcliffe. There couldn't be another explanation.

"Look," Gary started. "I'm sorry about that whole party incident at your buddy's place. I didn't mean to go off on you." It stung him to say those words, but he didn't want to offend Stan any more than he already had. If he'd had his way, he would have smacked Stan upside the head himself to set his brain straight. "It just really bothered me the way they were treating you, that's all."

"Don't worry about it," Stan said, but the clenched muscles in his face and neck contradicted him. Still, he wouldn't look at Gary.

Gary sighed. "All right, man. I just wanted to say I'm sorry. I'm sure they're all cool guys. I'll see you later."

He glanced at Stan once over his shoulder before disappearing over the hill toward the trees, but Stan hadn't moved at all.

There was something more than the Brubaker-Dorn incident going on with Stan, but Gary had too many other things on his mind to worry about it.

Chapter 15
Damnation

The next night at work, Gary scraped down the grill in long, slow strokes, brushing the hardened food crumbs off the side so he could sweep them into the garbage. He stared at the wall but didn't really see it. He didn't even notice the cheese in his better mousetrap had been licked clean by a sly rodent.

Rocky flitted in from the back alleyway, took his nip from the schnapps bottle, and slipped it back behind the wall of cheese cans. A thin, white bandage crossed his forehead diagonally.

"You're one hell of a kid, you know that?" Rocky raised his fist in the air, toasting with an imaginary drink in his hand. "I appreciate what you did for me the other night. I don't think many people would have done that."

Gary considered it was probably true. Most people might have called 911 for him maybe, but most people probably considered Rocky a big drunk. Even now, his eyes were glassy and practically dripping from their sockets. When he spoke, his head bobbed back and forth like a turkey.

"It's all right," Gary said.

Rocky staggered toward him, stumbled on his own feet but caught himself in time.

"I mean it."

Gary set down the spatula and faced his boss. "Are you okay, Rocky? Maybe that stuff's getting to you a little bit."

Rocky straightened himself and took a deep breath, trying to regain some of his dignity. "You're right. I have been drinking a little too much lately. I'll be cutting back soon."

He snatched his bottle from behind the cheese cans, downed a gulp, and set it back. The last shot seemed to click something on in Rocky's brain.

"You're doing a good job on that grill, sir!" His words slurred worse than usual. "That grill is like life. Yep, it sure is. You keep it clean and it will keep you clean. Stay clean, my friend, not like me."

Gary moved from the grill to the sink. He took a rag from the lower bin and began to wipe down the chrome of the sink, scrubbing the accumulated grease in the trap away. He didn't want to hear Rocky anymore. He felt some kind of a speech coming on, and even though he knew it would be different coming from Rocky, he didn't want to hear it anyway. It reminded him too much of his father.

Wasn't this just how his father started, before the violence began? He started out getting drunk and talking too much and getting all weepy like this. It made the familiar flames flicker in his chest, licking his muscles and lungs with heat, making him queasy. Rocky was different, sure, a nicer type of drunk, but a drunk all the same.

"Don't grow up like me," Rocky said behind him, a sniffle in his nose. "Don't own a pizza place. And don't go to war. If they try to draft you, don't go. Move to Canada or something."

Gary scrubbed harder. "I don't think they draft people anymore."

"Good! Because you don't want to do that shit anyway. All you do is run from people and hide from people and kill from people. I mean *kill* people."

The words bumbled out of his mouth, dragged through a swollen throat and around a paralyzed tongue. Gary turned his head to the man.

"Why don't you sit down, Rocky, before you fall and hurt your head again."

Rocky grabbed his bottle, downed another large drink. "I'm all right. I'm sorry."

He stumbled back a couple of steps and turned, as if to head back out into the alley, but as he approached the doorway, he stopped and his shoulders arched in a wince. Gary wondered if he were in sudden pain, but when Rocky turned back to him, his face lay slack and serene.

"You know what I figured out last night, Gary? I figured out something huge in my life, something that makes meaning of it all."

Gary dropped his rag. Maybe the man was drunk, but their lives were so similar in certain ways, he knew he had to hear what Rocky had to say.

"What's that, Rocky?"

"I'm damned."

His eyes fell to the ground and his shoulders slumped.

"What are you talking about?" Gary's throat was dry all of a sudden.

"I said I'm damned. I've killed people, so I'm damned. Once you kill someone, there ain't ever going back from that. Believe me, He knows."

Rocky pointed to the ceiling and crossed himself. He looked like a cardboard cutout, the way he stood there in that moment, motionless, comically serious, almost sober.

A moment later he was out the door and in the alley, no doubt sipping from another stashed bottle somewhere, thinking his drunken thoughts. Gary watched him disappear then glared up at the ceiling, considering what Rocky had just said. He wondered if it was true. He supposed it was, and hadn't he had similar thoughts of his own anyway? Why wouldn't it be true? Didn't one of the Ten Commandments say 'Thou Shalt Not Kill'? Wasn't that God's law? You couldn't get any more straightforward than that.

So there it was, like lightning jolting his brain, the truth from a drunken man who had also killed another human being. And there was no doubt in his head it was the Truth, Truth with a capital T.

He was damned.

After work, he trudged up Washington Street, absorbed in his own world. Rocky's words weighed on him like a ton of lead. He felt like he'd been run over by the train. Rocky told him not to grow up like he was, but it was already too late.

At the top of the hill, he glanced up at Beth's window, hoping to catch even a small glimpse of her, but it was dark. Seeing her might have made him feel better, but of course he didn't have such luck tonight. No such luck ever.

He stepped softly onto the porch, not wanting to make any noise, and opened the front door slowly. Inside, he slipped off his shoes and readied to sneak up the stairs, but Gail cleared her throat from the kitchen.

"Do you want something to eat?" She wore a red robe and a towel on her head, apparently just out of the shower. A cup of coffee steamed in front of her.

"No, thank you." He only wanted to hurry up the stairs and close the door behind him, shut out the world and go to bed and be left alone. He didn't think it was going to happen.

"Come on over and have a seat."

He slid over the linoleum on his socks and took the seat across the table, dropping his elbows at his side, looking down into his lap.

"That sure was a quiet entrance you made tonight," she said.

"I wasn't sure if you'd be sleeping or not. I didn't want to wake anyone up."

She took a quick sip of her coffee with a long, nearly unbearable pause. "That was awfully considerate of you. Thank you."

He said nothing, hoping the conversation would be over.

"Why don't you tell me what's wrong?" Her cup clinked as she set it down on the table.

"There's nothing wrong." He forced himself to look up, look into her eyes, show her nothing was wrong with him, but it only made things worse.

"Nothing?" She stared at him, through him, piercing.

"Nothing. I... just had a bad day today, I guess. I don't feel very well."

His eyes dropped back to his lap. She sighed with disappointment.

"I'm here for you, Gary. Anytime you want to talk. Just let me know."

He nodded and waited. When no more words came, he huffed to his room where he slept horribly, tossing and turning, dreaming of damnation.

Things weren't any better a few days later, as he sat on the uncomfortable stump in Beth's secret place, kicking at the dust. Things had grown worse after having those few days to let everything sink into his head, to settle into his nerves and his blood and his bones. He still didn't understand why Rocky's words rattled him so.

"I'm ready to tell you now," Beth said, her voice the wisp of a wraith's. She leaned at the edge of her plastic lawn chair, hands clenched over her knees, rocking. The sleeves of her bulky sweatshirt were more frayed than usual and her bangs obscured her eyes.

"What?" Gary asked, more a statement of disbelief than a question.

"I'm ready to tell you...."

He took her hand and knelt in front of her. He rubbed her knuckle with his thumb, not knowing how to soothe a woman, hoping it would help. Her oceanic eyes peeked through the strands of her bangs.

"It's...." she began, "my father."

Her head drooped, and even if Gary had been able to see into her eyes before that, there was no chance of it now. Confusion swelled as he waited for her to continue, but she sat silent. Confusion turned to frustration. Was he supposed to know what was wrong just from that? Was he supposed to guess?

"He touches me."

Like the sharp pain of fingers on a hot stove, he understood. It made sense—all of it—her father's protectiveness, the strangeness of their lovemaking, the secretiveness. He felt terribly sorry for her in that instant.

"I don't know how to stop him," she said.

Gary flushed with shock, and he took his hand away. It felt cold and limp to him. "I don't know what to say. I'm sorry." He couldn't see her eyes, but knew she was crying.

Dark shadows fell across her face. "It's been happening since I was six years old." She cleared the bangs from her forehead then, revealing her eyes; no concealment, no artifice, no hidden meanings, just deadpan eyes with a dark truth to tell, tears burning at the corners.

He felt the sting of tears that wouldn't come in his own eyes. Anger coursed through him like fire; he'd never felt such burning anger, *except for once....*

"Can't you leave?" he asked her.

Her eyes never moved away, which in itself was disconcerting, considering she'd never been able to look at him so directly before. "I can't. I'm afraid of what will happen to my mother."

The horror grew in Gary's mind. "Does she know?"

"I don't know."

Sticks of dynamite exploded in his chest. "That means yes. What the fuck is that?"

"You can't blame her! She's afraid of him. So am I. You don't know what he can be like. He's...."

"An asshole."

"The devil," Beth said.

"We should tell someone."

"Like who? The cops?"

Vedish's smug face materialized before Gary's eyes. It didn't feel like a viable option.

"What about my counselor? Ray?"

Beth squeezed her eyes closed. "Rubbin' Ray?"

"We could tell Gail and Don."

"Oh my God. Don't they have enough problems?"

He squeezed her to his chest, and her tears came stronger. She squirmed in his arms, as if trying to move closer to him, but then her hand came up from her pocket and she popped a little white pill into her mouth.

"You shouldn't take so much of that stuff," Gary said. "It dulls your brain."

"It's either that or suicide."

Images of Gail's wrist flashed in his head. "Don't talk about that. We'll get through this."

"Will you help me?"

"Of course I will. Anything. I'll help you. I'll take you away from him."

"Will you kill him?"

His body went cold, all the flames and explosions wrenching through his chest came upon a river of ice, and he shivered. The very question jabbed into his heart, the manifestation of all he was now, all he had become since he was that twelve-year-old boy who killed his father.

"You want me to kill him?"

"You have to. It's the only way."

"We need to tell someone."

"There's no one to tell."

"Are you serious? I don't know if I can do what you're asking." His voice came out weak and limp.

"Why not? You did it before." The words struck him like icy arrows in the center of a bulls-eye.

He stood and paced beneath the leafy overhang, kicking at stones, the anger in his chest slowly returning. "I shouldn't have told you about that."

"But you did."

"Is that your pills talking?" he asked, defensive, wanting immediately to take the words back.

"Fuck you."

"Do you know how hard it is for me to live with what I've done? Do you even understand what you're asking me to do? I killed a man, my own father!"

She stood and faced him, shoulders square, eyes blazing. "Don't you remember what it was like for you? Don't you remember your father beating you and your mother? Only imagine he's not only beating you, he's raping you, and he won't stop, no matter how much you beg him to."

Her tears poured over her cheeks, but she stood strong, defiant. He could only pray this was some cruel joke, a test he could pass by refusing to help her, but she was right. She struck a chord in him. He *could* imagine, and he understood how horrible it must be for her.

"Please," she said after a long silence. "It's the only way. I know."

His hands ached, burned. He had been clenching his fists and hadn't realized. He let them loose, blood trickled where the fingernails dug into the flesh. "Jesus, Beth."

For an endless hour they sat beneath the autumn gloom of the tree, the dark shadows of the place sinking into his bones, Beth's shadows. Neither of them spoke, the weight of their situation words enough.

Finally, Beth rose from her chair. "I have to go, it's late. He'll be looking for me."

The words bit him. "Don't go back there. Come with me."

"I can't go with you, I told you. Don't worry. He'll probably leave me alone for a little while. He's got something going on at work bothering him. He doesn't like to... when something is bothering him I guess."

He resigned himself, thrusting his hands into his pockets. He didn't know where he could take her anyway. *What can I do?* "Will I see you tomorrow?"

"Maybe. We should leave separately. I don't want us to get caught."

Of course he didn't want to get caught either, so why did she feel the need to remind him? She started to leave but turned to him.

"I love you, Gary."

Without hesitation, and without any joy whatsoever, he said it back. "I love you, too." He watched her leave. She grew tinier and more frail with each step. When she was gone, he leaned against the gnarled tree and bumped against the solid bark, taking in the hardness of it, the reality of it.

He was completely lost, and it was more horrible than ever.

He didn't take his usual way home this time. Instead, he walked further down the tracks, passing the trail near Beth's yard and to his foster home. He needed more time to think and absorb this new reality.

It was dusk, and Gail would be worried about him, but it didn't matter. If she saw him this way, she would certainly corner him into the kitchen or his room and press him to talk. She already suspected problems cropping up for him, leaking into his life like the ocean into a tiny lifeboat.

Was he drowning? It was starting to feel that way.

The evening breeze was cool, like wind blown over a cold pond. The sky was murky with gray clouds, a half moon barely shone through. He picked up a handful of rocks and tossed them one by one as he walked, clinking them onto the track rails.

The train approached and he watched it pass without any thrill, spitting the cold dust it threw at him from his lips. He threw a stone at the caboose. It bounced away with a distancing clang, practically mocking him.

He loved Beth, but now he hated Beth. He hated the childish fears she brought back to him. She wanted to bring back the part of himself he hated and tried to hide. It was the same with everyone he'd come to know.

He thought of Gail. He understood her now. She wanted to dig into the same part of Gary, into the abused little child to make her own past more bearable.

Then there was Rocky. Rocky didn't know about Gary's situation, but he might as well have. He latched onto Gary like a kindred soul, a *damned* kindred soul at that. Looking at Rocky was like looking into a mirror reflecting the future, and it scared the hell out of him. And there was Stan—what the hell was his deal? He was the only friend Gary had met in his time here. What was the deal with the cold shoulder at the fishing pond? That just added to the troubles. He'd only liked Gary because he was a juvie boy, someone he could show off.

And, coming full circle, there was Beth. He might have thought of her as the icing on the whole stinking cake, but wasn't she now the core of it all? No one had been so direct in their desire to use him for his wickedness, for that part of him that landed him in the worst place he'd ever known. *"Will you kill my father?" she'd asked.* You couldn't get any more direct.

He didn't want to do it again. He didn't want to go back to Radcliffe. He didn't want to spend the remainder of his days stuck in a jail somewhere, and he didn't want to live the life he'd lived up until now. He'd had a small taste of 'normalcy' and he wanted it to be *that* way from now on.

But he couldn't deny the fact that what Beth's father was doing was wrong. Wrong wasn't even the right word. Horrible? Terrible? Evil? He remembered when he shot his father, toying with the memory, replacing the image of his father with Beth's father, and it almost felt good to him. *How could a man do that to his own daughter and deserve to live? How could God allow such a thing to happen?*

He clenched his fist. It was the same argument in his head all over again. Why do these things have to happen, and why do these people deserve to live, and why do we have to be damned for doing what seems to be right?

His head ached. To his left, the thin trees rustled, beckoning him. He crossed through, heading over a makeshift trail that exited into someone's yard. Old wooden furniture covered the grass and a round, jelly-faced man working his grill noticed him. "Hey, what are you doing over there?"

Gary hurried his step. "I'm sorry. Just passing through."

"This isn't a trail, you know. This is private property." He shook his spatula in the air—a modern day, urban gladiator.

"Sorry." Gary quickly passed by. At the first cross street, he went straight toward Lincoln Avenue, figuring he'd do a once-around the northern section of town before heading home. His anger bubbled in him. He hoped it would settle down before heading back.

He was in for a huge letdown.

"There's the stud boy," a low voice called toward him. "Hey, man, the cops are looking for you."

Gary spun towards the voice. Brubaker and Dorn lurked at the corner, just beneath the streetlight, passing a cigarette between them. His first instinct was to run, but tonight he was angry and he couldn't give a rat's ass about these two.

"What the hell are you talking about?" Gary said.

"Didn't you hear, juvie? Somebody busted out some windows tonight. Rumor's going around you did it."

Gary thrust his hands into his pockets and started to pass them. "Screw you."

He didn't like the sound of the busted window thing, nor did he like the sound of their sneakered feet thumping the pavement after him.

"What's the matter?" Dorn started. "You like busting out windows, but you don't like us? Why don't you tell us where you were tonight?"

Brubaker hurried in front of Gary, blocking his path. He tried to go around him, but Dorn intercepted. They were like a wall, moving in to stop him.

"Get the hell out of my face." Gary's chest seared with anger.

Brubaker gave him a little shove on the shoulder and chuckled. "Maybe that little whore Beth will lie for you and say you were with her. She's in love with you right? Don't you love her, tough man?"

Gary stopped at the mention of Beth's name. He already knew whom they had been talking to in order to find out about Beth. He was a geyser of anger, ready to blow.

"What did you say? How do you know about her?"

Dorn grinned. "Ooh, I think he's mad now. I think you touched a sore spot. Little juvie boy's got himself a girlfriend. Maybe she'll be the one with some trouble next."

Gary exploded. He was back in Radcliffe again, lashing out against the idiot bullies who liked to pick on the smaller guys, who didn't know they were in for some trouble when they messed with Gary Sanderson. His fist connected with the bridge of Dorn's nose. Blood spurted out like juice from a crushed tomato. Dorn shrieked and grabbed his face, stunned. Gary wondered if the bully had ever actually been struck before and doubted it from his reaction. He didn't even hit him very hard.

Brubaker, having a bit more time to compose himself, rushed Gary, grappling him around the shoulders and waist. They crashed to the ground. Gary's face slammed into the street and stars erupted in his eyes. Brubaker brought his elbow down like a hammer, but Gary threw his leg over and took the brunt of the blow to his thigh.

He rolled, turning twice before landing behind the larger of the bullies, his greasy head gripped tightly in a headlock. Gary yanked him into a neat chokehold, body shaking with fury.

"If you fuck with Beth, I will fucking kill you! Do you understand?"

He didn't wait for a response, not even a grunt. He flipped the bully over and kicked him once in the face, aiming at the jaw like a punter. He struck him square, not even realizing what he was doing, and slammed Brubaker's jaw into his skull with a resounding thwack of bone on bone. Brubaker spit out blood and two chipped fragments of tooth.

Dorn was half way down the street, screaming, holding his nose, but Gary didn't hear him. He focused on the bloody mess of a face in front of him, and it didn't look near bloody enough for him at the moment.

"I'll fucking kill you!"

He pounded into Brubaker's face once more.

"Damn it! Why can't you leave me alone?" Gary cried, speaking to the world in general. "I'm not a juvie boy anymore!"

When he was done, Brubaker lay in a broken heap on the ground in front him, shattered teeth, busted nose, blood everywhere. Dorn was gone, who knew where. Gary stared at the mess he'd made and reality seeped in where his anger seeped out. His knuckles ached and his arms were streaked with Brubaker's blood.

To his right, a light splashed on, a woman's face peeked through her window. Then another light, and another face. He was an animal at the zoo.

He hurried toward home, afraid. *What have I done?* He'd completely lost control, and this is what happened when he lost control.

The streets were a blur of November, of blue chill and yellow leaves and dying grass. The sidewalks were cracked under his feet, threatening to spread open and send him straight to hell.

It didn't take long for a floodlight to burst to life behind him, flashing onto his back with the red and blue cherries. The voice that called out through a blaring speaker froze Gary's bones. It was Officer Vedish.

"Hold it."

Gary stopped. He didn't bother to say a word. The floodlight shone over his bloody hands and bloody shirt, and he was sure

Vedish had already found Dorn and Brubaker, or at least the broken heap of Brubaker where the faces in the doorways on that street had directed him.

The car pulled up to the curb with a squeak of the breaks and hum of the engine fan, and Officer Vedish stepped out, squawking something into the CB on his shoulder. He stopped a few feet in front of Gary and his eyes moved up and down.

Gary knew he was in trouble.

"Get in the car."

He did so without a single word.

The police station was as dark and oppressive as a dungeon. The faint odor of cigarette smoke permeated the air, trickling out from the break room. Gary sat alone in what Officer Vedish called the Holding Area, a tiny cubicle of a room with a single mahogany desk and a rollaway chair with one squeaky wheel. The walls were painted a dull yellow, and a pale green chalkboard, on which someone had begun a game of hangman, covered the wall to the right.

Gary stared at the back wall, seeing nothing. A female officer named Rebecca Sojin had bandaged his hands before they threw him into the Holding Area, and the bandages itched where the skin had been broken. He scratched at his knuckles with the tips of his fingers, waiting. A healthy bruise bloomed on his cheek.

Finally, after nearly an hour, Officer Vedish came into the room and closed the door behind him. He hiked up one leg of his pants and planted himself on a corner of the desk, staring at Gary. He stank of a cologne that reminded Gary of wood stripper.

"So where were you tonight, Gary?"

"Just out." He couldn't tell him he was with Beth. That would make things even worse.

"Were you at work? I don't think so because I talked to your drunk of a boss and he said you didn't work tonight. Not that he'd know the difference."

Gary boiled. "Rocky's a good guy. He's a lot better than you."

Officer Vedish croaked an amused laugh. "Yeah, I'm a real bad guy. Why don't you tell me about those windows? Someone busted out about twenty windows at the Tool and Die shop. Know anything about that?"

"I don't know what windows you're talking about. Whatever happened, it wasn't me and you know it. Those idiots did it."

"You mean those 'idiots' you attacked and kicked the hell out of tonight?" Vedish's voice dripped with sarcasm.

"Hey, it was the other way around. They jumped me. I was just out walking."

"Doesn't matter how it went down. You put somebody in the hospital. No matter how you look at it, it's a serious offense."

"Look, I don't know anything about the windows, and I'm telling you the truth. Those two guys came up to me and started in about some windows or something, and then they tried to shove me around, so I fought back. That's it."

Officer Vedish stared at him a good long moment, not breathing, then finally slid off the desk, facing Gary. He put his thumbs in his belt. "All right, so that's how it's going to be."

"It doesn't have to be any way. I didn't do anything wrong."

Officer Vedish opened the door. "Your dad's on his way to pick you up."

Gary's heart sank into his gut. "He's not my dad."

He waited in silence for another half an hour until Don arrived to pick him up. Vedish tapped on the door to get his attention.

"Your daddy is here. Let's go."

He led Gary to the front door where Don was finishing up paperwork. He wasn't happy. He handed the forms to the desk officer and glared at the floor, unable to look at Gary directly. He chewed his upper lip.

Vedish crossed his arms and nodded. "Like I said on the phone, this isn't a good situation for the kid to be in."

Don only nodded.

"I don't know what else to say about it. You'd think he'd of wised up a bit from Radcliffe, but I don't see it. He's got an attitude problem to boot."

Don nodded, cleared his throat. His face was red.

"I'm going to look into those windows. All I got is hearsay right now, but you'll be hearing from me if I find anything else. And

I'll let you know if any of those boys wants to press charges. He hurt one of them pretty bad."

"I didn't break any windows...." Gary started.

"Shut up," Don barked at him.

Vedish eyed Gary with satisfaction. "You can go now."

Gary followed Don out to the parking lot and stepped up into the truck. The night was dark now, November dark with just a slit of moon lighting the dashboard. Don's knuckles were white on the steering wheel. He still chewed on his upper lip, as if chewing on the words he wanted to say. Gary felt the urge to brace himself for a strike.

"I don't even know how to begin to tell you how disappointed we are in you right now," Don said after they had pulled onto the main road.

Gary said nothing. His entire body ached with disappointment, as if he'd been tied up and wracked for days.

"I can handle this kind of shit, but Gail can't do it. You're turning her into a nervous wreck. Do you know that?"

Gary glanced sideways at Don. His anger burned in his ears. "Me? *You're* the one making her a nervous wreck."

"What did you say to me?"

"You never give her the benefit of the doubt." Gary tried to keep a civil tone and almost achieved it. "You don't listen to her, just like you're not going to listen to me."

Don slammed a hand down on the dashboard. "You busted out windows and you put a kid in the hospital tonight, Gary. Don't turn this around on me."

Gary shook his head. "I already told you I didn't bust out any windows, and those two guys attacked *me* first. I didn't do anything wrong."

"Fine," Don said, but Gary could tell Don's mind was made up. "You know, we took you into our house and gave you food and clothes. We helped you go to school, and look what you gave us."

It felt like an elephant sat on Gary's chest.

"This is shit," Don went on. "This is real shit. Kids like you can't change. You'll never change. You'll always be this stupid little punk that has to fight with people. What good are you?"

Gary turned away. He wanted to cry, but he knew he wouldn't. In the window, his distorted reflection glared back at him. It was ugly and warped.

"I don't know. I've been asking myself that for years." In his own mind, he wasn't any good, except maybe for one thing.

Don snorted. "What?"

"Nothing," Gary said, and they rode in silence the remainder of the way home.

Gail was waiting for them when they pulled up. She opened the door and let them pass. Don huffed in and headed straight for the basement, but not before barking, "Deal with this," and slamming the door. Gary kicked off his shoes and stood before her, stark and as emotionally naked as a wounded child.

She inspected the cuts on his hands and his face. Her soft fingers were warm and soothing. "Are you all right?"

Gary cleared his throat. "I'm sorry about this."

"Well, there's nothing we can do about it now." She removed the bandages from his hands. "Let me put some Bactine on these."

She led him to the kitchen and produced a bottle from one of the cabinets. The liquid burned over the open cuts, but the stinging didn't last long.

"Do you want to tell me about it?"

"They said I busted out some windows, but I swear to God I didn't do any of that. It wasn't me."

Gail searched his face, her eyes locking with his. After a long moment, she looked back down and proceeded to rewrap his bandages.

"I believe you, but it's more complicated that that. It isn't enough that I believe you."

"I know." He felt like someone held him under water. The events of the past twenty-four hours raced through his mind. He only wanted to escape it all. "I don't think it's working out for me here."

Gail dabbed his bandages, making sure they were loose enough. "Don't give up on us, Gary, and we won't give up on you."

Gary nodded.

"We have to talk about this. You have to let me in, and I can't wait any longer for it. Don't you see what happens when you leave things bottled up inside of you for this long?"

"I don't want to talk about it." He bit at his lip. "I don't know what to say."

"Anything, anything at all. Tell me why you got in a fight tonight, or why you fight at all. Tell me why you think those windows got broken, or why you don't want to talk to anyone about what is bothering you. Anything. I want you to tell me anything at all about what makes you tick so I can help you. Damn it!"

It wasn't so much the word that shocked Gary, but the tone of it. For the first time Gail had become angry with him, and it was the one thing he thought would never happen.

He backed away and hurried up the stairs to his room. He couldn't bring himself to slam the door, even though he wanted to. He didn't want to shut himself off from her, not from Gail. He secretly wished she would run up the stairs after him, tell him it was all right, everything was going to be all right. He wished he could tell her about Beth.

In his room, he took Butchy from his drawer and stared at it. Part of the paint had worn away on the face. He gritted his teeth and glanced out the window. Beth's dim light bled through the drawn shade. He wondered if her father was with her. It made him sick to his stomach.

"What should I do, Butchy? What the hell am I supposed to do here?"

Gail appeared in his doorway. He retreated to the center of the room; weak, angry, sad, disheveled, a gigantic and erratic mixture of emotional uncertainty. He wiped a tear from his cheek with his sleeve.

"Can I talk to you?" she asked.

"I didn't mean to run away from you."

"I know that you want to get away from me, but you can't anymore. We need to talk."

He flopped onto the bed. She was right, but where to begin? He was able to talk to Beth, but this was different. Fresh, new scars formed in him, aching, bleeding. He needed to tell Gail about Beth.

"I know what you're going through," Gail said. "I know it's hard."

"You don't know what I'm going through."

"Yes, I do. I told you about my mother, didn't I? I know how angry I was and how I hated everything about everything for the longest time. I hated everything about myself, too."

Gary sat up in the bed, turning his pillow over in his hands. "It's not just that."

"I know, but we have to start somewhere. You need to talk about it."

His body pulsed with tension. His teeth nearly shattered against the force of his jaw. His anger and confusion were a hot rose, blooming in his chest. "Why does everyone have to talk about this crap? That's what started this whole thing in the first place."

"That's not true."

He looked at her, his eyes awash with tears, yet none fell. He felt trapped with nowhere to go. "Do you know what I want to talk about? I want to know why there has to be so much abuse everywhere. So much shit."

Gail's face dripped with sympathy. "I don't know."

"And why the hell do people have to hurt other people all the time? What gives them the right to live?"

Gail dropped to her knees in the middle of the room. She ran her fingers along the carpeting, staring into Gary's eyes. "We can't just take a person's life, Gary, no matter what they've done. It's just not right."

"But why do they deserve to live when every day *we* want to cry? What gives them the right to do what they do to us?"

"They have no right."

Gary clenched every muscle in his body to hold his tears back. They wanted to come so bad but he wouldn't allow them. "What good am I? I already know I'm going to Hell for what I've done."

Gail rose and threw her arms out to him, but he backed away. He couldn't take it.

"You're not going to Hell. You were just a boy."

"I knew what I was doing." He glanced at Butchy, admitting it to himself for the first time in his life.

She sobbed with soft tears, aching tears.

He clenched his fists on his knees. "Didn't you say you had a sister?"

"Yes, a younger sister."

"If you could go back to when you were a little girl and you had to do it all over again, what would you do?"

Gail's lips twisted with confusion. "What do you mean?"

"I mean what if you had to take all that abuse again? What would you do? Would you run away? Would you kill your mother and make her stop?"

A long tear streamed onto Gail's chin. Gary wondered if this was how she thought their talk would go.

"I'd run away," she said. "I wouldn't let her hurt me."

He stood up from the bed and paced the room, more animated, upset, worried.

"You mean you would just run away and leave her with your sister? Someone you loved, who you were supposed to protect? What gave her the right to do that to you and your sister? What gave her the right to live?"

Gail shook her head, tears streaming, her mouth working to form words, yet nothing would come out but muffled squawks.

"Would you just sit by and watch or would you do something about it? Wouldn't you kill her? Or would you just try to kill yourself?"

He pointed to Gail's wrists and the scars there glowed in the dim light. She froze. Not even a breath stirred within her as her gaze burned into him. He immediately regretted the question, but he had to know, had to find out if she was right or wrong, had to show her the consequences of all this.

"What's worse? Doing that to yourself or doing nothing? Why did you even want me here? Was it so you could build some perfect little world to hide in all by yourself? Is turning me into the perfect little boy with no problems and no past going to make you all better?"

Gail sobbed deeply. "Isn't that what you wanted?"

"Yeah," Gary said. "And now I know it doesn't work that way at all. There's always someone around asking you to pay up for what you did, always someone around to remind you so you never forget."

Gail lowered her head in the ensuing silence. "Yes."

"What?"

"I said yes," she breathed, tears streaking her face. "If I could go back I'd kill my mother for what she did and I wouldn't think twice about it. Is that what you wanted to hear? Are you happy now?"

With that, she broke down in a heap. She drooped against her knees and cried deep, powerful tears, tears that had probably been there for ages and never had a chance to get out.

"I would kill her a thousand times over for what she did to me and my sister."

Gary stood, wracked with pain, pounded with rage and tears. He felt sorry for Gail. He felt sorry for what he had just done to her. He readied himself to tell her about Beth and prayed she could help her.

The door burst open and Don's angry frame stood in the doorway, eyes wide, absorbing the scene. "What the hell are you doing?"

He crossed the room in an instant and struck Gary once on the corner of his cheek, the same place his father had struck him those years ago. Lightning streaked through his head. He dropped to the ground and thwacked his head against the dresser. The picture of his mother fell, cracking the glass in shards. He covered his face, expecting more blows, but none came.

"Stop!" Gail called. "It's not Gary's fault. I asked for this. I wanted him to open up to me and he did."

Don fumed, his entire body shaking. "You call this *opening up?* Goddamn it! This is ridiculous!"

With that, he picked Gail up and helped her out of the room, slamming the door behind him, leaving Gary in the saturated silence. Alone, he tried to put the glass of his mother's picture back in place, but he cut his finger. The edge of the photo was torn and the picture was nearly sliced in half. It was the only picture he had of his mother.

He laid his arms over the top of the dresser, letting it take his full weight, and he allowed himself to cry at last. To him, this was probably the worst thing that could have happened. He didn't blame Don for hitting him. It probably looked pretty bad from his perspective, Gail lying on the floor in a heap, crying, with Gary standing over her. His throat clenched shut. Radcliffe wasn't so far away anymore.

Downstairs, he heard yelling. The sounds were muffled, but he could tell it was Don starting in on Gail. He went to the door and cracked it open.

"Now will you listen to me?"

"I don't want to hear it. Just leave me alone," Gail cried.

"Damn it, I told you this would happen. We can't take much more of this, I'm telling you. I told you something was going to break, and now it's broken."

After a long pause, Gary cringed when he heard Gail say, "I know."

"I know you wanted to help him, Gail, but you aren't capable of doing that. Neither of us is. He's got more problems than you can even think about and it's going to take a lot more than a stint in some caring foster home to help him."

"I know."

"I think it's about time we start talking about sending him back to Radcliffe."

No response from Gail but a horrible silence.

Gary didn't want to hear anymore. They couldn't help Beth, or him. He could see where it was going. He quietly closed the door and did his best to shut out the world.

CHAPTER 16

When All the Doors Are Closing

Monday was hell. Gary awoke to a dim room and cool rain tapping against his window. The cold reached into his room like ghostly fingers and shook his bones. He showered and dressed quickly, rummaging through his dresser for something warm to wear. He selected a gray sweater and pulled it over his head, mussing his hair.

The sweater screamed Don's words at him. "We took you into our house and gave you food and clothes." And this is what they get for their efforts.

Atop the dresser, the shattered picture of his mother glared back at him, another reminder. When he left for school, no one greeted him at the door. Don had gone to work early, and Gail never came out of her room. He could have knocked on her door, but he didn't think she wanted to see him. His heart felt ready to burst and drip into his stomach.

In English class, Stan didn't say a word to him, but it was all right. He didn't have anything to say to Stan except that he deserved to get clocked in the head for his part in the whole Brubaker-Dorn thing. He barely even heard the teacher's lesson for the day. He kept thinking of Old Eben Flood standing on the hill, staring down into the town that no longer welcomed him. That was how it was for him now. The doors were closing fast, and he didn't know what to do about it.

He actually even looked forward to talking with Counselor Ray after school, and that was a first. Not that they'd do tons of talking, but the entire weekend worried him, and he hoped Ray might have some more information and insights about it all. He hoped he might be able to help Beth.

He crossed through the hall toward Ray's office, running his fingers along the cold, corrugated lockers. The ceiling light that had blinked for so long had finally died, leaving the hallway dark and black. Ray sat in the office, flipping his cards in his fingers. He wore dress shoes today, black and polished, and a long sleeve button-down shirt with thin red stripes. His hair was neatly combed back and even his ponytail had been clipped down. His knees poked through his pressed slacks like wire hangers. It didn't seem like Ray at all.

"Gary." He leaned forward on the desk. "Have a seat."

Gary dropped his book bag under the chair with a grunt. He let out a deep breath and threw up his hands, having no clue where to start.

Ray stared at him with an odd look in his eye. "Nice shiner you got there. Rough weekend, huh?"

Gary nodded.

"Well, I heard all about it already," Ray said, flipping, flipping, fingers constantly moving. "Not too good."

"Not really."

"So, tell me about it." He folded his hands finally and propped himself to listen.

Gary shifted uncomfortably in his chair. "I don't know what to do. It's like everything is falling apart."

"Why do you think that is?"

His head pounded like bongo drums. He thought of everyone who had come into his life since Radcliffe, but mostly he thought of Beth. Every thought of her now crushed him. He thought of how he could tell Ray.

"I don't know where to start, I guess. It's my foster parents, and it's my job, and my friends, and those two guys I beat up. And this girl."

"Sounds like it's everything."

"Yeah. Pretty much. I'm afraid of going back to Radcliffe. I can't go back there."

Counselor Ray angled up from his desk and clicked along the floor with his new leather shoes. He slipped behind Gary and began to rub his shoulders. *Rubbin' Ray.* "Don't be afraid, Gary. I can help you. Go on."

Gary tightened, unsure of how to react. Why was Ray touching his shoulders? It made him uncomfortable, but he needed Ray's help. The whole *Rubbin' Ray* conversation with Stan flashed in his mind.

"I... I've got these problems."

Ray's hands slipped down onto Gary's arms. "Go on."

"Something happened," Gary said, "with this girl I know. I...."

He shuddered. Ray's hands slipped down too far, practically falling into his lap. He shot up from the chair and shoved Ray backward. The counselor slipped in his new shoes and bumped into the closed door.

"What the hell are you doing?" Gary demanded. His body shook.

"Whoa." Ray held his hands up. "Relax, man. Just relax."

Gary backed away until he hit the desk. The cards fell onto the floor, scattering. "What the hell were you doing?"

Ray, with his hands still up, clicked back behind the desk and scooped the cards back into a deck. It only took him moments to rearrange them in his slick, disgusting fingers.

"Just hold on now," he said. "Come on, talk to me."

Gary took his backpack from beneath the chair and flung it over his shoulder. "We're done."

"You better hold on, Gary." Ray leaned back in his chair, and his voice took on a more authoritative tone, the first time Gary had heard such a thing from the man. He wasn't the friendly Counselor Ray anymore. "This is ridiculous you know. I don't know what you imagined happened just now, but it was nothing. I'm just trying to help you."

"I know how you were trying to help me. Jesus!"

"Look, can you please relax," Ray said. His voice was smug. "It never happened, all right? It never happened. Just clear your head and sit back down. Please."

Gary opened the door and started to leave.

"You know, I can send you back to Radcliffe with a phone call."

Gary slammed the door behind him and hurried up the hall. He didn't want to be in the same room with Counselor Ray ever again, and now there wasn't a doubt in his mind he was going back to Radcliffe. He didn't know when, but he figured it would be soon. The doors were closing. There weren't many of them left.

At home, Gary didn't say anything about his counselor. Don hadn't come home yet, and Gail said she didn't feel so well. He sat in the kitchen with her, wondering what he might say to her, worried she might hate him now for what he'd said and done to her.

"I feel really bad about everything," he began, fumbling over his own words. "I mean, I feel like an idiot about making you cry like that. Don probably hates me now."

She looked up at him, and her eyes lingered at the bruise Don had given him. He rubbed it with his hand.

"I don't really know what to say," he said.

"I don't know what to say either. I'm very confused right now. I don't know what to do anymore."

She began to cry, and her breath grew shallow, rapid.

"Gail?"

"It's so hard doing this, you know, being like this all the time, living with myself all the time. You were right about me. What was I thinking? I thought I could bring you here and help you and that would make everything perfect."

Her breath came faster, shallower. She drew her knees up to her chest and wrapped her arms around herself.

"Gail, are you all right?"

"I'm a terrible person, aren't I? I couldn't help you. I couldn't even help myself. I'm an idiot! An idiot!"

She screamed the words through what little breath she had left then clawed at the table suddenly, slamming her fists down. Gary flew up and tried to stop her, but she tore away and fell to the floor.

"Gail! Gail!"

The front door opened and Don rushed in, just like the night before. Gary backed away quickly, holding his hands up. "I didn't do anything, I swear! She just started acting like this. I don't know if she can breathe!"

Don rushed to her and took her in his arms. He cradled her, hushing softly. "She's having a panic attack. She used to have them all the time. It's been a while now."

Gary stepped forward, but Don pulled her away. "She'll be fine. Just go to work or something. I'll take care of her. Please."

He ran up the stairs and shut himself up in the painting room. *What's happening to Gail? What am I doing to her?*

Before him, the canvas was black. He glared out the window, but Beth's light was off, the shade drawn. Images of her flooded his brain. He thought of her father and wanted to vomit. That would make an interesting piece of artwork, wouldn't it?

He was lost.

Without thinking, he scraped the paint brush along the canvas with white paint, forming a dull, chaotic line. He rubbed the paint with a paper towel into a smooth smudge, giving it a bleeding, shadowy feel. Soon he had an outline of something even he himself didn't recognize right away. When he did, he ripped the canvas from the easel and crumpled it into the garbage. It looked a little too much like Butchy the Cowboy for his own liking.

Things were looking bad for him. Very bad.

Gary served customers with all the zeal of a zombie. His legs were like two cinder blocks he was forced to drag around and his eyelids were like lead. He was tired from everything, dead tired, but not the kind of tired where you want to fall onto a soft couch and pass out until morning. He was tired in his bones and in his brain.

He hadn't seen Beth in two days—not since she'd asked him the critical question that had been crushing him. He wanted to see her, but he also didn't, and it drove him insane. He knew he couldn't ignore the fact that she desperately needed his help, and now time might be running short for him, considering his run in with Brubaker and Dorn, Officer Vedish, and Gail and Don. It was all a nightmare pressing itself into reality.

Radcliffe was coming, he felt it. Counselor Ray would see to it, and if Gary spoke up, it would be his word against the school counselor. Who would believe a stupid juvie boy who killed his father and just kicked the crap out of two guys? Oh, and busted out a bunch of windows, too.

And then there was Stan. *That* particular betrayal hurt him the most. There was no way Brubaker and Dorn could have known about Beth if Stan hadn't told them, and he was sure they were the ones who busted out the windows to get him in trouble. Why did they hate him so much? Why did they want to screw with him like that? Because he had the balls to stand up to them? Probably. Not like Stan.

He could almost understand Stan's motivation in helping the bullies, with his desperate hope to become a bad-ass in the eyes of the world and his inane need to please his bullying friends. Hell, that was what drew him to Gary in the first place, the fact that he had come from Radcliffe. To Stan, there was little else as prestigious as juvie, so he had sacrificed one friend to please the others. An understandable concept. Stupid, but understandable. Gary just didn't like being that one friend.

He worried about Gail as well. She'd torn herself up trying to help him, and look what she got? He was like a poison to everyone around him.

In the kitchen toward the end of the shift, he worked the grill with the scraper, cleaning off the residual gunk. The kitchen practically gleamed now, but he found no joy or pride in it this time. It didn't matter anymore. Everything had become tainted and dirty.

Rocky staggered in from the front, eyes glossed over, flecks of spittle on his chin. "Think you can lock up here tonight?"

Gary bobbed his head. "Sure, I can handle it."

Rocky tipped his paper hat. "Thanks, friend. You really are a good kid."

Under his breath, Gary said, "Yeah, right."

The boss staggered through the back door and closed it behind him. *He didn't even take a nip from his bottle,* Gary noted.

In another hour, he'd be done. The only things left were to finish the grill and mop the floor, and then....

Something clunked in the kitchen, startling him. He paused, holding the scraper up to his chest, and listened. Faint scratching sounds. At the far wall, the coffee can lay flat on the floor, held down by the can of jalapeno cheese. *His better mousetrap had caught the mouse.*

He couldn't believe it. He finally caught the little bastard. From the cheese shelf, he ripped off a small piece of cardboard and slid it beneath the can so the mouse wouldn't escape, then flipped it upright and peeked inside. The tiny body of the mouse shook like a baby's rattle, its dark, frightened eyes glaring up at the slice of light entering its prison.

"How does it feel to be stuck somewhere?" Gary asked the mouse. "No way out, is there?"

He pictured the dank walls of his room and the oppressive hallways of Radcliffe.

"They're going to send me back, you know. So nothing really matters anymore, does it?"

Rocky popped into his head, asking what he would do with the mouse if he actually caught it. Was he going to let it go? Was he going to kill it? Did he really think he could kill something like a mouse?

"I'm just a killer, you know," he told the mouse, heat welling up in his chest again, the flames licking his lungs and his shoulders. "I guess you can't fight what you are, isn't that right?"

He stared down at the partially rusted can and considered the thing, and the thing within the thing, as if it might hold some answers for him, some reason for his life in general, some rationality for why things had unraveled the way they had.

He never received an answer.

With everything he had, he slung his arm back and heaved the can into the wall. The can bounded off the wall, chipped the paint where it struck and dented in the entire side of the can. It arced back toward him, bounced once against the hard floor then landed, rumpled, at his feet. He gazed down at it with new consideration, the brute force in himself oozing through his pores like sweat, staring down at the results of his actions.

The can revealed nothing, not even a sound. He nudged it upright with his shoe and bent over, peering into it. The tiny, furry thing was no longer breathing. It was dead, crushed along with the can. He had killed it, which confirmed everything he knew about himself and left him with no other reasonable choice. At that moment, he decided to give up, to quit fighting the killer he was.

Before leaving work, Gary took the gun from the front drawer, checked to make sure it was loaded, and slid it into his pocket. The heaviness of it brought back memories he didn't think he could deny any longer.

Beth sat glued to the stump beneath the tree, knees drawn up to her chest, sleeves bunched up over her hands. She leaned her chin onto her right knee and watched Gary through her unkempt bangs.

The gun weighed Gary's pocket down. He clenched the handle in his fingers, afraid it might disappear if he let go of it, or that it might turn into a dark metal monster and consume him for losing control.

"I'm afraid," he said.

She rocked herself forward and back, slowly, watching him. Her face was slack, no doubt from her pills. "Me, too."

"Are you sure you want to do this?"

"Yes," she said without hesitation.

He paced the ground, wearing a path in the dirt. "We can still just run away."

Her head shook. "I can't. You know you can't just run away from this. Besides, I have to help my mother."

He fell against the table and sighed, still gripping the gun, while she watched him with her dull eyes.

"What happened to your hands?" she asked.

He held them up for inspection, aware that his hand was no longer touching the gun. The bandages were gone, but the scabs and swollen knuckles were still there.

"You mean you haven't heard? I got in a fight."

"Are you serious?" More animation in her voice this time, worry. "What happened?"

He told her about Brubaker and Dorn. Her eyes widened in disbelief.

"Are you all right?"

"I'm all right, but they aren't. One of them had to go to the hospital with a busted nose. I guess I knocked him out."

Her gaze shifted to something resembling awe. He didn't like it.

"I hate those guys," she said. "Everybody does."

"I shouldn't have done it like that. I couldn't help it. I'm in big trouble now. But it's nothing compared to...." He let the sentence hang there, all fat and ready to explode.

She said nothing.

"You know what'll happen to us when we do this, don't you?" he asked her.

She stopped rocking. "Maybe."

"Maybe, meaning yes, or maybe meaning you have no idea."

She shrugged dully.

"I don't know either." He thought of Rocky. "It's not so easy to kill a person, you know. It does something to you."

She picked at the denim on her knees.

He pulled the gun out of his pocket so she could see it. "I got it from work. I don't think he'll miss it for awhile, not that it matters anymore."

She stared at the gun, mesmerized by it. "When do you want to do it?"

"I don't know."

It felt like two giant hands had seized him, trying to tear him in half. What was she asking him to do? He didn't want to do it, yet he had no other choice. What were the options? Either kill the man, or let the man continue to rape his girlfriend. Sickening either way he looked at it.

There was no choice. *I love her, don't I?* He couldn't let it continue, for her sake, no matter what the sacrifice. Even Gail had agreed with him, in a roundabout way. He'd asked her if she would have killed her mother for what she had done to her and her sister, and she said yes. It was the right thing to do. Wasn't it?

He aimed the gun at the tree and pulled the trigger. It kicked back some against his palm, but not too hard. The bullet splintered the side of the tree, throwing out shards of fresh bark and wood. A dozen birds flew up from the branches, startled, a cacophony of wings and feathers.

Beth didn't move, not surprised in the least. Apparently, she was ready right now.

"Soon," he said. "We'll have to do it soon."

He sat in his room on the bed, face in his hands, hunched over like an old bum. It felt like entire worlds were draining from his brain, falling out of him like sour liquid, running down his hands and arms to his feet, congealing there in sticky pools. He stashed the gun under his mattress at the pillow end and swore he could feel it there, like the princess and the pea, though he was sure it was all in his mind.

He thought of Beth. He still wasn't sure if he could help her. His every thought was a marathon runner, sprinting back and forth between edges of his dilemma. Should he do it or shouldn't he? He needed to help her, but should he murder for her? His mind grew dull from the pressure.

The rain had stopped, even though the forecast called for it, replaced by a sharp, bleating wind wrapping its knuckles against the window. It howled through the windowpane, a dull, pained murmur. His homework lay open on the bed next to him, but he found it impossible to concentrate. The only thing stuck in his head was the poetry assignment for English class. It was a poem by T.S. Eliot called *The Hollow Men*. The final lines haunted him.

This is the way the world ends
This is the way the world ends
This is the way the world ends
Not with a bang but a whimper.

That was how it would be for him. He was a hollow man, a stuffed man, his head was filled with straw. And this would be how his world would end, with a lousy whimper.

"Can we talk downstairs?" It was Don. Gary hadn't even heard him open the door.

He followed Don into the kitchen where Gail sat, waiting for them, her face limp as a dying flower. She looked like a woman beaten down, defeated, tired of fighting and clawing her way to the top of the heap. He knew exactly how she felt, and he had a good idea of what was about to happen.

He took his normal seat and clenched his hands together in his lap, waiting for the blow to land. He wasn't disappointed.

"We've decided to send you back to Radcliffe," Don said. "We've already called them, and they're expecting you back."

So that was it, like a shotgun to the chest. He glanced at Gail but she couldn't look at him, not in the eye at least, and he understood it all. This was entirely Don's decision, and Gail knew it was a fight she couldn't win. She'd lost already in so many ways. She shouldn't have bet on him. It would always be a losing bet.

"It's just not working out here," Don went on. "With all this fighting and busting out windows and hurting Gail, we just can't handle it. We think you need more time to learn to adjust with, well, with what you've done in your life."

Gary thrust his arms over his chest, as if he could contain everything raging within him. "And I'm sure you talked to my counselor, too, right? I'll bet he had a lot to say about this."

Gail turned away.

"That's right," Don said. "He said your sessions were going nowhere, that you were only interested in playing cards."

Flames spat. "I'm sure that's what he said. So when do I leave?"

"As soon as I can get you down there, probably Saturday."

Gary stood up from the table upset, but without a single tear in his body. The flames in his chest had burned them all away. "I don't blame you for sending me back," he said. "It's good to know when to give up."

He had four days left, four whole days remaining in Winsbury, Illinois. It wasn't so long ago that he sat in his dank, little room in Radcliffe, listening to Hector's dire warnings that seemed ludicrous at the time. "Just don't let those *suburbios* screw you up."

Too late.

What would Hector say to him now, limping back to Radcliffe with his tail stuck between his legs like a beaten puppy? He wouldn't rub it in his face, at least. He knew that much. Hector wasn't the type. At least in Radcliffe, you didn't have to wonder what people were about. They either liked you or hated you, and they told you so pretty much up front. It wasn't like that in Winsbury.

All of this came to him on Saturday morning as he wandered the town, up and down the streets, through the parks and the fields.

Don told him not to go, but he didn't listen. He didn't care now, and there wasn't much anyone could do about it anyway. It wasn't in his bones to be so blatantly defiant, but what the hell? He was going back to Radcliffe. There wasn't much else they could threaten him with.

What would Old Eben Flood do? The idea made him chuckle. He'd slam down a jug of whiskey, that's what he'd do.

He had unfinished business waiting before he could leave, business that would probably cause him to skip Radcliffe altogether. He might wind up in some other jail that wouldn't let him work in a kitchen, that might weigh him down with bricks and cinders and kick him in the face at every turn. He knew this, but it didn't matter. He knew what had to be done now.

He had been appointed by fate, perhaps. It almost made sense. Who knew why? Did it matter? He was already a killer. That wouldn't change, no matter what. Somebody up there must have known all about what he'd done. Why else would they bring him to this dinky little town and mix him up with Beth, make him fall in love with her, and then throw him in the face of her rapist father?

It all came down to one question: *Who deserved to live?* His own father sure as hell hadn't, and he took care of that pretty well, didn't he? Beth's father didn't deserve to live either, and he'd take care of that, too. Maybe that was what he was created for, to take all the assholes to Hell with him. Hell was a real place, and he was headed straight for it, just like Rocky.

There was one bit of unfinished business he was about to deal with right away. *Stan.* He'd had time to cool off a bit and wasn't quite as ticked off at the guy, but he was still disappointed in him. He circled through town and headed through the forest preserve, coming out at the pond, hoping to find Stan there fishing.

Stan stood on the bank, casting his plastic flies out across the water like he'd taught Gary. He turned when he heard Gary's approach, and Gary sensed the apprehension in him, noting the look of surprise washed across his friend's face.

"Hey, bro," Stan said. "What are you doing here?"

Gary stopped at the bank, kicked a stone into the water. A slight breeze flopped his bangs into his eyes. He quickly brushed the hair away. "I pretty much figured out how it all happened, Stan. Those idiots got to you. Am I right?"

Stan reeled in his line, then set the pole down on the dirt, facing Gary. "I'm sorry."

Gary couldn't help but note the sincerity. He almost felt sorry for Stan.

"I didn't think it would be like this. I didn't think you'd get in so much trouble."

"Why didn't you tell me what they were going to do?"

Stan's eyes dropped away like a fallen ocean sail. "I don't know."

"They want to send me back."

"To Radcliffe?"

"Yeah," Gary spat. "I hate that fuckin' place, but you want to know what I hate more?"

Stan's guilty eyes rose once more. "What?"

"*This* fuckin' place. You know, I can take the shit from guys like Dorn and Brubaker, but what happened to you? Did you think they'd think you were all cool by bringing a juvie boy around? Are you trying to buy your friends? They're not even worth your time."

Stan thrust his hands into his pockets, practically naked without his trusty leather jacket. "I'm sorry. I just wanted to be in their group. I wanted them to stop whacking me in the head every time they wanted a stupid beer. You saw how they treat me. I'm like their idiot mascot."

Part of Gary wanted to haul back and slam his friend in the head for that statement, but looking at him, at his raw, naked honesty, brought forth more pity than anything.

"So you just threw me to the dogs, man. You can take the knife out of my back any time, you know. Acting like those guys doesn't make it better. All they want to do is scare people. Why do you think they keep you around? Because they scare you and they smell it. They like it. It makes them feel good. It's like that everywhere."

Stan cocked his head, exhaled. "I don't know what to say."

"You have this idea that you want to be a bad ass, that I'm some kind of bad ass dude because I was in Radcliffe, but that's bullshit. Do you know what I did to get in there? I fuckin' killed my father when I was twelve. How bad is that? How bad ass is a twelve-year-old kid that pulls a trigger because he's scared shitless of his father?"

Stan's mouth fell agape. His face cringed. He stared at Gary as if he'd just spit on him.

"Do you even understand how screwed I am?" Gary asked. "Forever. Don't waste your time with Brubaker and Dorn. You're better than they are. A lot better."

Gary turned away and headed toward the trail, doubting he'd ever see Stan again in his entire life. He turned back with an afterthought. "You should go fishing with your Dad once in a while, man. You got it lucky and you don't even know it."

He turned away again and stomped down the trail.

He had the gun in his pocket. It was with him all day, like a brick. It had plenty of bullets. Maybe enough to use on himself when he was done with Beth's father. Who knew how he'd feel when this was all over? Maybe he'd want to end it all. He practically did now.

He wished he could have said goodbye to Rocky. He'd considered it, but it would have been too risky. What if he knew the gun was missing? He didn't want to take the chance.

It was getting late. A pale outline of the moon had risen over the trees. The early evening was gray and dim. The air smelled faintly of burning leaves. There would probably be snow in less than a month. He wondered what Winsbury would look like with snow. He pictured a little, snowy village trapped in a snow globe with fat, wet snowflakes swirling in the air around houses with white roofs and yards sporting giant snowmen. There would be children building forts and having snowball wars in the parks and hot chocolate brewing in all the bright kitchens. He longed for it.

He went to the railroad tracks and followed them down, hoping he might spot a train passing, but there was none. He took the trail to Beth's hiding place and slipped under the tree, surprised when he found Beth there, crouched up like a little ball on the stump she liked to sit on.

"Beth, what are you doing here?"

She didn't look up, only rocked herself to some invisible rhythm. Her notebook lay on the ground in front of her, several pages torn in half.

"What's wrong? Are you all right?"

Nothing. He went to her and placed his arms around her shoulders, drew her into himself. Her body shuddered as she cried. He took her chin in his fingers and turned her face up so he could look into her eyes, so he could help her. What he saw stunned him.

A thin line of blood colored her bottom lip and she had two scratches on her left cheek.

"Oh my God, did he...."

Her eyes fell and she nodded, once, almost imperceptibly.

A nuclear explosion flashed in Gary's chest. "That son of a bitch."

She sobbed, trying to catch her breath, body shaking. "He came to me earlier today when my mother went to the store. I told him I didn't want to do it anymore and this is what he did. He never hit me before. It's getting worse."

"Is he still home?"

She nodded, and he stormed through the low branches, in an instant making the decision that antagonized him for so long.

"I'm going to kill him now."

Chapter 17
The Choice

Time and the world grew foreign to Gary, foreign, as if darkly filtered through a kaleidoscope. In the back of his head, an ice pick of rage stabbed him, and he knew he wasn't thinking straight. The familiar burning rose up in his chest, though he welcomed it this time. He had something terrible to do, and he wouldn't be able to do it without that blinding anger.

What kind of cowboy do you want to be, Gary?

He was the murdering kind.

"Shut up," he said.

He was only faintly aware Beth still followed him. He glided over the ground. He barely felt the earth beneath him. His body wasn't his own, invaded by some dire spirit thrusting toward its new objective. If there had been a train coming, he could have run it down, stopped it with his rage.

Up the trail, through the grass, through Beth's front door. Mrs. Carter, Beth's mother, nodded on the living room sofa, a tall glass of bourbon in front of her. A half knitted sweater rested in her lap. She jolted awake when the door slammed. Her drunken eyes flew open, and she glared, disoriented, at Gary. She eventually focused on the gun in Gary's hand.

"Oh, my God!" She froze.

"Where is he?" Gary thrust himself into the living room.

Beth cowered behind him.

Mr. Carter bounded down the stairs so quickly he nearly fell, but caught himself with the railing. He wore a dark t-shirt and gray sweatpants. The sight of him made Gary's stomach curdle.

"What the hell is going on?"

Gary pointed the gun at the man's chest. "Why don't you tell me, you son of a bitch?"

Mr. Carter's eyes locked on the gun, as if nothing else existed. He paled as the blood left his face. He glanced to Gary's left. Gary followed his eyes to the telephone. He kicked it over.

"Look at her," Gary said, pointing to Beth. "What did you do to your daughter?"

Mrs. Carter shook, horrified. "Don't do this! Leave him alone!"

"Shut up!" Gary cried. "Do you even know what he's been doing to your daughter?"

Beth sobbed and slumped to the floor.

"Beth?" Mrs. Carter said.

Beth heaved enormous tears and scratched at the carpet, weak, powerless. Gary went to her, holding the gun on her father. He dropped to one knee and draped his arm around her, making the critical error of taking his eyes away from the man he had come to kill.

Mr. Carter rushed him. Mrs. Carter screamed. Beth's father was a large man with a hefty gut, but he moved faster than Gary expected. He crossed the room in a flash, swatting his robust arms like an ape. His left hand struck the gun, knocking it from Gary's grip.

He fell on top of Gary, knocking the wind out of him. The acrid smell of his terrified sweat bit Gary's nostrils. Gary strained to push the man off of him, but he couldn't muster the strength. Mr. Carter was too heavy and too slippery from sweat.

"Oh, my God!" Mrs. Carter screamed from somewhere in the room. Beth screamed too, but it was all ringing in Gary's ears.

"I told you to stay away from my daughter!" Mr. Carter yelled as he maneuvered himself atop Gary. Gary struggled, but wasn't strong enough. Fists rained over Gary's face.

He drew his arms up to fend off the blow but they kept landing, slamming his cheeks, his nose, his jaw, his forehead. But the rage sustained him.

He reached out, blindly, searching for anything to help. He knew he wouldn't last much longer. His hand came up with something, he didn't know what, but it was heavy enough. He threw his arm and the newfound object struck Mr. Carter square on the temple.

Stunned, the man went limp for a moment and fell backward with a thud. Gary scrambled to his feet, face bloody and swollen, rage chewing him up, spitting him out, chewing him up again. He panted and gripped the object in his hand, looked down at it finally.

It was a clay ashtray. Horrified, he threw it across the room. It shattered into a dozen pieces against the wall. Mr. Carter stirred on the floor, opened his eyes. He scowled with hate.

Gary rushed him and drove his knee into the man's gut. Then he saw the gun. It had fallen beneath the couch. He dove and came up with it, aimed it at Mr. Carter's head.

Mr. Carter shuddered, beet red with pain. The two women cried and screamed.

"Don't kill him!" Mrs. Carter implored. "Beth, do something!"

Beth pushed away from her mother and squared herself for the event. Mr. Carter's eyes flew wide as softballs as he stared death in the face.

"I want him dead, Mom," Beth said.

"Why?" Mrs. Carter screamed.

Horror and disbelief stretched Beth's face. "How can you ask me that? Don't pretend you don't know why. Why do you keep buying my stupid pills? Why do you let him tuck me in every night? Why do you keep yourself drunk? So you can ignore what he does to me! Let's just kill him. Kill him now!"

"Oh, my dearest God in Heaven." Her mother threw her glass of bourbon across the room. It splattered over the wall.

"God doesn't hear you, Mom," Beth said. "He doesn't hear me at all, and I was the one who needed Him."

Gary cringed. He felt true hatred for the man before him, and for the woman on the couch who knew about everything he'd done. He pressed the gun into Mr. Carter's forehead, the pressure of his skull pushing back against the gunmetal. "Tell me why you should live."

Mr. Carter stammered something, but the words spilled out as garble.

"What good are you!? You're the one that needs to be put away, not me! Why do I have to suffer for what you did?"

Gary no longer saw Mr. Carter beneath him. He saw the snarling face of his own father, the hateful look in his eyes at that moment he struck Gary's mother down.

Gary pressed the gun harder. He gripped the trigger and tensed with renewed anger and despair. The room grew silent. The scene unfolded in slow motion over the length of an eternity.

Gary's whole life ran through him. He pictured his mother dying in the hospital bed, her body arching and kicking, knowing she was dying yet helpless to stop it. Killing Beth's father wouldn't only be vengeance for Beth, it would be vengeance for himself, for his mother, for Gail, and for every other victim in the world forced to deal with their own Mr. Carters. It would all be over in an instant.

He tightened his finger on the trigger, then paused when he saw Mr. Carter's eyes. Somehow, they pierced Gary's shroud of anger. They were the eyes of a monster, true, but they were also the eyes of a man. They reminded him of Rocky and of damnation. He considered life and death, Heaven and Hell. He thought of his grandfather and Butchy the Cowboy.

Come on Gary, a voice rang in his head, a mixture of all the individuals who ever mattered in his life. *It's now or never. Make the choice. Really, what kind of cowboy do you want to be?*

A single tear rolled across the bridge of his nose.

He couldn't pull the trigger. In that briefest of moments, Gary Sanderson knew he wasn't a killer, never was, never could be. At least not anymore.

He stood, stunned, simultaneously torn to pieces and enormously relieved. He threw the gun behind him, away from Mr. Carter.

"I can't do it."

Mr. Carter slumped to the floor, his eyes shut. Mrs. Carter fell in a heap on the couch, staring at the ceiling she crossed herself.

Gary fell to his knees and wept. His tears were stark and deep, pulled from deep wells he never knew he had. Every cell in his body joined in, throwing out tears and pain and anguish that had built up in them over the eons of his life. His soul lurched beneath his skin. The world rumbled.

"Oh, Beth, I'm so sorry," Mrs. Carter sobbed. "I'm so, so sorry. I'm so sorry."

Gary slumped against the wall, exhausted. He started for the front door, but a violent *boom* exploded in his ear, then another, and another.

Beth held the gun in both hands. She pulled the trigger with two fingers and the bullets tore into her father as he lay prone on the floor.

Mrs. Carter began screaming maniacally, curling into a ball on the couch. Gary threw himself back, afraid Beth might fire on him as well.

"I hate you, I hate you!" Beth cried over and over as she squeezed the trigger.

Gary reached for the gun, knowing there were still bullets in it, but she clutched it to her chest like it was her journal.

"You were right! He doesn't deserve to live. I hate you, Dad!"

Gary watched her, afraid. She was over the edge; her voice no longer her own, it became a freakish, maniacal version of her, a person gone mad with what she had just done.

"Why didn't you just kill him? Why didn't you just shoot him?"

"I couldn't do it. We have to get out of here. You're going to be in trouble."

"Don't say that! He deserved it for what he did to me!"

Gary searched the room. A set of car keys rested on the table. One single thought rang in his head: *Get Beth the hell out of there.*

As if reading his mind, Mrs. Carter fell off the couch, screaming. "Get out of here now! Get out! Get out! Get out!"

Beth winced. "Mom? I did this for you too...."

"Get out, now! I said *now!*"

Beth cringed. She wouldn't loosen the grip on the gun.

Gary grabbed her arm. "I have to get you out of here. Come on."

He led her to the yard, unlocked Mr. Carter's car, and jumped into the driver's seat. Beth fell into the passenger seat, eyes washed-out, zombie-like, and they sped away down the street.

At the main road, Gary slowed down, doing his best to stay at the speed limit, trying not to draw attention to himself. Now he had another reason to be nervous. He'd never driven a car on his own before and it confused him. It kept veering to the right for some reason and he kept jerking it back to the left to stay on the road. The pedals were foreign objects.

He headed toward the main highway, having no idea where he was going. He needed time to think. He kept his mind on the gun in Beth's lap.

"Can I have the gun?"

She drew it tighter, protecting it. Her eyes were becoming more irrational.

"It's so beautiful outside tonight, isn't it?" she said. "The sky is like a giant blanket of stars."

"We're going to figure out what to do."

"God, I can stare at the sky all night."

"Are you listening to me? Don't lose it on me."

She began to cry. She thrust her hand into her pocket and came out with her pill bottle. She did her best to unscrew the top but it was awkward with the gun in her hand. It popped off suddenly, and she yanked the bottle up to dump all of the pills in her mouth. Gary slapped the bottle away before she could do it. The pills bounced along the floor like hail stones.

"What the hell are you doing?" Gary asked. "Stop it."

"I don't want to go to jail."

"You won't go to jail. People will understand what you did. Look at what he was doing to you."

She twisted the metal of the gun barrel in her hands, staring out the window at the sky. "I'm afraid."

Gary eyed the gun. "Can I please have that?"

"No."

He turned onto the main highway and sped up, gripping the wheel with both hands. Scenarios rifled through his mind. *What am I doing? Why am I running?* Wasn't that the dumbest thing to do?

They'd follow him, and there wasn't anywhere he could go. The best thing would be to talk to the police, explain what happened and why. Let them make their judgments on their own.

"It'll be all right," he said. "Please."

She relaxed and slowly, finally, began to slide the gun toward him. He reached for it and nearly had it in his hand when the sudden blare of sirens burst out behind them. Beth recoiled with the gun and spun, frightened, shaking like a beaten dog.

"Shit! We're going to have to stop, Beth. We shouldn't have tried to run away. It's my fault."

"No! I have to get away from here. Now!" She aimed the gun at Gary now. Her eyes darted back and forth.

To their right, a train rushed through the night, its bright light like a beacon, calling them.

"You're not going to shoot me, are you? I love you, Beth."

The gun shook in her hand. She wouldn't, or couldn't, move it away.

"We'll get through this. I'm going to pull over. Just give me the gun."

He stopped the car on the side of the road, slamming it into park, and reaching out toward the gun, afraid she might actually pull the trigger. "Please."

Beth leapt from the car. She ran toward the train tracks, her grip not loosening at all from the gun handle.

"Beth!" He ran after her.

Behind them, a police car screeched to a halt in the gravel, then another. Gary saw Don's truck behind them.

"Gary!" someone yelled and he cringed. It was Officer Vedish.

"Gary, wait!" came Gail's voice.

But Gary continued toward Beth. His foot came down in a rut and twisted his ankle, slowing him down. The train approached through the darkness. The knee high grasses snapped at his legs.

Finally, Beth stopped on the railroad tracks and stood there, gripping the gun to her chest.

Gary paused ten feet away and held up his hands. "What are you doing?"

"It wasn't supposed to be like this," she said. "I didn't want it to turn out like this."

She put the gun to her head.

Gary's heart stopped. "Don't do that."

"Why didn't you tell me this would happen?"

Officer Vedish arrived, panting, gun drawn. Don and Gail appeared behind him.

Vedish aimed his gun at Beth. "Put down the gun! Now!"

The train rushed toward them.

"What are you going to do?" Gary said to Vedish. "You going to shoot her if she shoots herself?" Then he turned to Beth. "Please come off the tracks. The train is coming. You're afraid of the train."

Beth began to dance, bouncing on one foot, then the other. "I don't have to be afraid of the train anymore, right Gary? All I have to do is get off the tracks, right? I'm sure off now, huh?"

She stepped off the tracks, then back on again, off, on, off, on. "See? It's easy."

The train whistle blew. The light bore down on her. Gary snatched his hand out to grab her but she shoved the barrel of the gun to her head again.

"Stay away!"

Vedish slapped at his thigh. "God damn it, get off the tracks!"

Gail stepped forward. "Beth, honey, please don't do this. Let us help you."

Vedish growled. "What the hell happened here?"

"I shot my father," she said.

"What?"

"He was molesting her," Gary said. "She had to do something."

"Oh, my God," Gail cried.

"Jesus," Don breathed.

"How do you rape your own daughter?" Gary asked them.

"I don't want to go to jail." Beth no longer danced.

"You won't go to jail," Gail told her. "We'll get help for you. We'll help you if you want us to."

"Please, Beth," Gary implored. "I love you."

The train was almost upon her, horn blaring in their ears. Vedish backed away, yelling something, but the sound of the train's horn overpowered his voice. Gary readied himself to charge her. If she didn't get off the tracks, he was going to barrel into her. He might get shot or he might hurt her, but it was better than the alternative.

But suddenly, Beth stepped off the tracks, and handed the gun to Gary. "I love you too." Her eyes were red, dripping with tears. "Always."

Gary sighed with relief, but before he knew what happened, she stepped backward, directly into the path of the train, and closed her eyes.

"No!" Gary screamed and started for her, but a pair of hands yanked him backward.

In an instant, the train rushed through in a gigantic huff of wind and metal, like a mythical beast come to claim its sacrifice. It struck her down without relent, without remorse.

It was what she wanted. It was over.

CHAPTER 18

A New Beginning

Two Years Later

Gary wasn't the same person who had gone back to Radcliffe at sixteen, yet he wasn't entirely different. He'd grown three inches in the past two years and had broadened in the face, chest, and shoulders. His blonde hair no longer flopped over his head, but lay close cropped as a soldier's.

Today was his eighteenth birthday. He was free to go, though he was required to have strict court supervision and regular visits with social workers and a court appointed officer. That didn't matter to him—he was leaving Radcliffe again, heading back out to the world that had screwed him up twice before. He was far more prepared this time.

Through her office window, Ms. Sanchez waved. Gary waved back. Before long, a Greyhound bus pulled up to the main curb, and Gary hopped in, plastic bag full of clothes slung over his shoulder. He had a cheap bouquet of orange and yellow flowers in his lap that Mrs. Sanchez agreed to purchase for him. He didn't tell her what they were for. He didn't have to. He had told her everything about Winsbury, and about Beth and Rocky and Gail, and everything else bothering him in his life. He finally opened up to her and it helped a great deal. He only wished he could have done so much earlier.

He leaned his head on the window and slept until the bus arrived at his stop.

He hopped off and soaked in the green of the park. At the top of a hill sat the cemetery where Beth slept. He strolled through the sidewalks and breathed the crisp air. He crossed a black steel gate and wandered among the rows of headstones until he found Beth's—a tiny, gray little thing neatly trimmed into the grass.

He laid the flowers there, reached into his pocket, and pulled out a piece of paper. It was her poem.

"Hi, Beth. It's been a while. I got out for good this time. Eighteen today. I thought I'd stop by and say hello. Or goodbye, that is."

He shifted in his shoes, uncomfortable, thinking.

"I guess what I really wanted to say is I'm sorry I couldn't help you. I hope you'll forgive me. But I also wanted to say thank you for helping me. I don't think I'm afraid to talk to people now about what happened to me. I owe that to you. I... just hope you'll forgive me."

He yanked something out of his bag. "I got something else for you." He propped it up on the grass beside her grave. It was Butchy the Cowboy.

"I don't need this anymore."

He folded up the poem and set it back into his pocket. "This, I'll keep forever."

He closed his eyes and pictured her face like he'd done a thousand times. He wished he could speak with her for real.

"I'm sorry you couldn't step off the tracks. I wish you could have. That's what I'm going to do now. I'm taking my own advice. I'm stepping off the tracks. I'm starting over. I hope I do it right this time."

A few minutes later, a car pulled up, and the driver stepped out. It was Gail Morgan.

"Happy Birthday, Gary," she called.

He left the cemetery through the gate. "How've you been?" He hadn't seen her in two years but they had kept in touch by letter. Her hair had grown out. She wore a bright yellow coat.

"All right, I guess. I'm glad to see you, though."

He understood. "How's Don?"

"Better." She paused. "*We're* better if that's what you mean. Counseling helps. He's really stuck with me through everything, now that I've... well... opened up to him."

"I guess that was the hard part. It feels good, doesn't it?"

"It does. Speaking of counseling, they fired Counselor Ray."

"Finally?"

"I talked to the Principal last week. He said your letter to Mr. Reynolds helped. I wish you would have told me sooner."

"I wanted to. Things were different then."

"I know." She mussed his hair. "Can I take you to lunch?"

He gave her a quick hug and she squeezed him back. It was a pleasant, familiar feeling.

"That would be great," he said.

He took up his backpack and dropped it in the back seat. They drove through the park while the sun warmed their faces as they drove toward Winsbury.

"Where to?" she asked.

"How about Rocky's?"

"He's already got the pizza ready."

In his bag sat the last letter he'd received from Rocky. It read, *"I quit drinking, kid. Cut back at least! Feeling a lot better. You're welcome back any time. I know what you did and why and I'd have done the same. Don't worry about Heaven and Hell. You're a real angel, kid."*

Gary smiled. Everything would be all right.

About The Author

Michael J. Hultquist is a screenwriter and author working in the Midwest, currently near Chicago. He is an active member of the Horror Writers Association and writes mostly dark fiction. He is also a chili pepper enthusiast, deeply devoted to the jalapeno.

Visit Mike's web site at: *http://www.michaelhultquist.com.*